Bar-el, Dan,
Dog night at the Story
Zoo /
[2017]
33305240673859
ca   03/16/18

NIGHT

at the

STORY ZOO

*Written
by*

DAN BAR-EL

*Illustrated
by*

VICKI NERINO

TUNDRA BOOKS

For Colonel Scruffington the 3rd (and Sam), who get the jokes and the other stuff —DB

To all the snuggly, as well as the resistant-to-snuggles creatures (and people), out there. And also to Mom and Popps. —VN

Text copyright © 2017 by Dan Bar-el
Illustrations copyright © 2017 by Vicki Nerino

Tundra Books, an imprint of Penguin Random House Canada Young Readers,
a Penguin Random House Company

All rights reserved. The use of any part of this publication reproduced, transmitted in any form or by any means, electronic, mechanical, photocopying, recording, or otherwise, or stored in a retrieval system, without the prior written consent of the publisher—or, in case of photocopying or other reprographic copying, a licence from the Canadian Copyright Licensing Agency—is an infringement of the copyright law.

Library and Archives Canada Cataloguing in Publication
Bar-el, Dan, author
Dog night at the story zoo / Dan Bar-el ; illustrated by Vicki Nerino.
Issued in print and electronic formats.
ISBN 978-1-101-91838-8 (hardback).—ISBN 978-1-101-91839-5 (epub)
I. Graphic novels. I. Nerino, Vicki, illustrator II. Title.
PN6733.B37D64 2017   j741.5'971   C2016-905229-X   C2016-905230-3

Published simultaneously in the United States of America by Tundra Books of Northern New York, an imprint of Penguin Random House Canada Young Readers, a Penguin Random House Company

Library of Congress Control Number: 2016948349

Edited by Samantha Swenson
Book design by Kelly Hill
The artwork in this book was created with pens, paper, computers and dog hair.
The text was set in Kidprint.

Printed and bound in China

www.penguinrandomhouse.ca

1   2   3   4   5   21   20   19   18   17

TUNDRA BOOKS | Penguin Random House

CAFETERIA
STORY ZOO TONITE!

STARRING BOOMER!

FETCH!
PAGE 10

STARRING EMMA!

THE STORM
BEFORE THE CALM
PAGE 32

STARRING WALTER!

TENDER
ON
THE INSIDE
PAGE 57

STARRING WILMETTE!

THE HOUND
OF
BAKERSVILLE
PAGE 71

THE AUTHOR AND ILLUSTRATOR

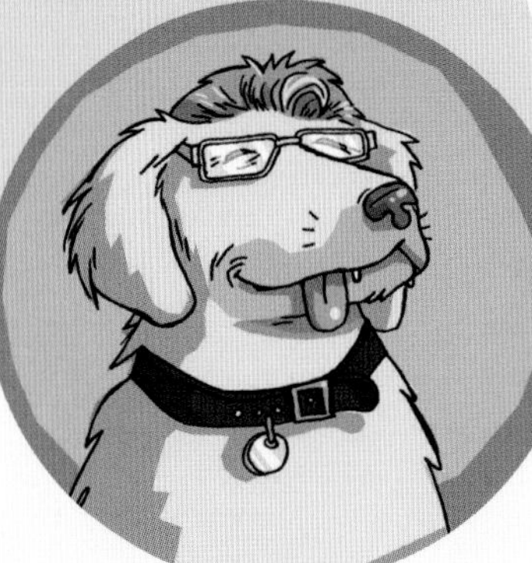

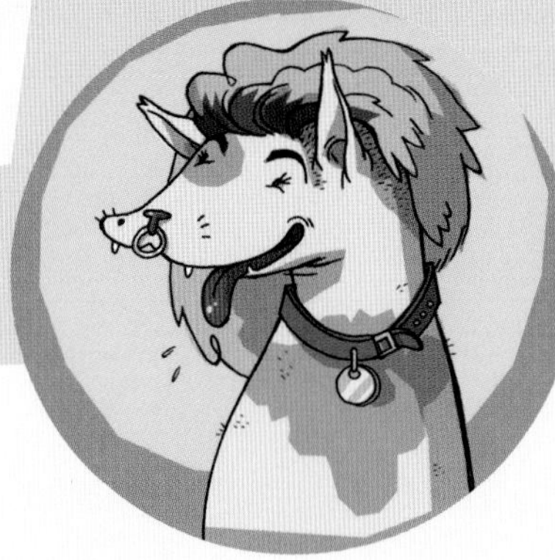

DAN BAR-EL is an award-winning children's author, educator and storyteller who has published chapter books, picture books and graphic novels. Over the past twenty-one years, he has worked with children ages 3 to 13 as a school age childcare provider, a preschool teacher, a creative drama and a creative writing teacher. Dan is the author of *Audrey (Cow)*, *It's Great Being a Dad*, *Nine Words Max* and many other books. He lives in Vancouver with Dominique and Sasha, the best cat in the known universe.

♥

Dan would like to thank the SPCA, its staff and volunteers. It was through this organization that he was introduced to Sasha, who admittedly is a cat, but often thinks that he's a dog. A pet is part of the family, or in his case, it completes a family, so he'd also like to acknowledge the veterinarians who provide care for these vulnerable creatures when it is needed.

Classically educated and poorly socialized, VICKI NERINO likes to make a mess of things like comics, illustrations and paintings. She smears paint with her fingers and scratches ink off with her nails, but holy smokes does she ever clean up nice. She has a thing about tigers. *Dog Night at the Story Zoo* is her first book for kids.

♥

Vicki would like to thank all the dogs she has met who have enriched her life, in alphabetical order so no ones gets jealous: Bamboo, Barley, Ben, Chaniel, Charlie (the little one), Charlie (the big one), Chrystal + her 13 pups, Colonel Boomer Scruffington, Cookie (aka Pickle), Dallas, Dudley, Dylan, Gary Panter, Jackson, Kaiser Ribwich, L'orso, Lupé, Moe, Monty, Niki, Oscar, Peanut, Precious, Princess, Sheeba, Simpson, Splinter, Stella, Summer, The Gracie, Thunder, Wally, that amazingly stubborn basset hound who lives across from her house and every single one of the hundred million pups she's pet on the street.*

*She'd also like to thank a few cats because they are also four-legged pet-able creatures and she don't discriminate: Fizzgig, Greta, Honey, Lucy Fur, Merlin, Mia, Milo, Misty, Mitten, Mordecai, Panties, Peaches, Quincy, Rico, Skillet, Sylvia Plath, Turnip and all of the street cats who have rubbed all up on her ankles.

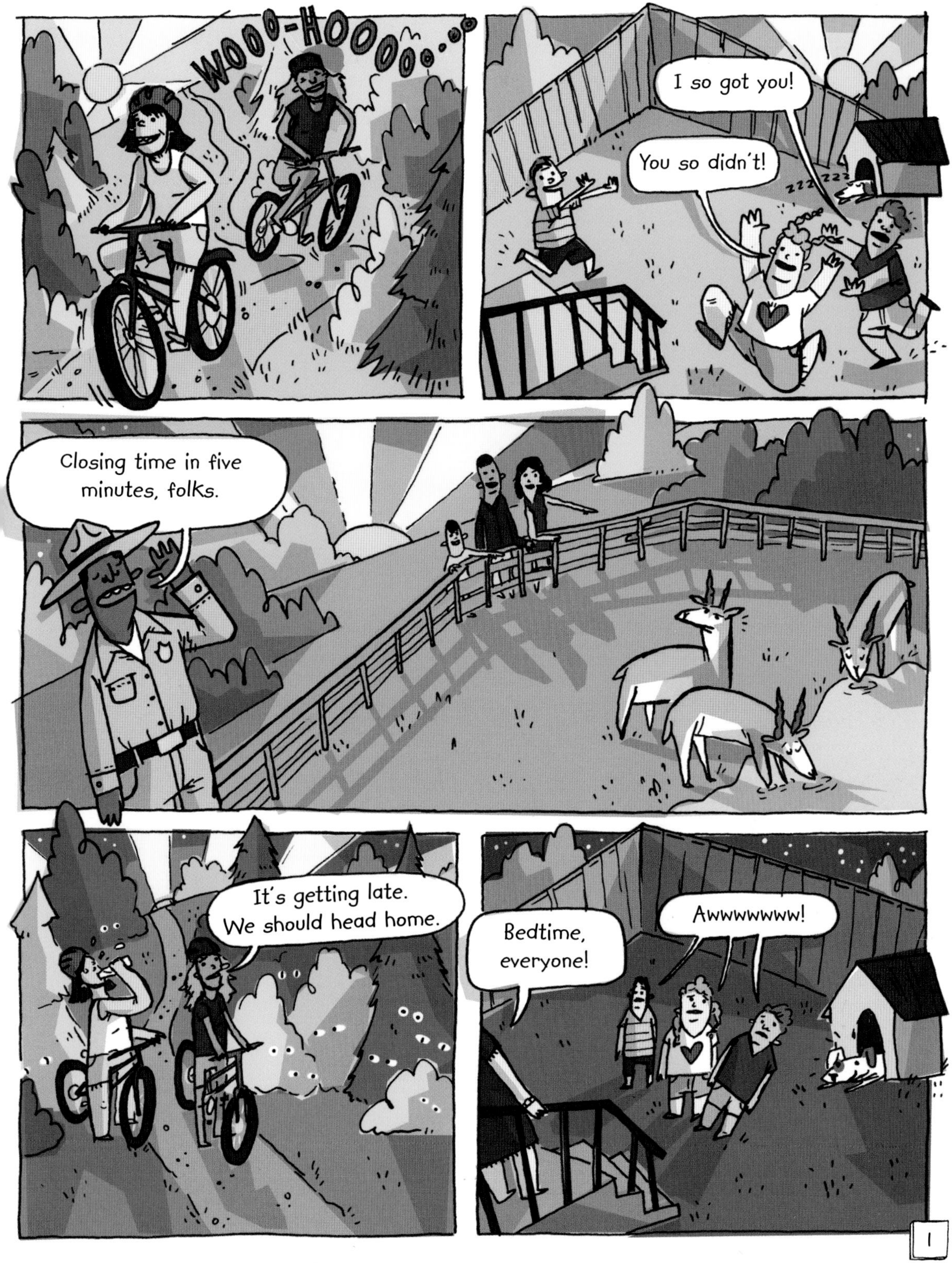
WOOO-HOOOOO...
I so got you!
You so didn't!
Closing time in five minutes, folks.
It's getting late. We should head home.
Bedtime, everyone!
Awwwwwww!

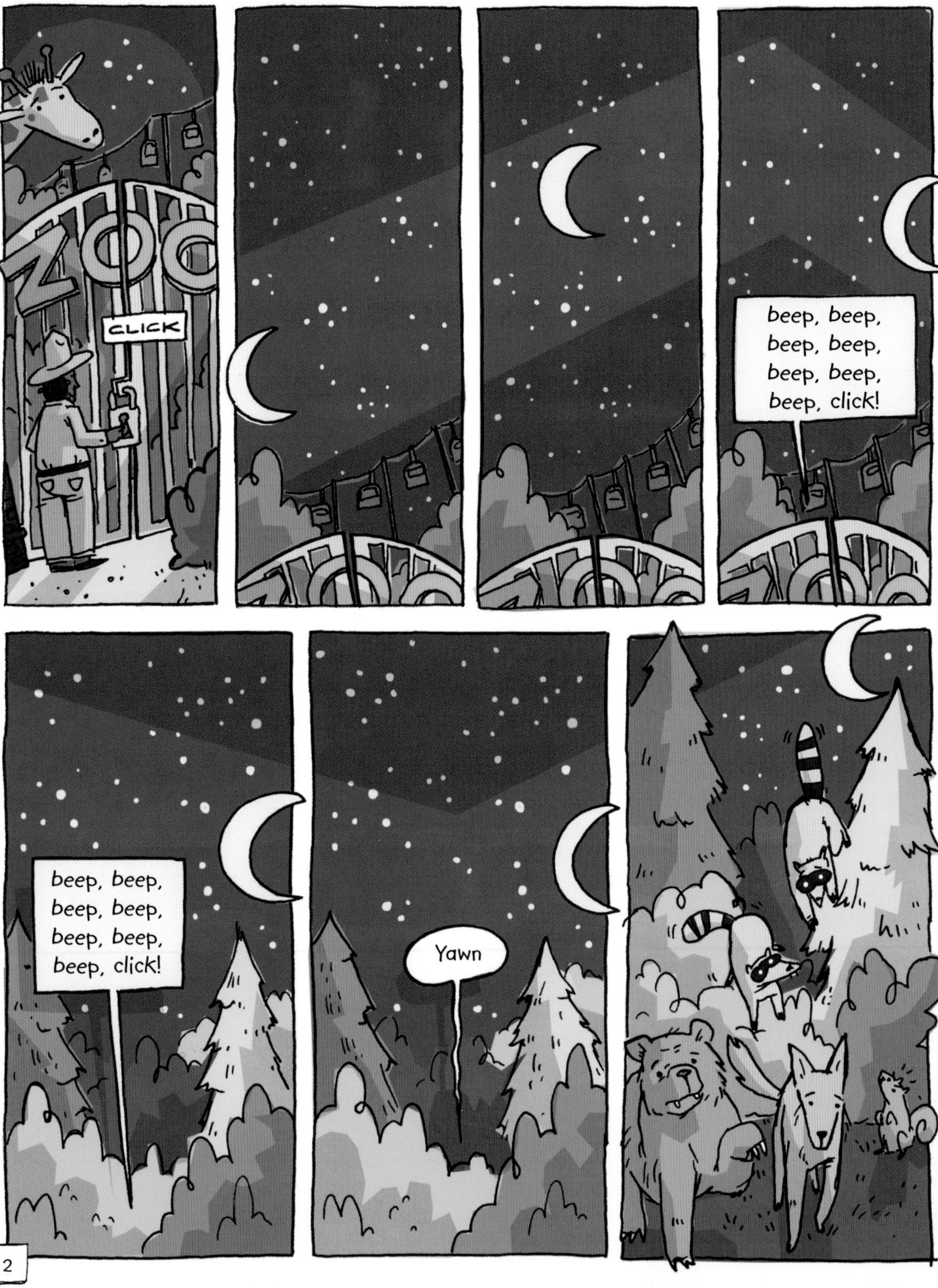
ZOO
CLICK
beep, beep, beep, beep, beep, beep, beep, click!
beep, beep, beep, beep, beep, beep, beep, click!
Yawn

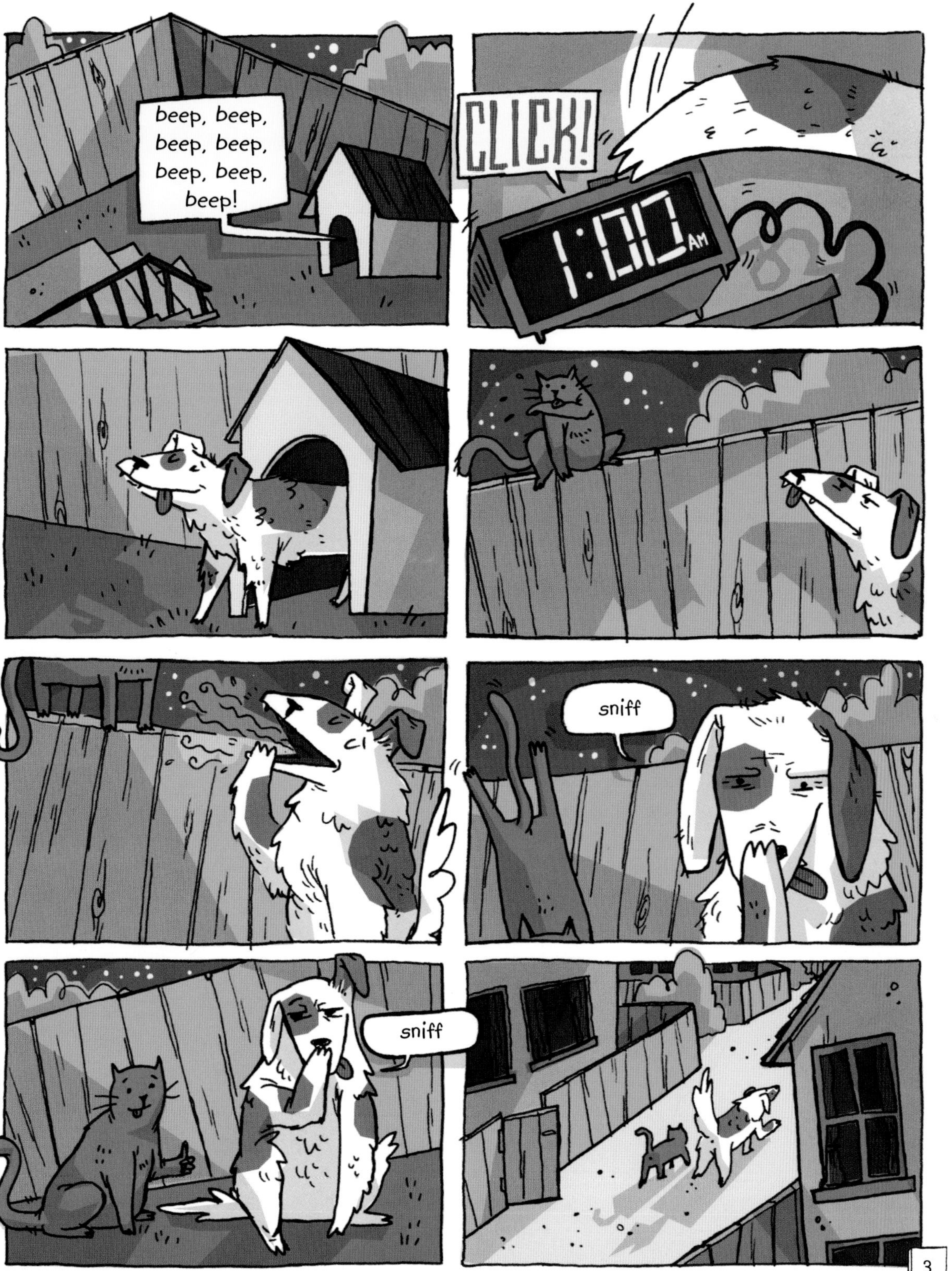
beep, beep, beep, beep, beep, beep, beep!
CLICK!
1:00 AM
sniff
sniff

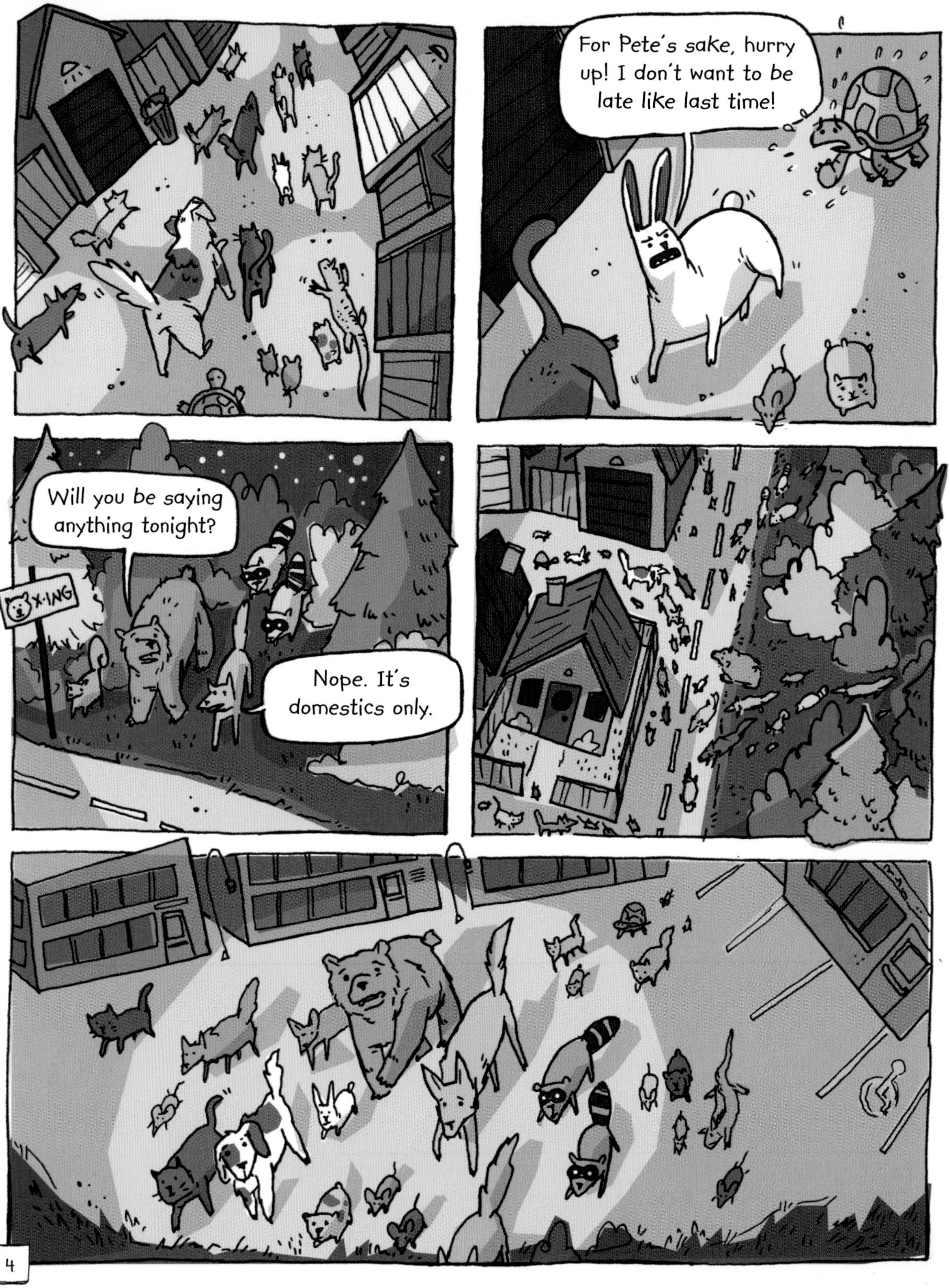

For Pete's sake, hurry up! I don't want to be late like last time!
Will you be saying anything tonight?
X-ING
Nope. It's domestics only.

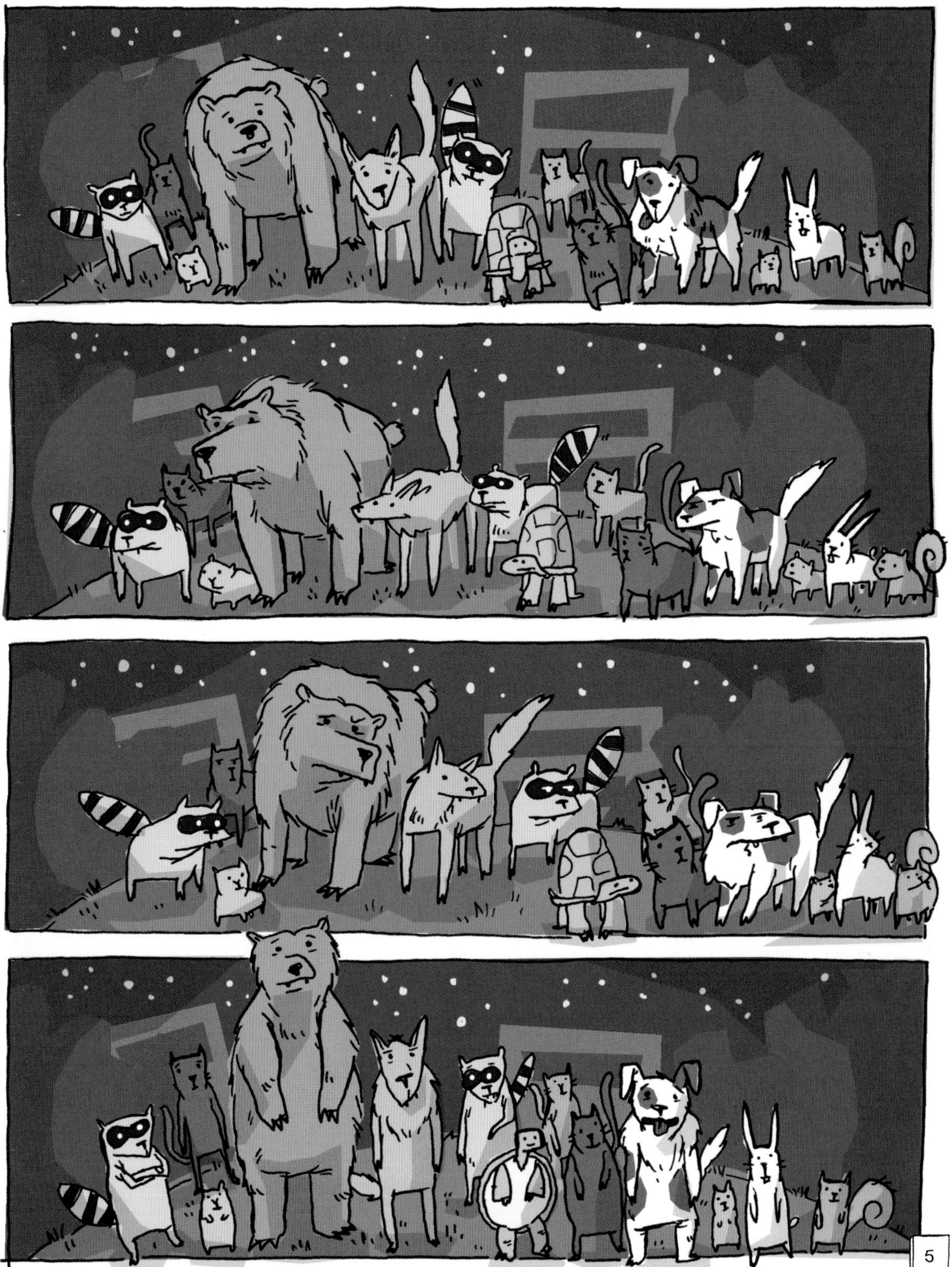

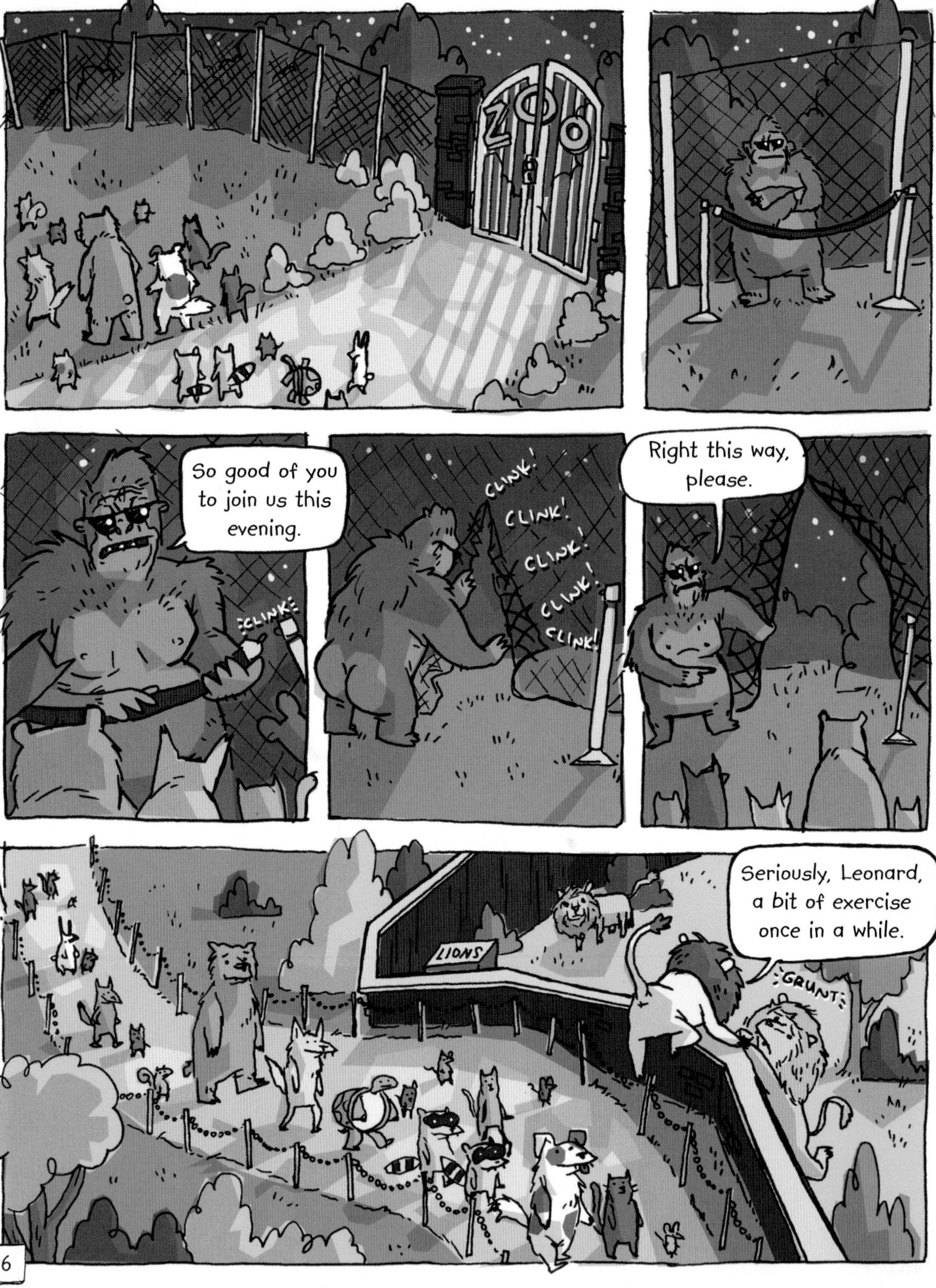
ZOO
So good of you to join us this evening.
CLINK
CLINK!
CLINK!
CLINK!
CLINK!
CLINK!
Right this way, please.
LIONS
Seriously, Leonard, a bit of exercise once in a while.
GRUNT

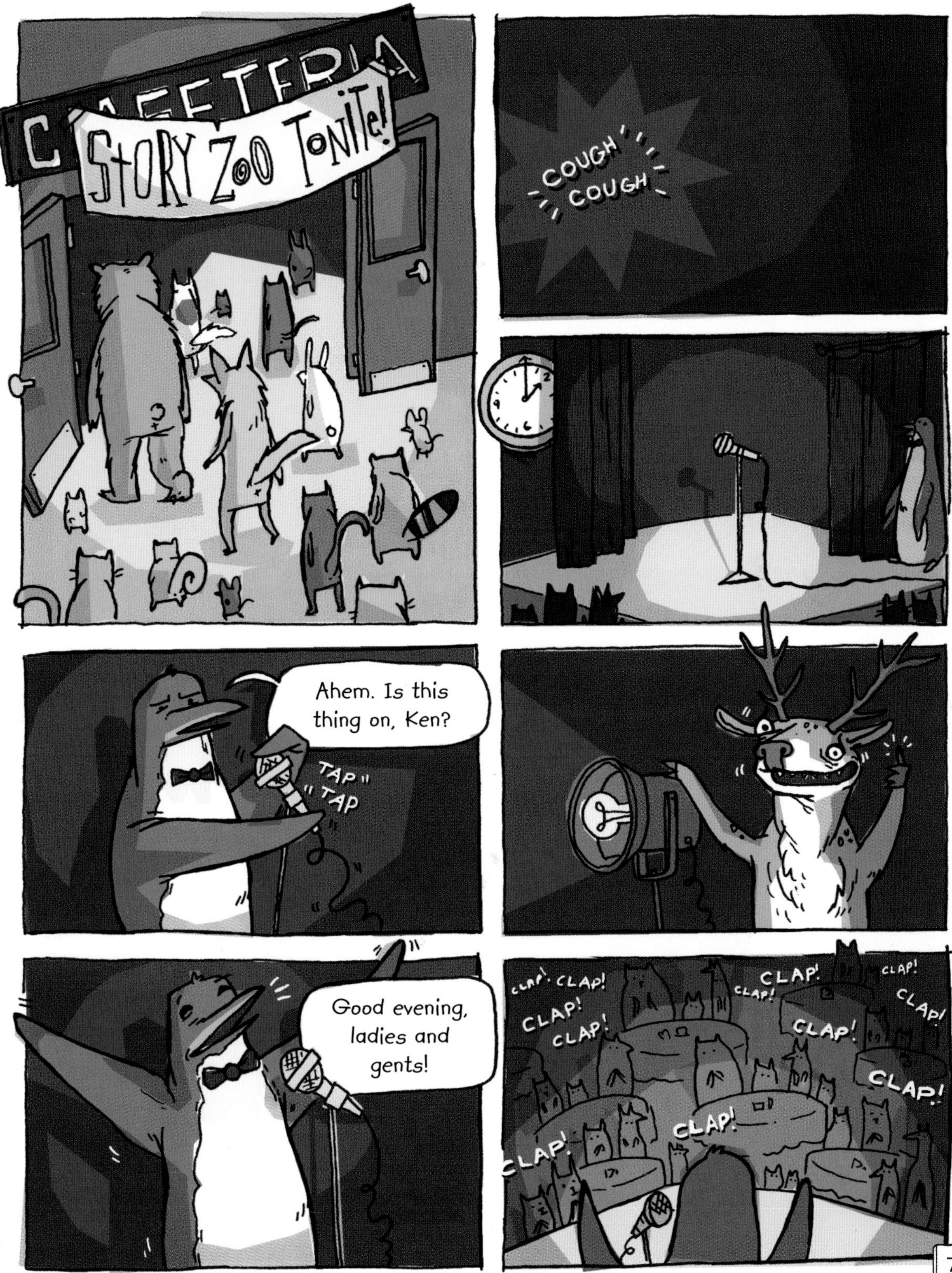
CAFETERIA
STORY ZOO TONITE!
COUGH COUGH
Ahem. Is this thing on, Ken?
TAP TAP
Good evening, ladies and gents!
CLAP! CLAP! CLAP! CLAP! CLAP! CLAP! CLAP! CLAP! CLAP! CLAP! CLAP! CLAP!

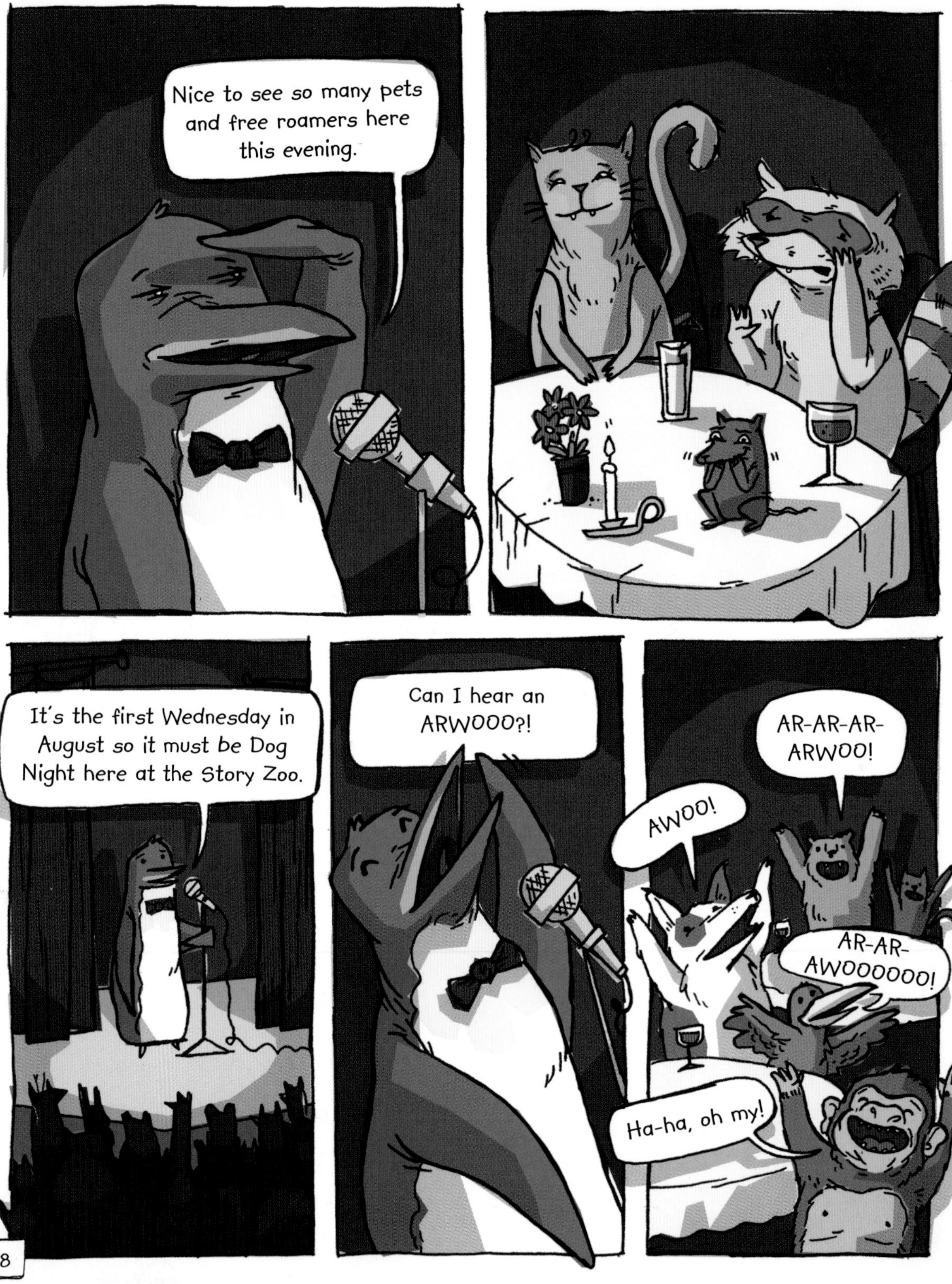
Nice to see so many pets and free roamers here this evening.
It's the first Wednesday in August so it must be Dog Night here at the Story Zoo.
Can I hear an ARWOOO?!
AR-AR-AR-ARWOO!
AWOO!
AR-AR-AWOOOOOOO!
Ha-ha, oh my!

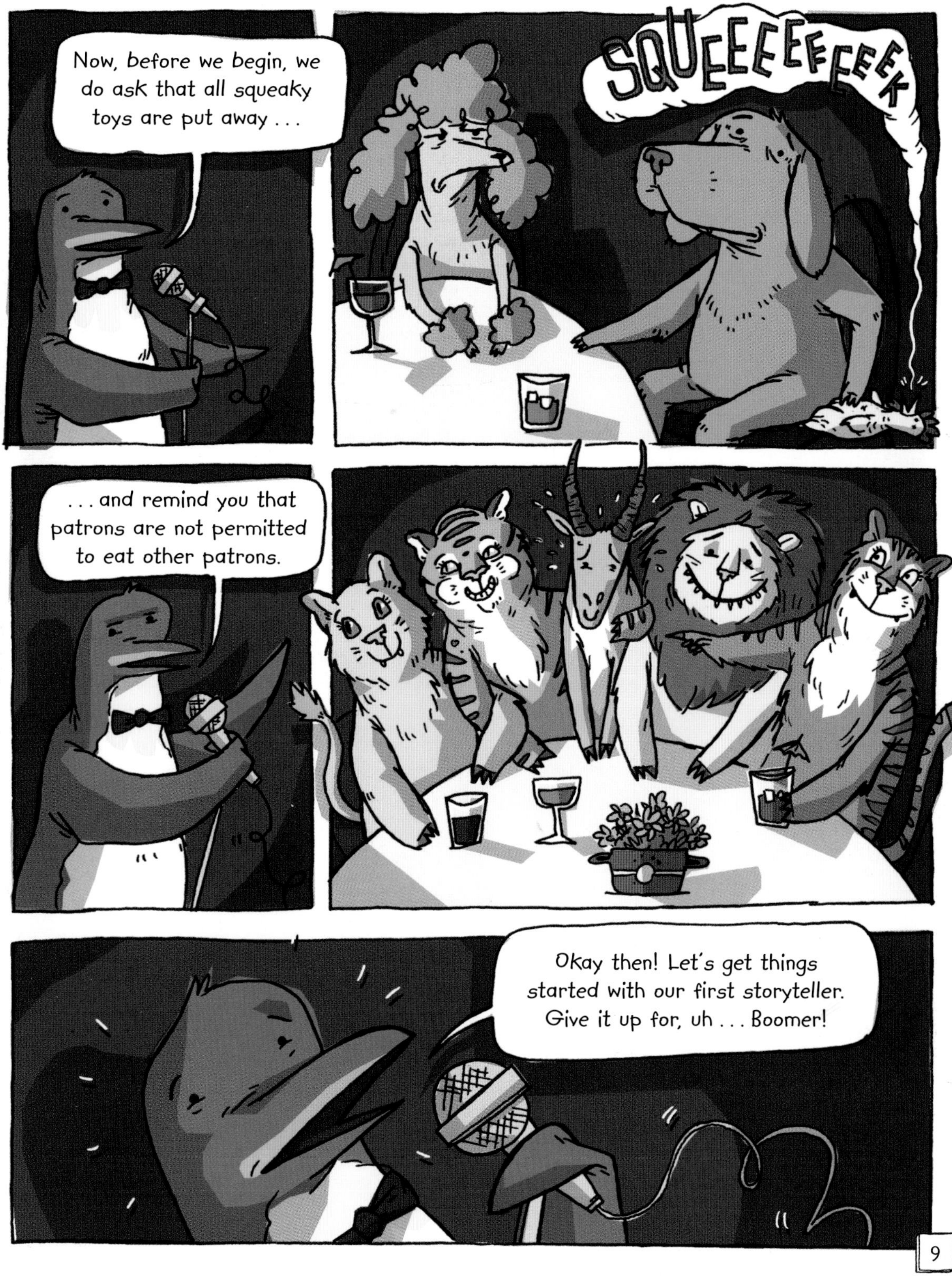
Now, before we begin, we do ask that all squeaky toys are put away . . .
SQUEEEEEEEEK
. . . and remind you that patrons are not permitted to eat other patrons.
Okay then! Let's get things started with our first storyteller. Give it up for, uh . . . Boomer!

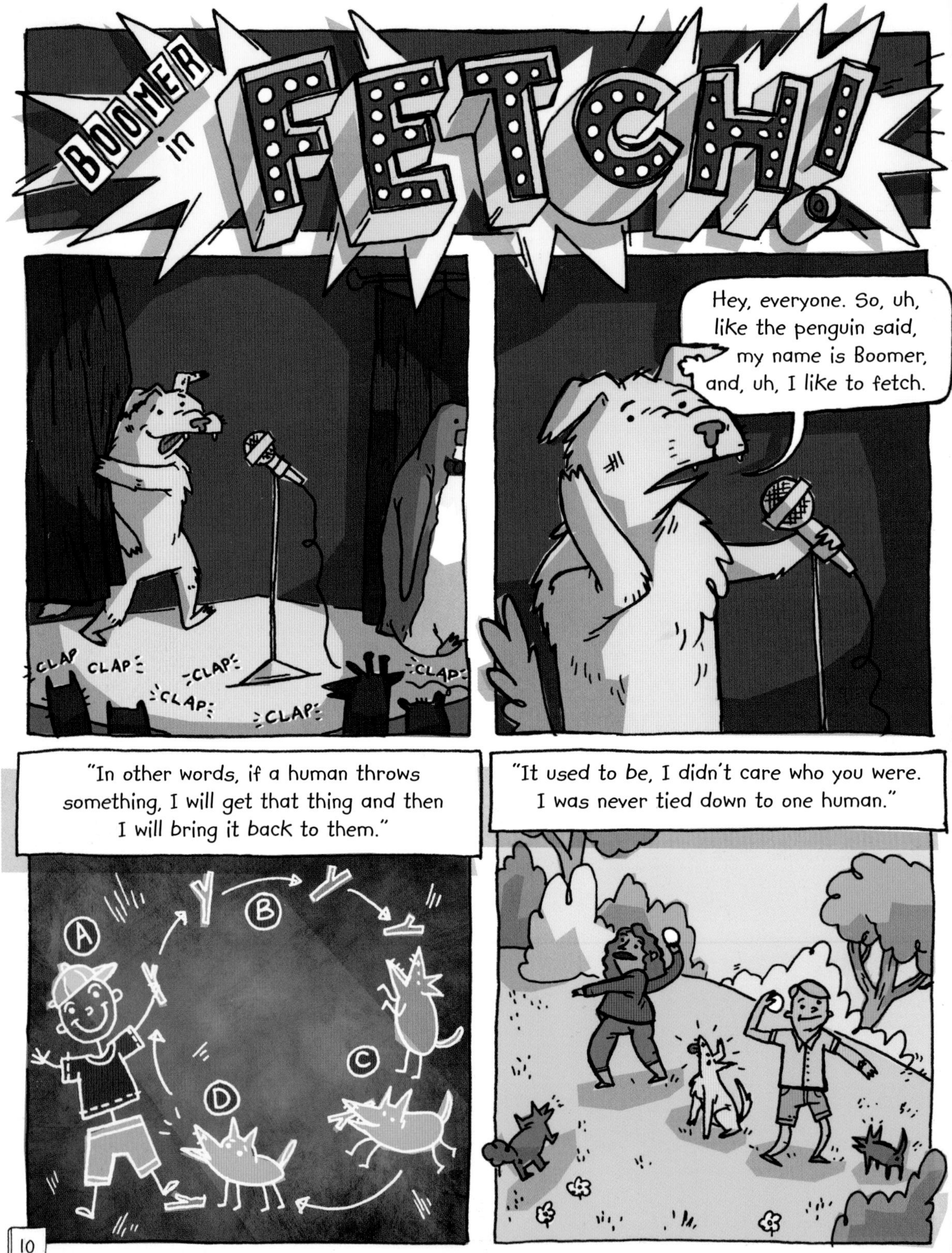
BOOMER in FETCH!
CLAP CLAP CLAP CLAP CLAP CLAP
Hey, everyone. So, uh, like the penguin said, my name is Boomer, and, uh, I like to fetch.
"In other words, if a human throws something, I will get that thing and then I will bring it back to them."
A
B
C
D
"It used to be, I didn't care who you were. I was never tied down to one human."

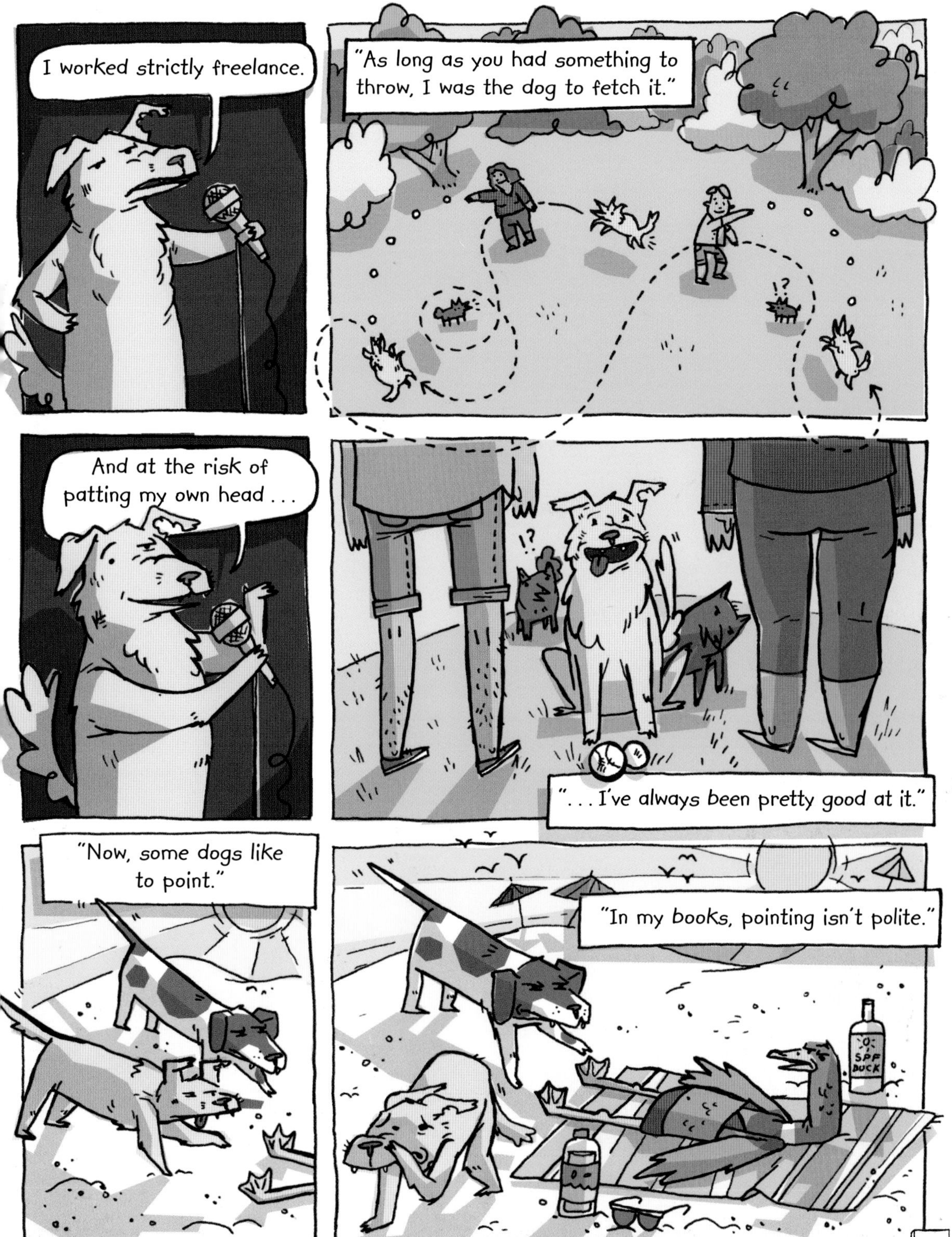
I worked strictly freelance.
"As long as you had something to throw, I was the dog to fetch it."
!?
And at the risk of patting my own head . . .
!?
". . . I've always been pretty good at it."
"Now, some dogs like to point."
"In my *books*, pointing isn't polite."
SPF DUCK

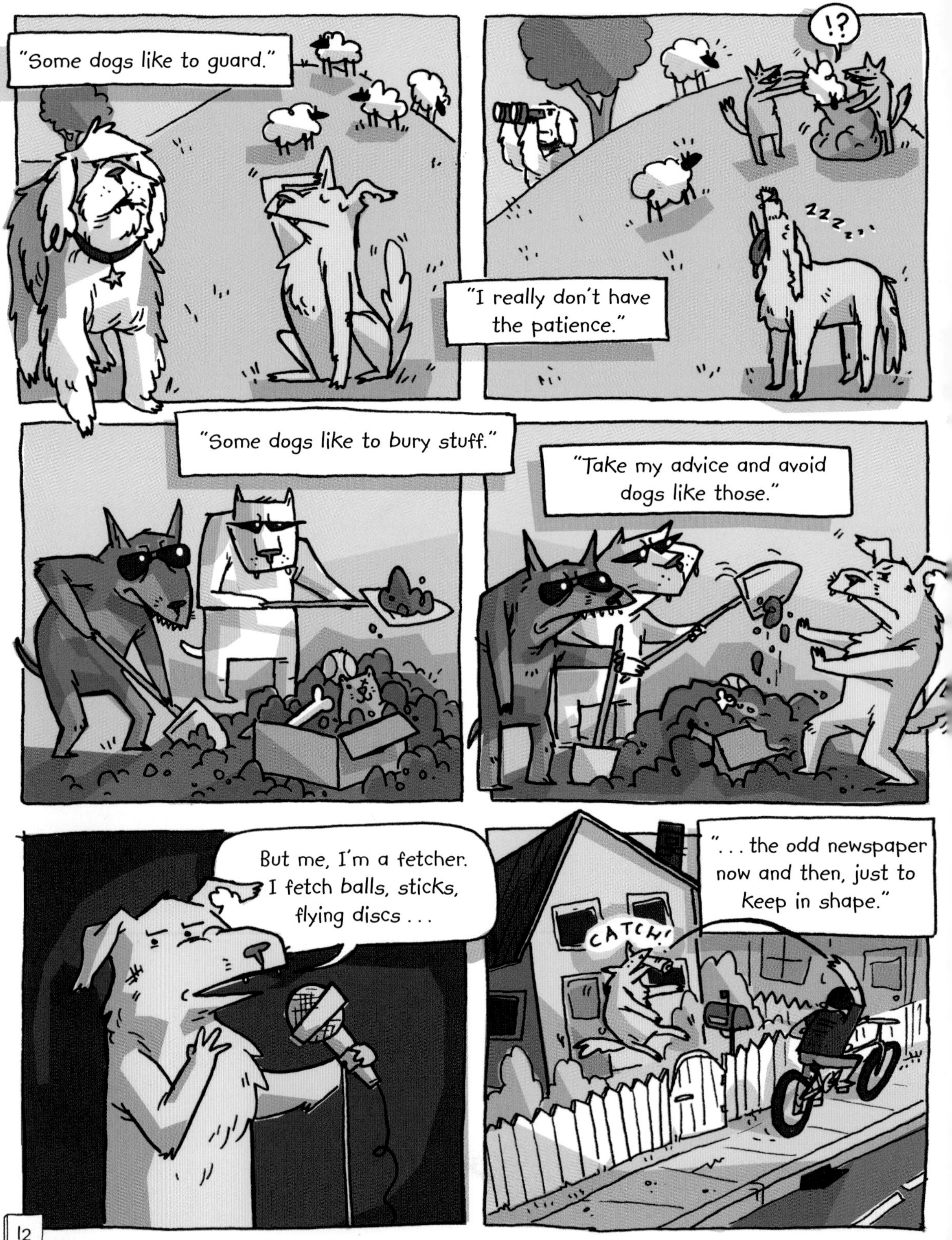
"Some dogs like to guard."
!?
ZZZ
"I really don't have the patience."
"Some dogs like to bury stuff."
"Take my advice and avoid dogs like those."
But me, I'm a fetcher. I fetch balls, sticks, flying discs . . .
CATCH!
". . . the odd newspaper now and then, just to keep in shape."

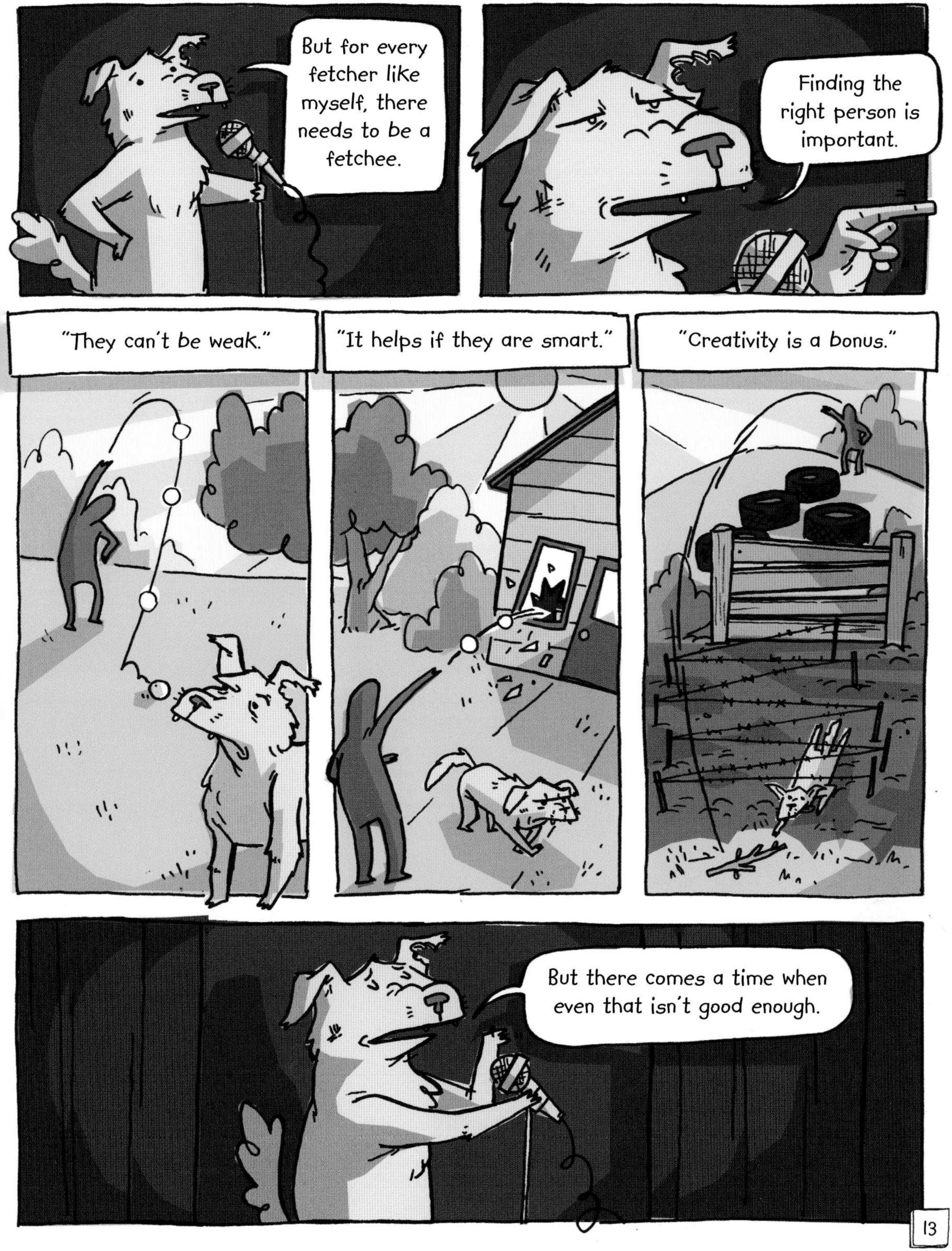
But for every fetcher like myself, there needs to be a fetchee.
Finding the right person is important.
"They can't be weak."
"It helps if they are smart."
"Creativity is a bonus."
But there comes a time when even that isn't good enough.

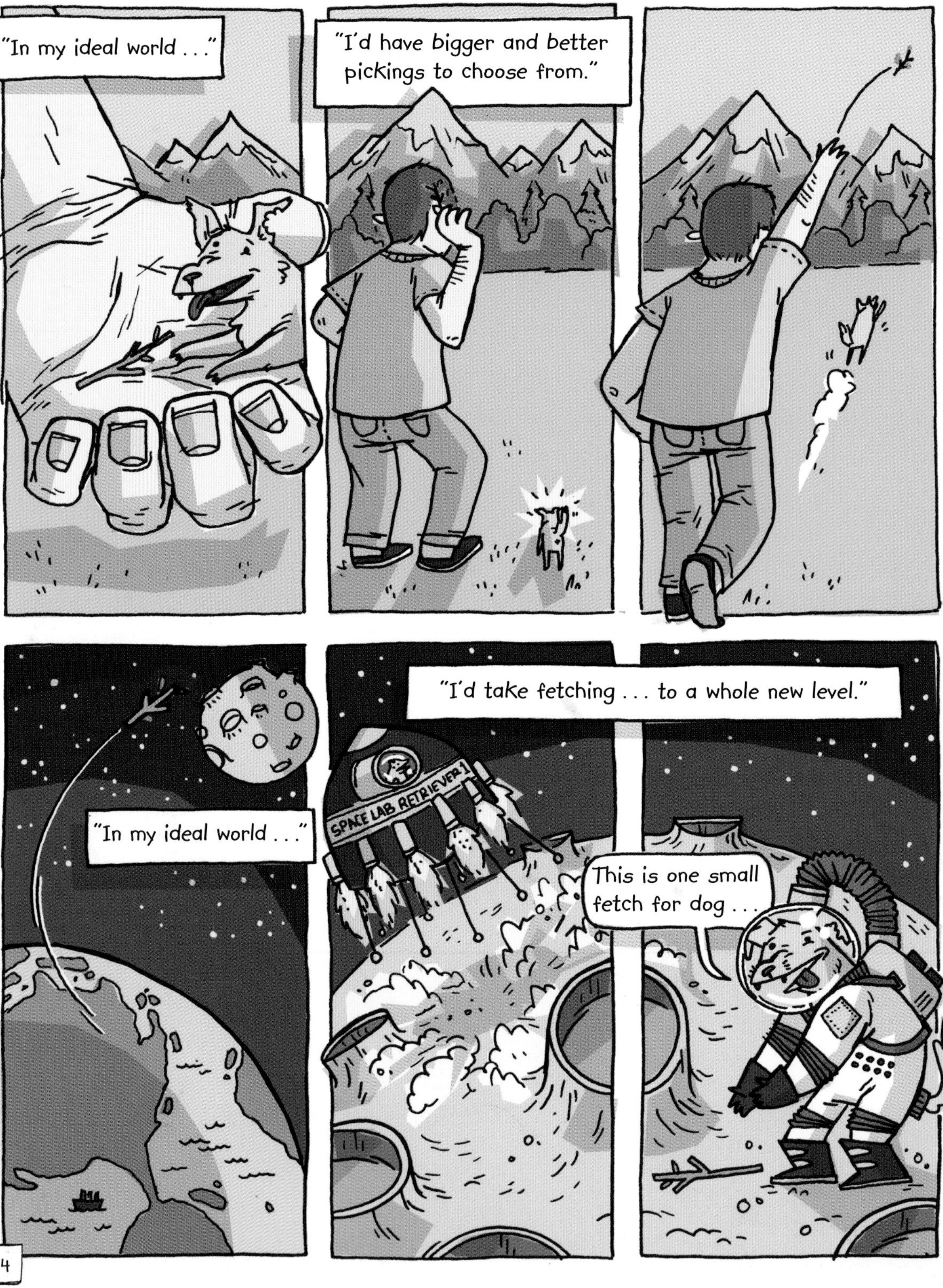
"In my ideal world . . ."
"I'd have bigger and better pickings to choose from."
"In my ideal world . . ."
SPACE LAB RETRIEVER 1
"I'd take fetching . . . to a whole new level."
This is one small fetch for dog . . .

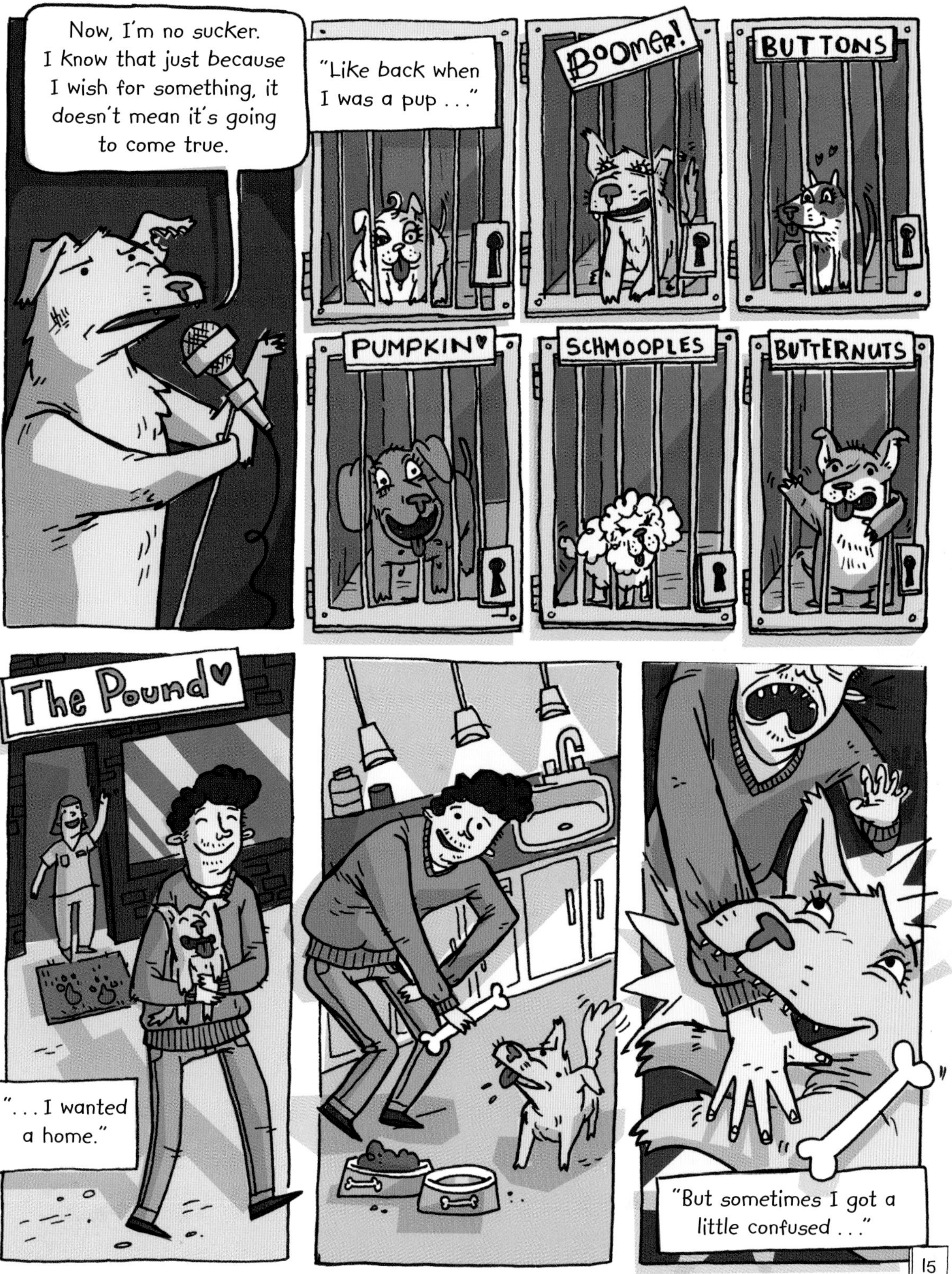

Now, I'm no *sucker*. I know that just *because* I wish for something, it doesn't mean it's going to come true.
"Like *back* when I was a pup . . ."
BOOMER!
BUTTONS
PUMPKIN♥
SCHMOOPLES
BUTTERNUTS
The Pound♥
". . . I wanted a home."
"But sometimes I got a little confused . . ."

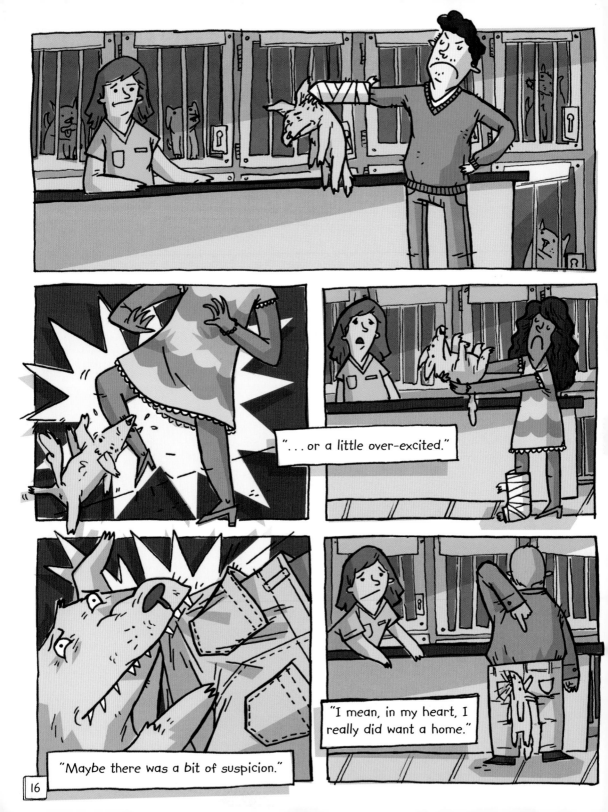

"... or a little over-excited."

"Maybe there was a bit of suspicion."

"I mean, in my heart, I really did want a home."

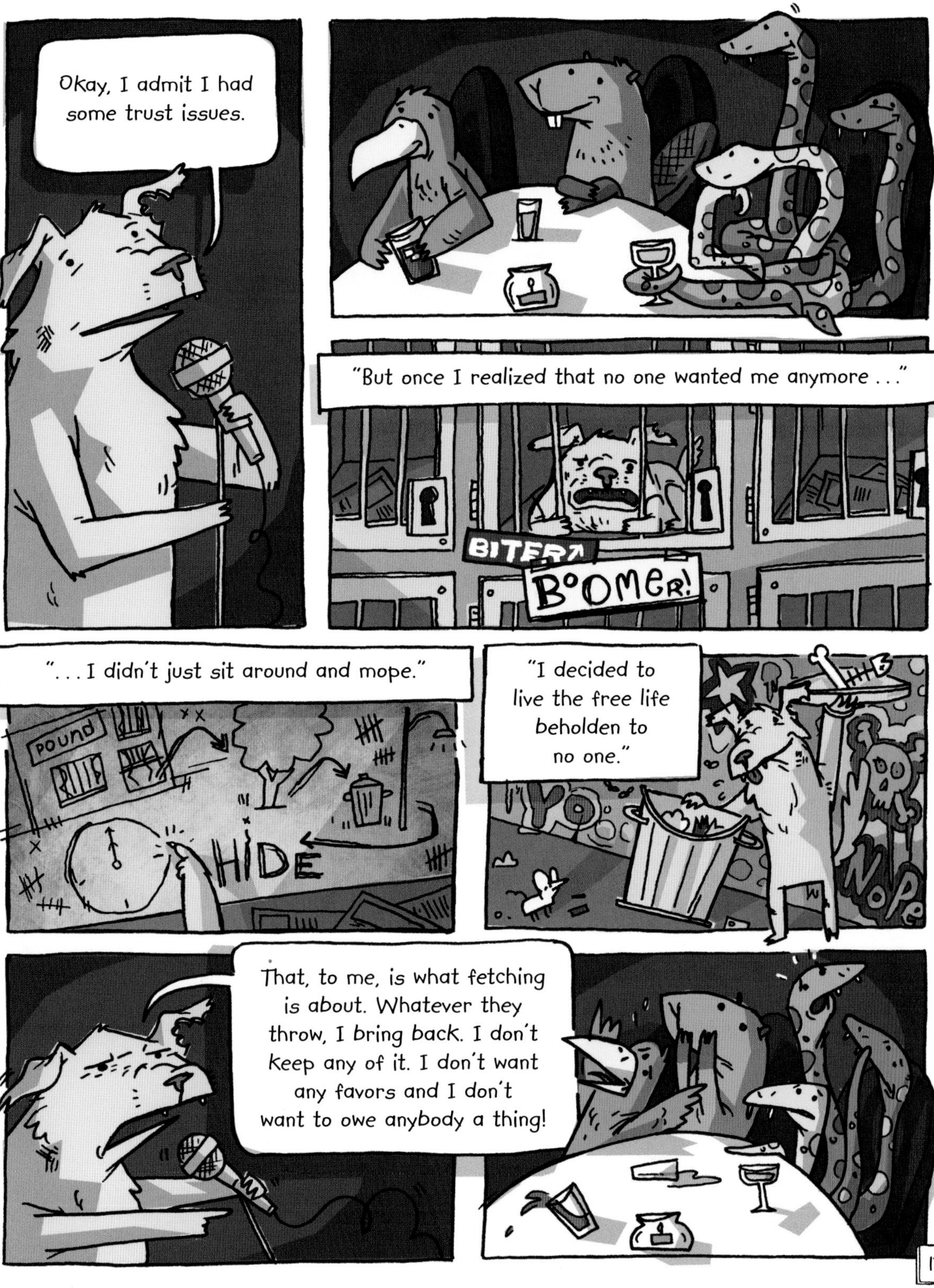
Okay, I admit I had some trust issues.
"But once I realized that no one wanted me anymore . . ."
BITER
BoOMER!
". . . I didn't just sit around and mope."
POUND
HIDE
"I decided to live the free life beholden to no one."
YO
NOPE
That, to me, is what fetching is about. Whatever they throw, I bring back. I don't keep any of it. I don't want any favors and I don't want to owe anybody a thing!

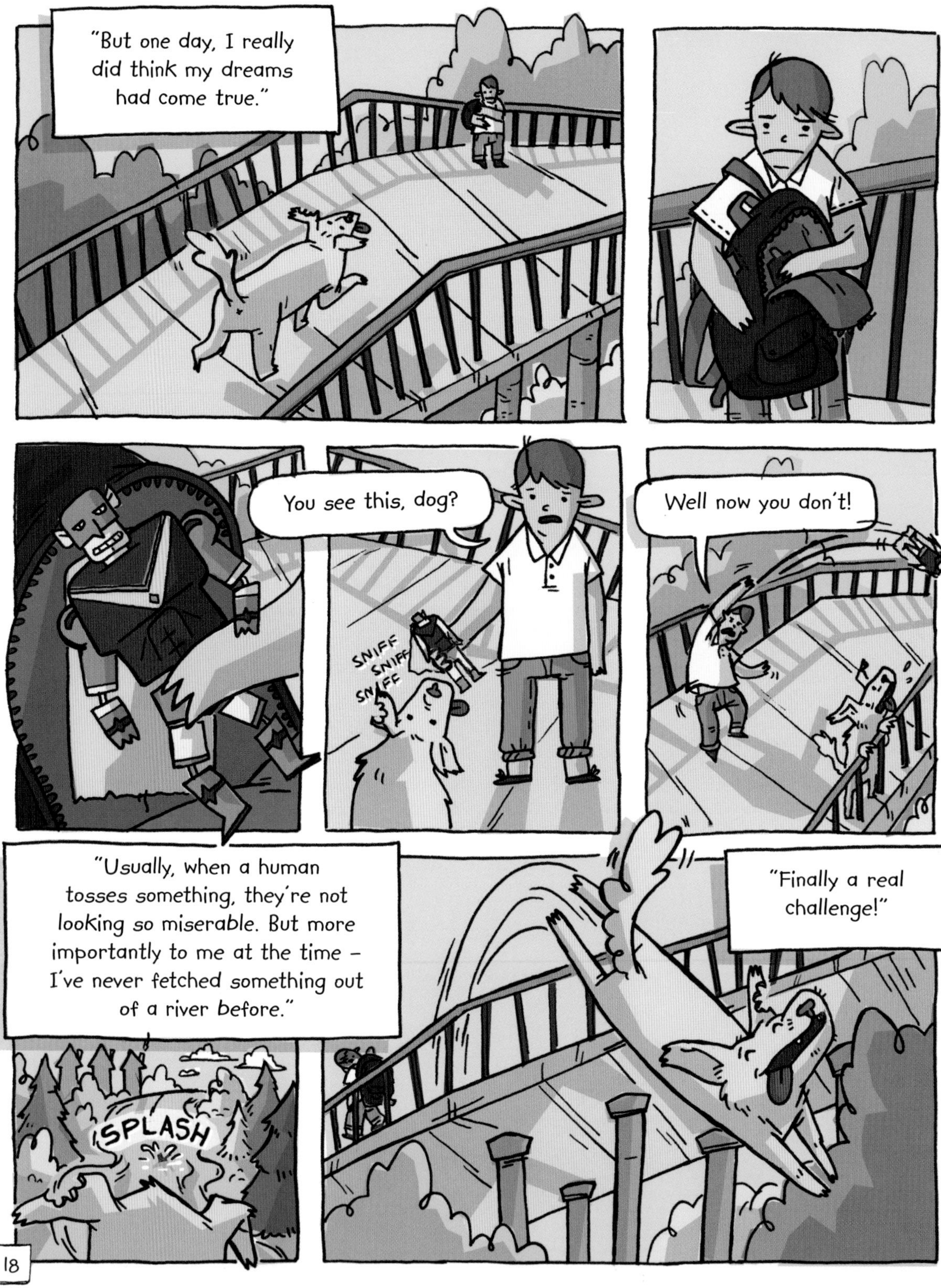
"But one day, I really did think my dreams had come true."
You see this, dog?
SNIFF SNIFF SNIFF
Well now you don't!
"Usually, when a human tosses something, they're not looking so miserable. But more importantly to me at the time – I've never fetched something out of a river before."
"Finally a real challenge!"
SPLASH

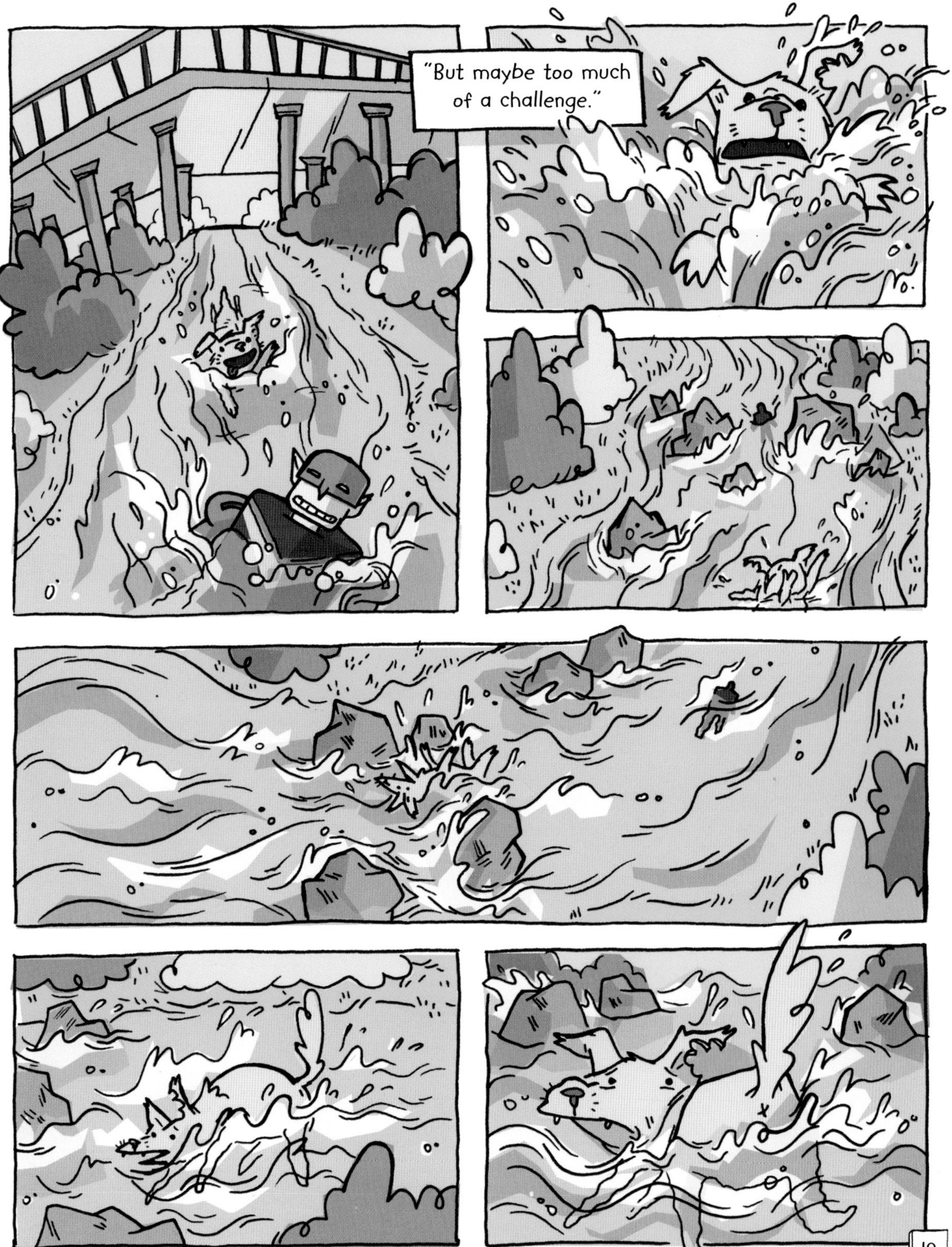
"But maybe too much of a challenge."

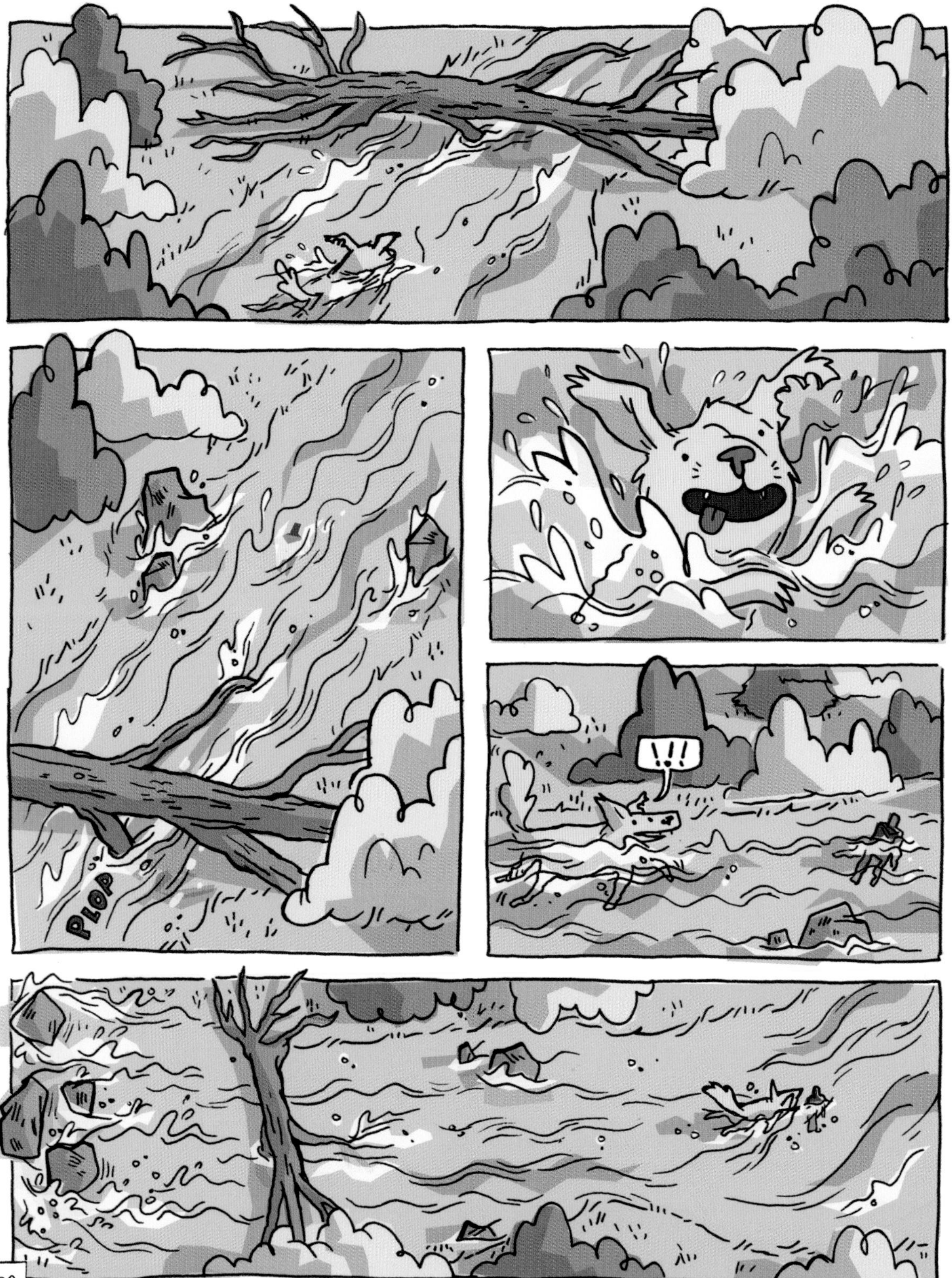
PLOP
!!!

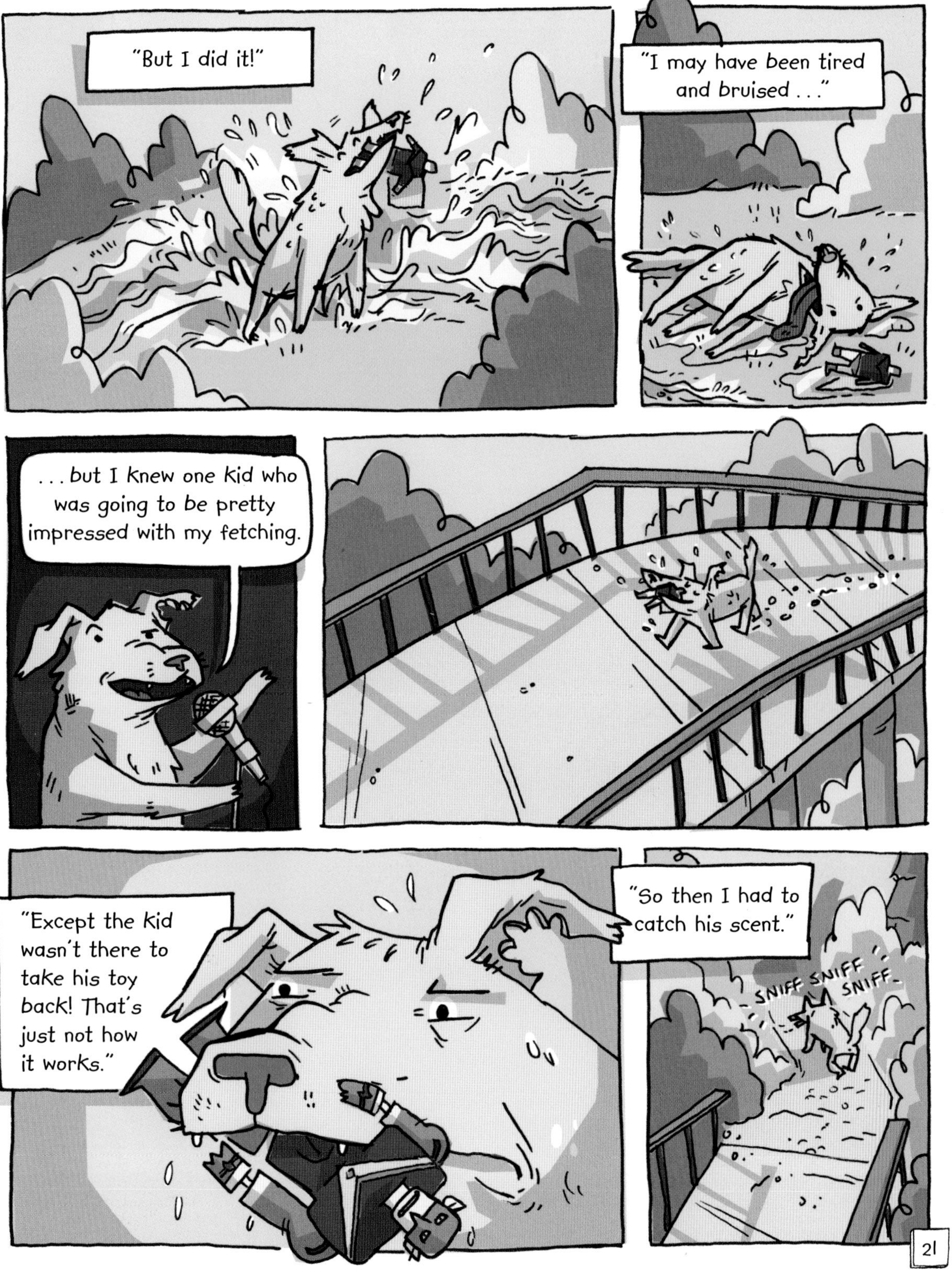
"But I did it!"
"I may have been tired and bruised . . ."
. . . but I knew one kid who was going to be pretty impressed with my fetching.
"Except the kid wasn't there to take his toy back! That's just not how it works."
"So then I had to catch his scent."
SNIFF SNIFF SNIFF

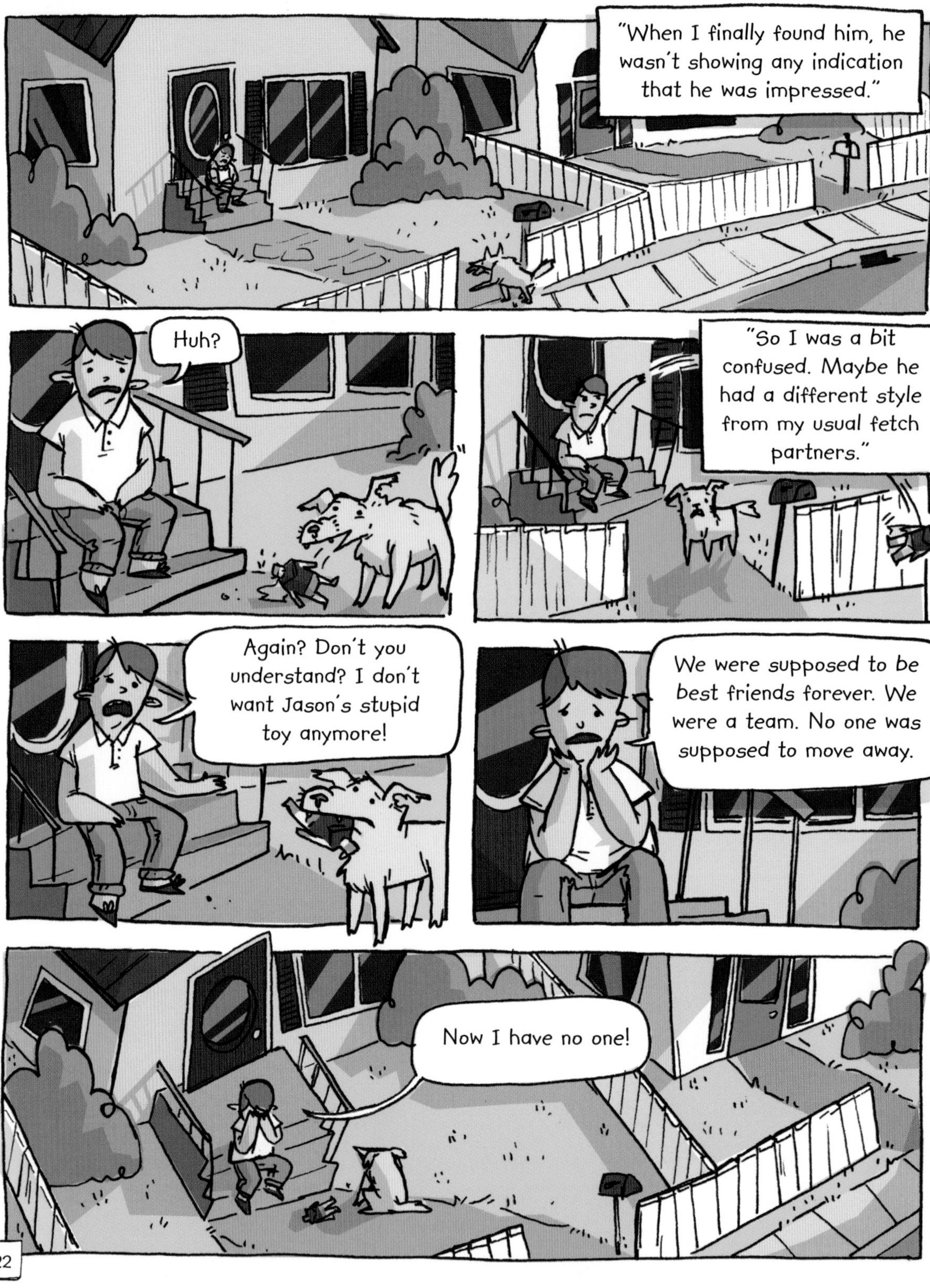
"When I finally found him, he wasn't showing any indication that he was impressed."
Huh?
"So I was a bit confused. Maybe he had a different style from my usual fetch partners."
Again? Don't you understand? I don't want Jason's stupid toy anymore!
We were supposed to be best friends forever. We were a team. No one was supposed to move away.
Now I have no one!

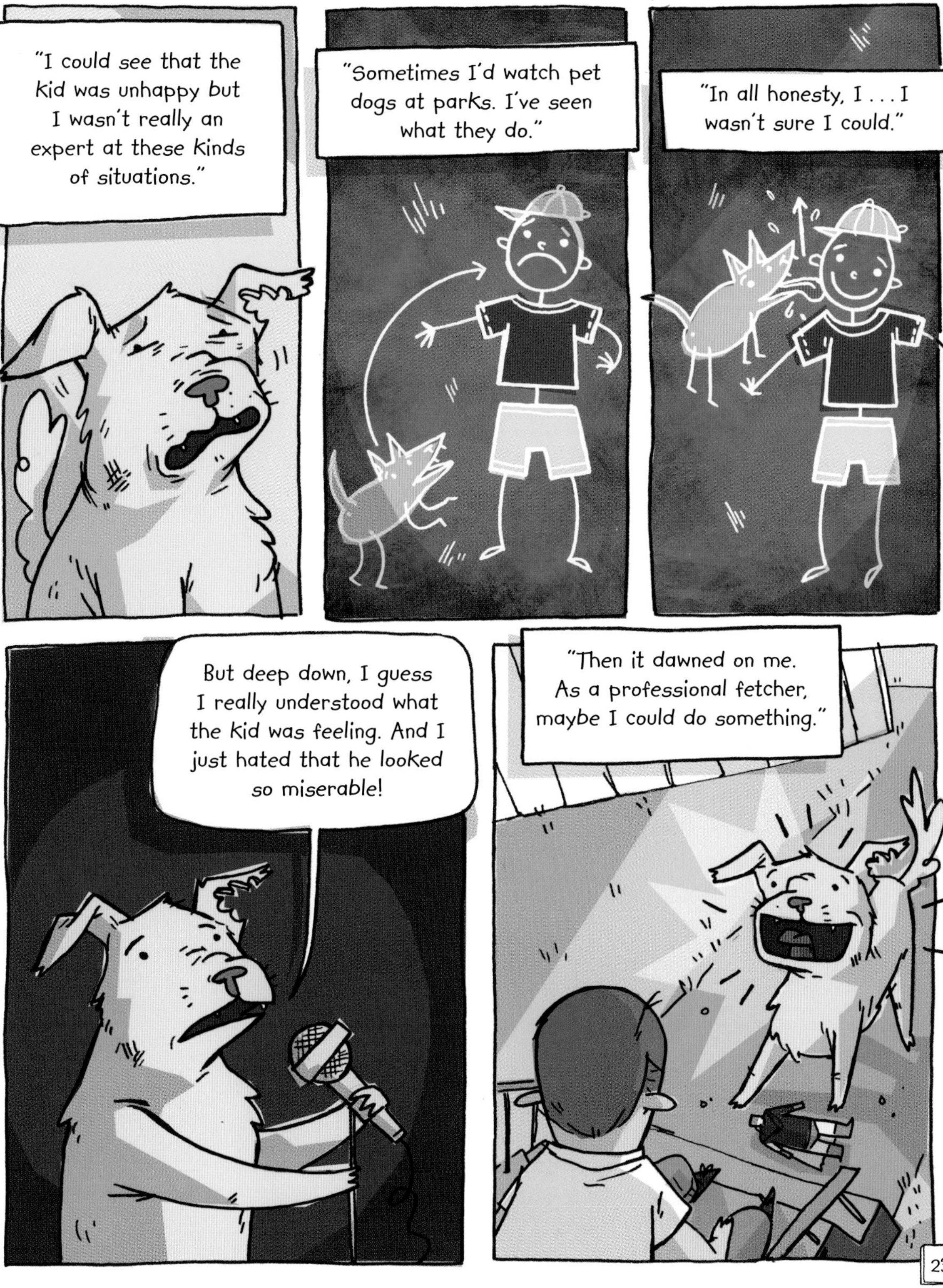

"I could see that the kid was unhappy but I wasn't really an expert at these kinds of situations."
"Sometimes I'd watch pet dogs at parks. I've seen what they do."
"In all honesty, I . . . I wasn't sure I could."
But deep down, I guess I really understood what the kid was feeling. And I just hated that he looked so miserable!
"Then it dawned on me. As a professional fetcher, maybe I could do something."

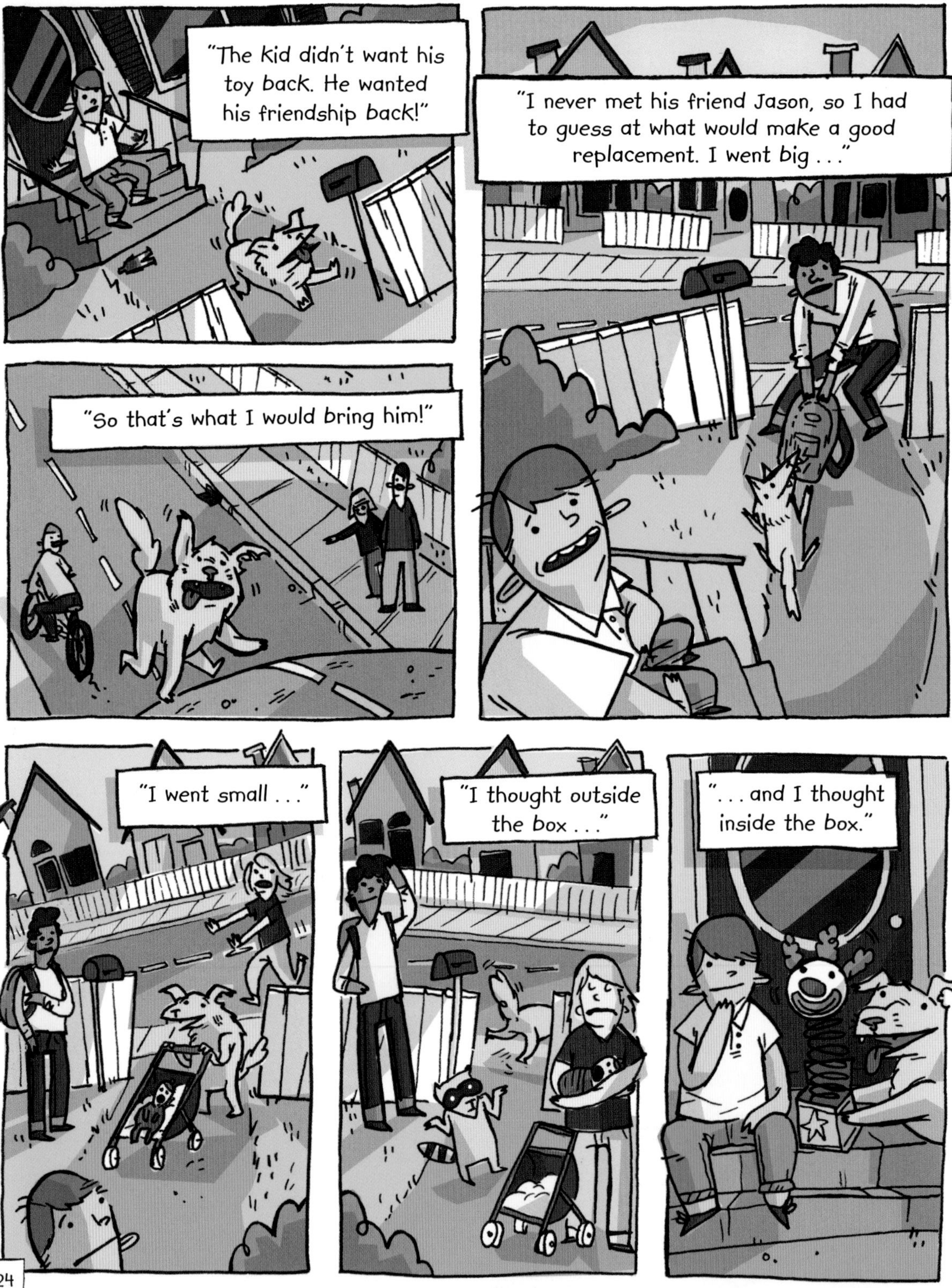
"The kid didn't want his toy back. He wanted his friendship back!"
"I never met his friend Jason, so I had to guess at what would make a good replacement. I went big . . ."
"So that's what I would bring him!"
"I went small . . ."
"I thought outside the box . . ."
". . . and I thought inside the box."

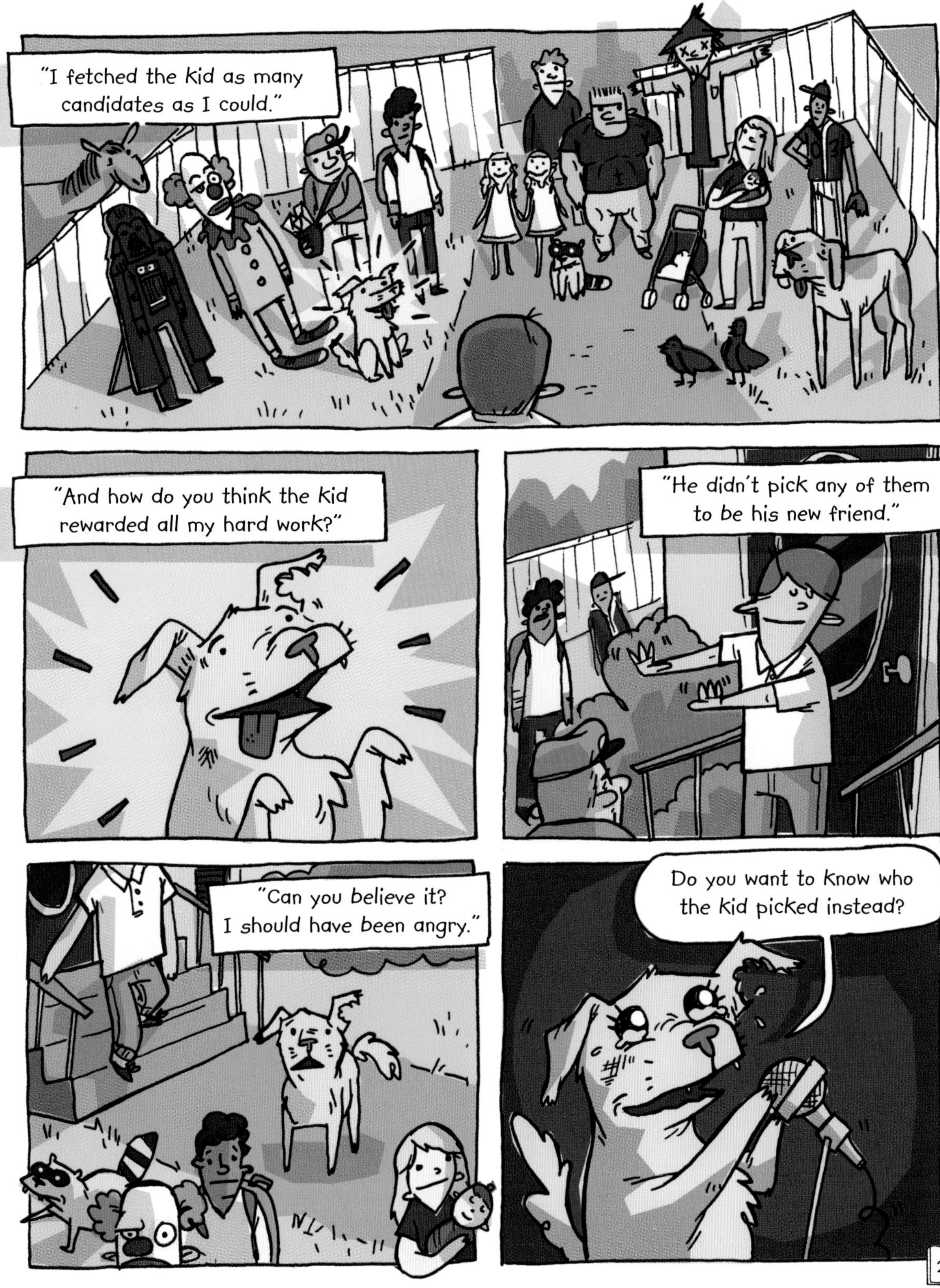
"I fetched the kid as many candidates as I could."
"And how do you think the kid rewarded all my hard work?"
"He didn't pick any of them to be his new friend."
"Can you believe it? I should have been angry."
Do you want to know who the kid picked instead?

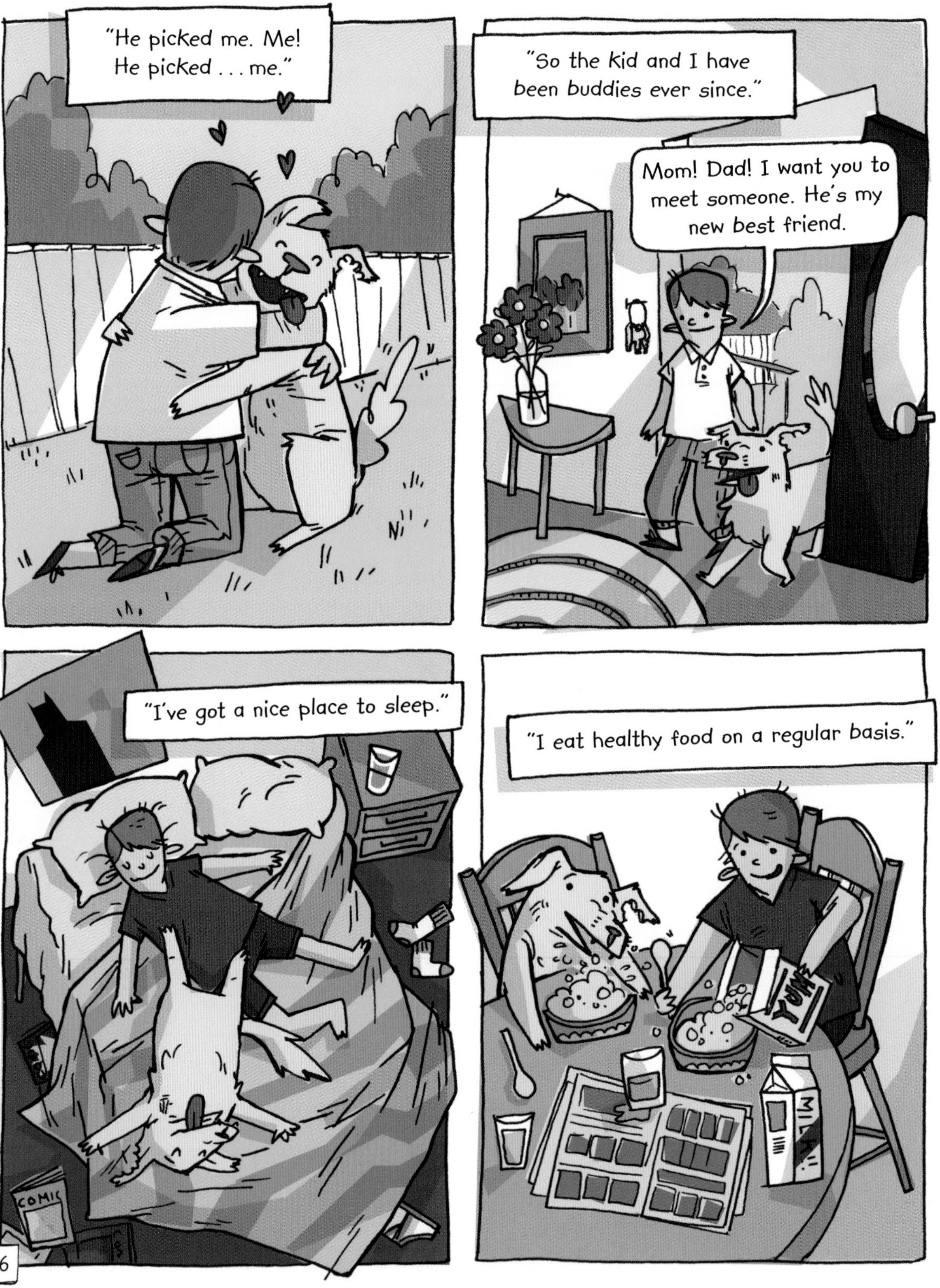
"He picked me. Me! He picked . . . me."
"So the kid and I have been buddies ever since."
Mom! Dad! I want you to meet someone. He's my new best friend.
"I've got a nice place to sleep."
COMIC
"I eat healthy food on a regular basis."
YUM
MILK

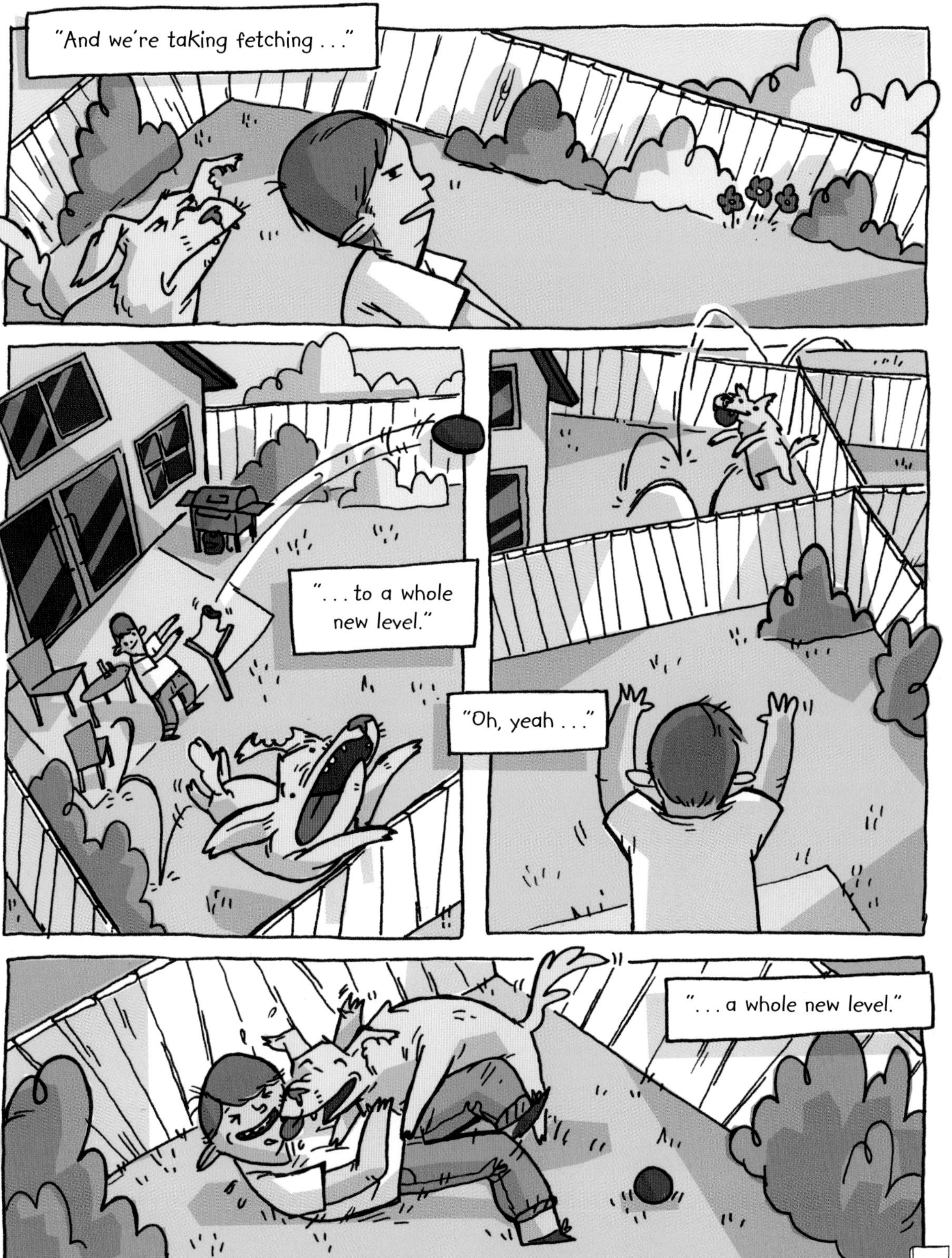
"And we're taking fetching . . ."
". . . to a whole new level."
"Oh, yeah . . ."
". . . a whole new level."

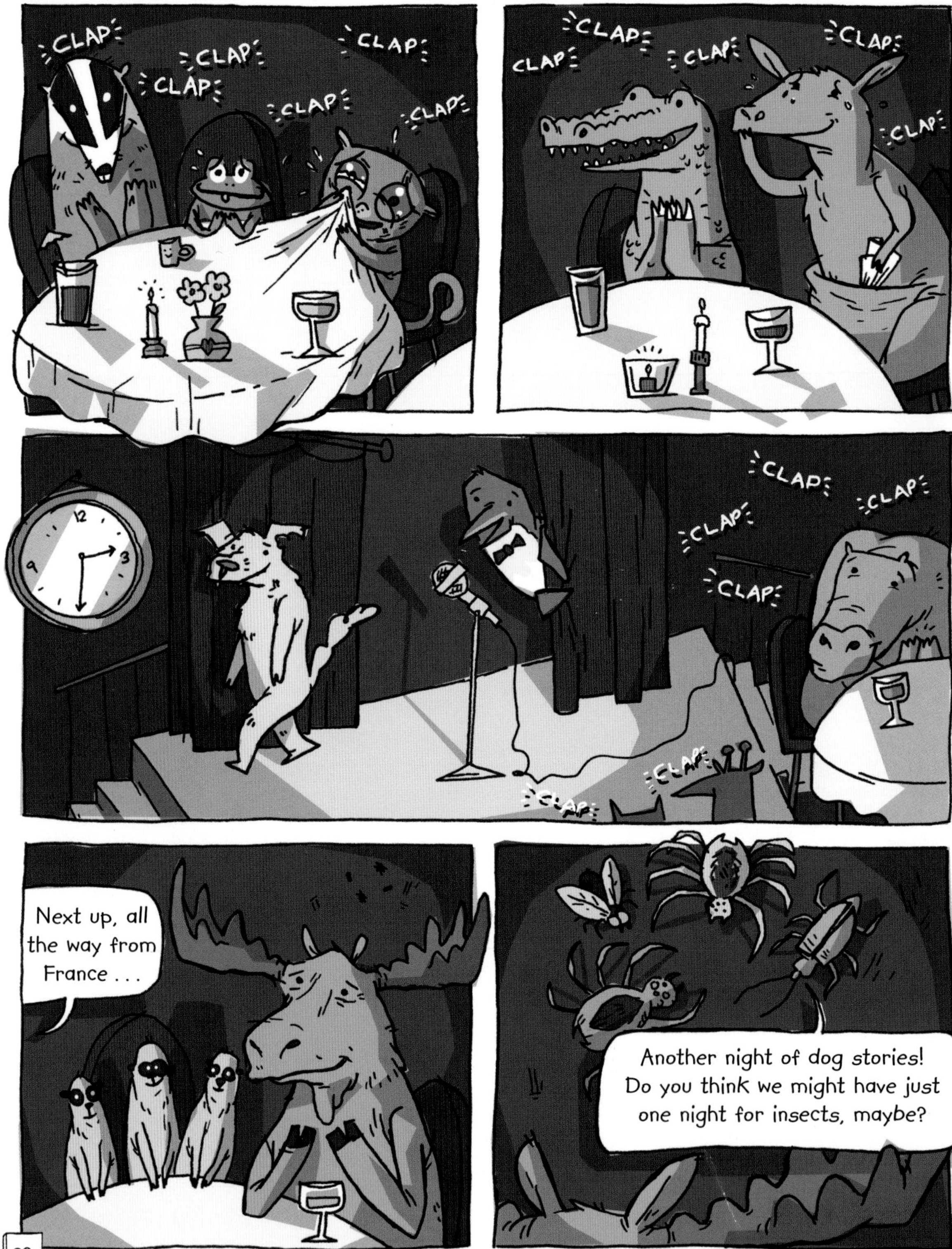
CLAP
CLAP
CLAP
CLAP
CLAP
CLAP
CLAP
CLAP
CLAP
CLAP
CLAP
CLAP
CLAP
CLAP
CLAP
CLAP
CLAP
Next up, all the way from France . . .
Another night of dog stories! Do you think we might have just one night for insects, maybe?

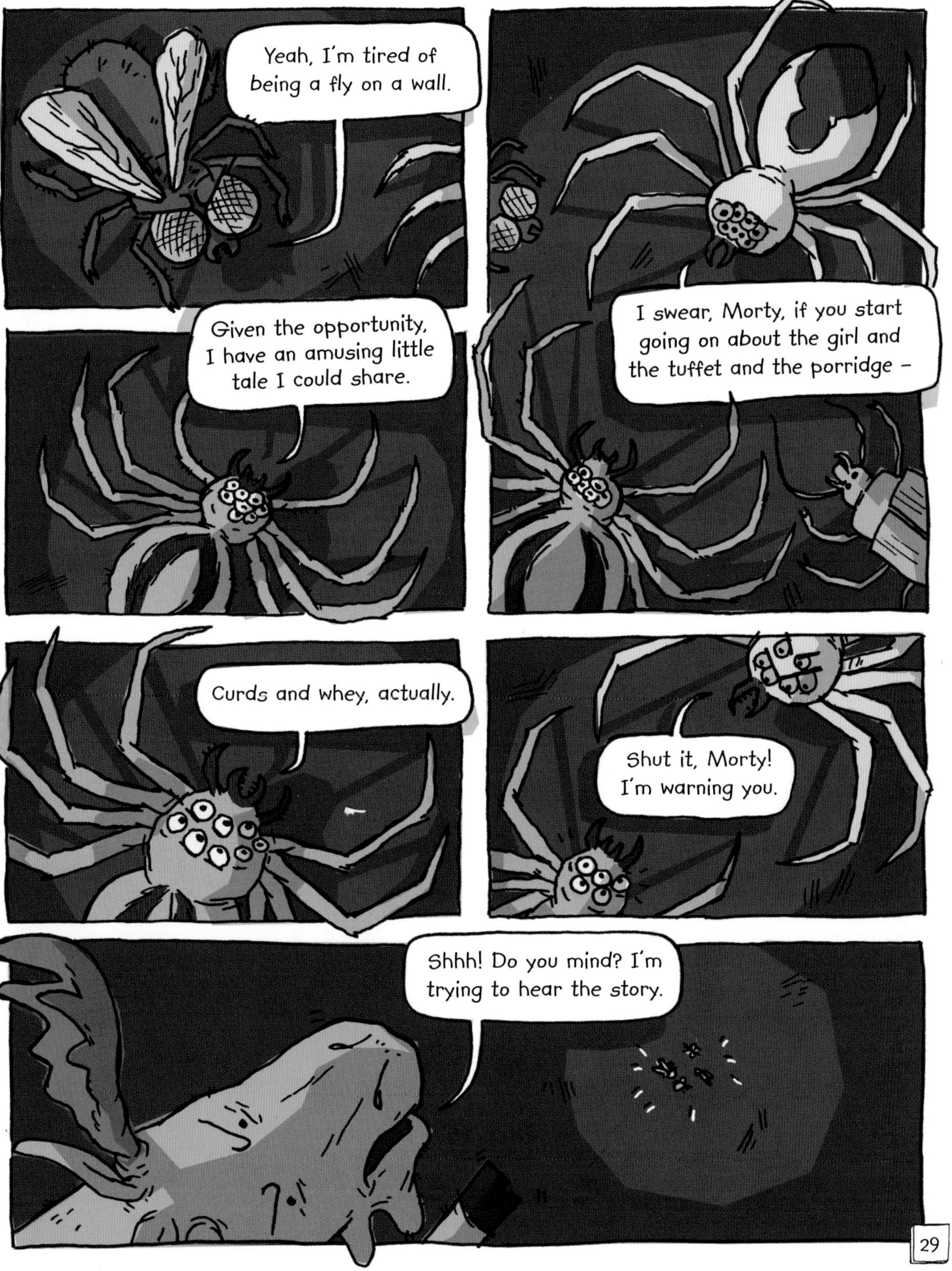
Yeah, I'm tired of being a fly on a wall.
Given the opportunity, I have an amusing little tale I could share.
I swear, Morty, if you start going on about the girl and the tuffet and the porridge –
Curds and whey, actually.
Shut it, Morty! I'm warning you.
Shhh! Do you mind? I'm trying to hear the story.

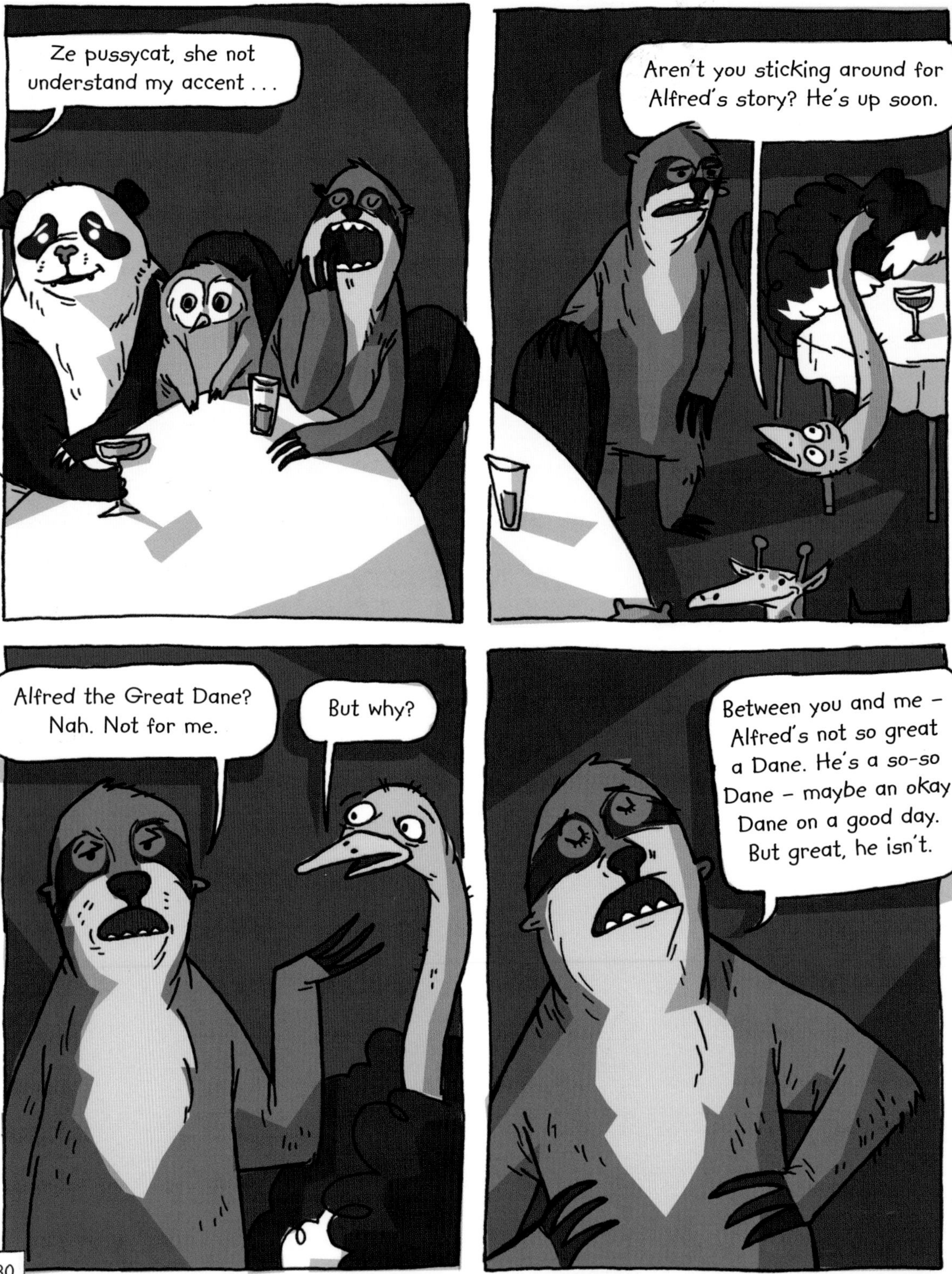
Ze pussycat, she not understand my accent . . .
Aren't you sticking around for Alfred's story? He's up soon.
Alfred the Great Dane? Nah. Not for me.
But why?
Between you and me – Alfred's not so great a Dane. He's a so-so Dane – maybe an okay Dane on a good day. But great, he isn't.

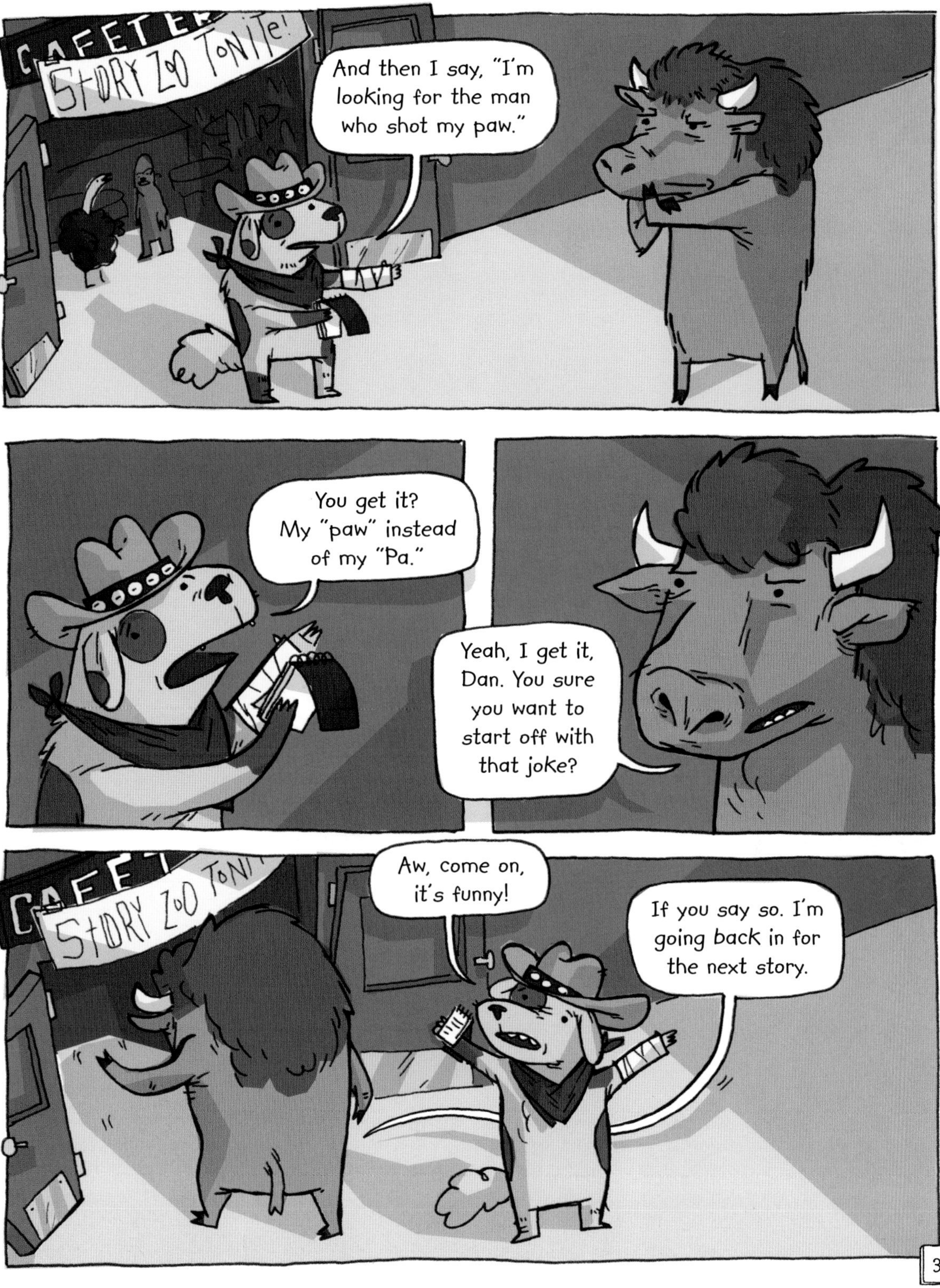
CAFETER
STORY ZOO TONITE!
And then I say, "I'm looking for the man who shot my paw."
You get it? My "paw" instead of my "Pa."
Yeah, I get it, Dan. You sure you want to start off with that joke?
Aw, come on, it's funny!
If you say so. I'm going back in for the next story.

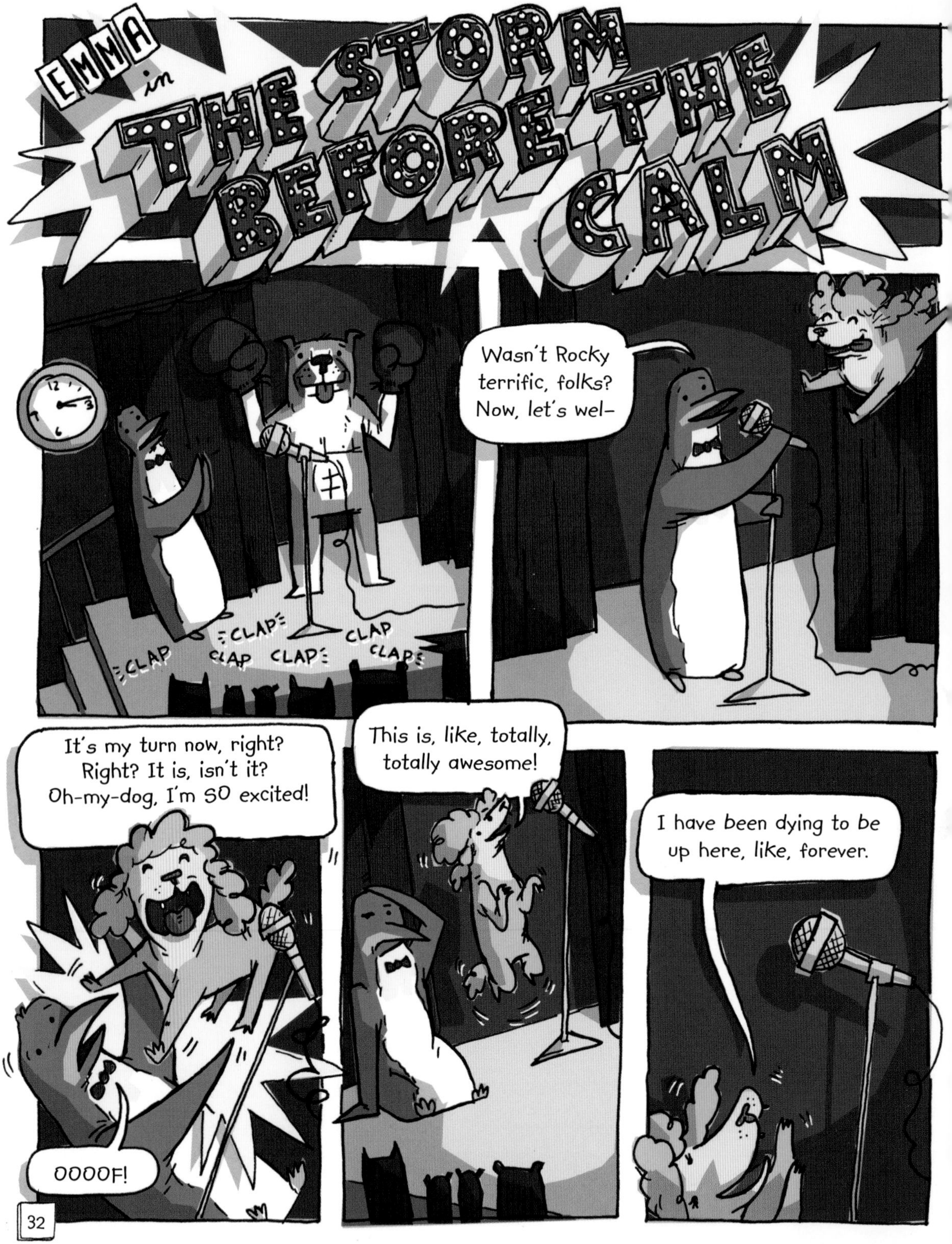
EMMA in
THE STORM BEFORE THE CALM
CLAP CLAP CLAP CLAP CLAP CLAP
Wasn't Rocky terrific, folks? Now, let's wel–
It's my turn now, right? Right? It is, isn't it? Oh-my-dog, I'm SO excited!
OOOOF!
This is, like, totally, totally awesome!
I have been dying to be up here, like, forever.

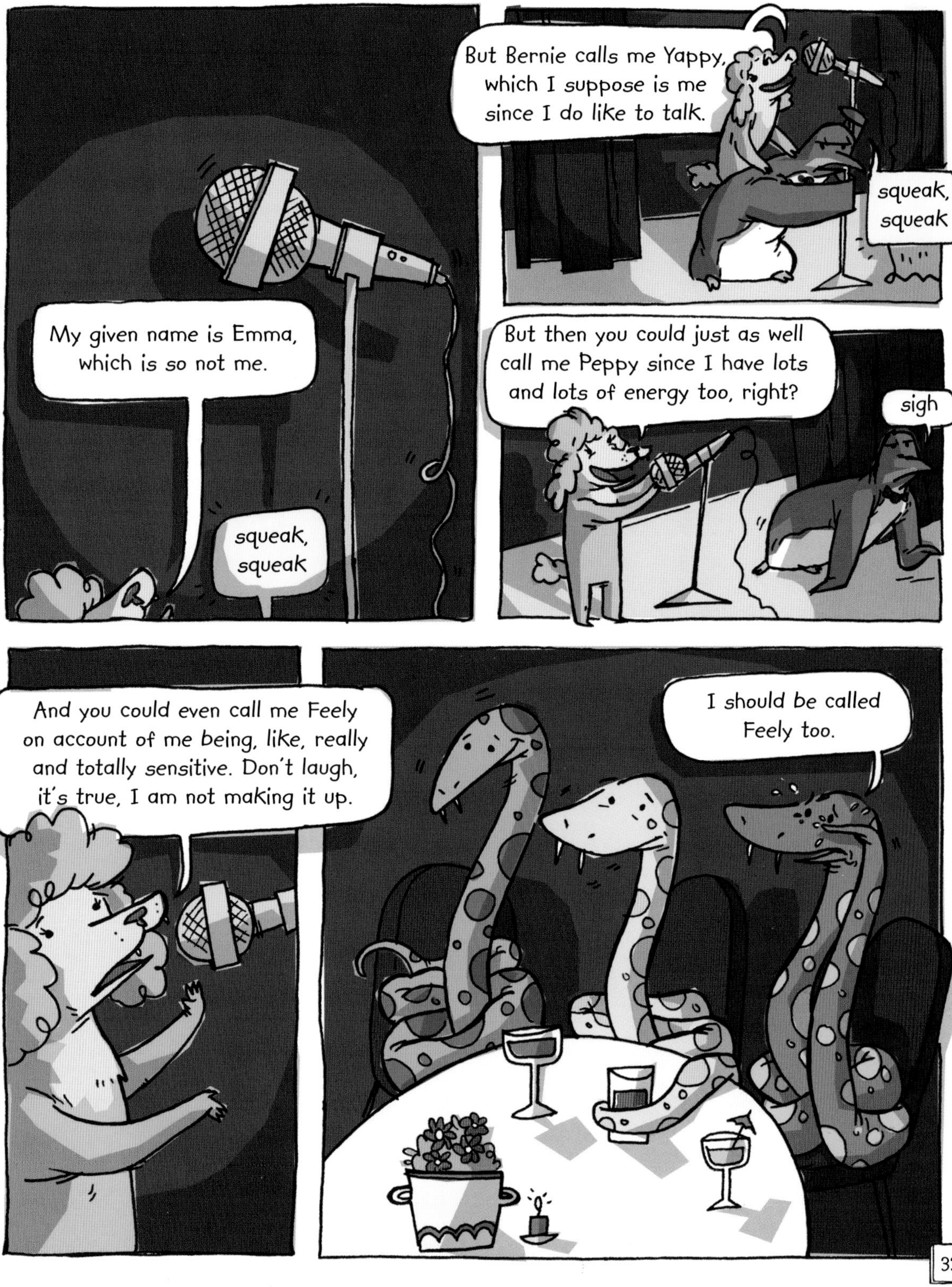
My given name is Emma, which is so not me.
squeak, squeak
But Bernie calls me Yappy, which I suppose is me since I do like to talk.
squeak, squeak
But then you could just as well call me Peppy since I have lots and lots of energy too, right?
sigh
And you could even call me Feely on account of me being, like, really and totally sensitive. Don't laugh, it's true, I am not making it up.
I should be called Feely too.

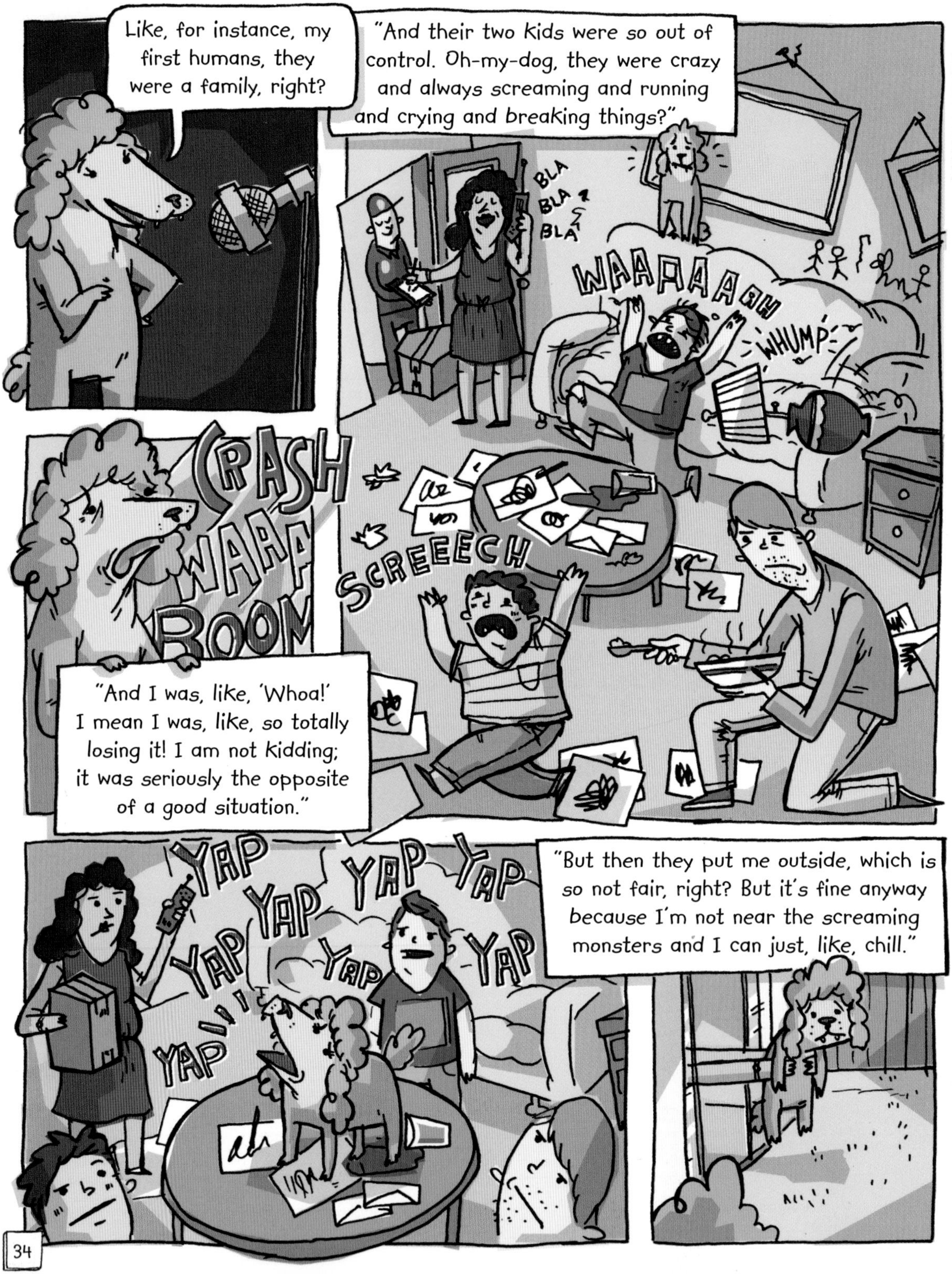

Like, for instance, my first humans, they were a family, right?
"And their two kids were so out of control. Oh-my-dog, they were crazy and always screaming and running and crying and breaking things?"
BLA BLA BLA
WAAAAAAGH
WHUMP
CRASH
WAAP
BOOM
SCREEECH
"And I was, like, 'Whoa!' I mean I was, like, so totally losing it! I am not kidding; it was seriously the opposite of a good situation."
YAP YAP YAP YAP YAP YAP YAP YAP
"But then they put me outside, which is so not fair, right? But it's fine anyway because I'm not near the screaming monsters and I can just, like, chill."

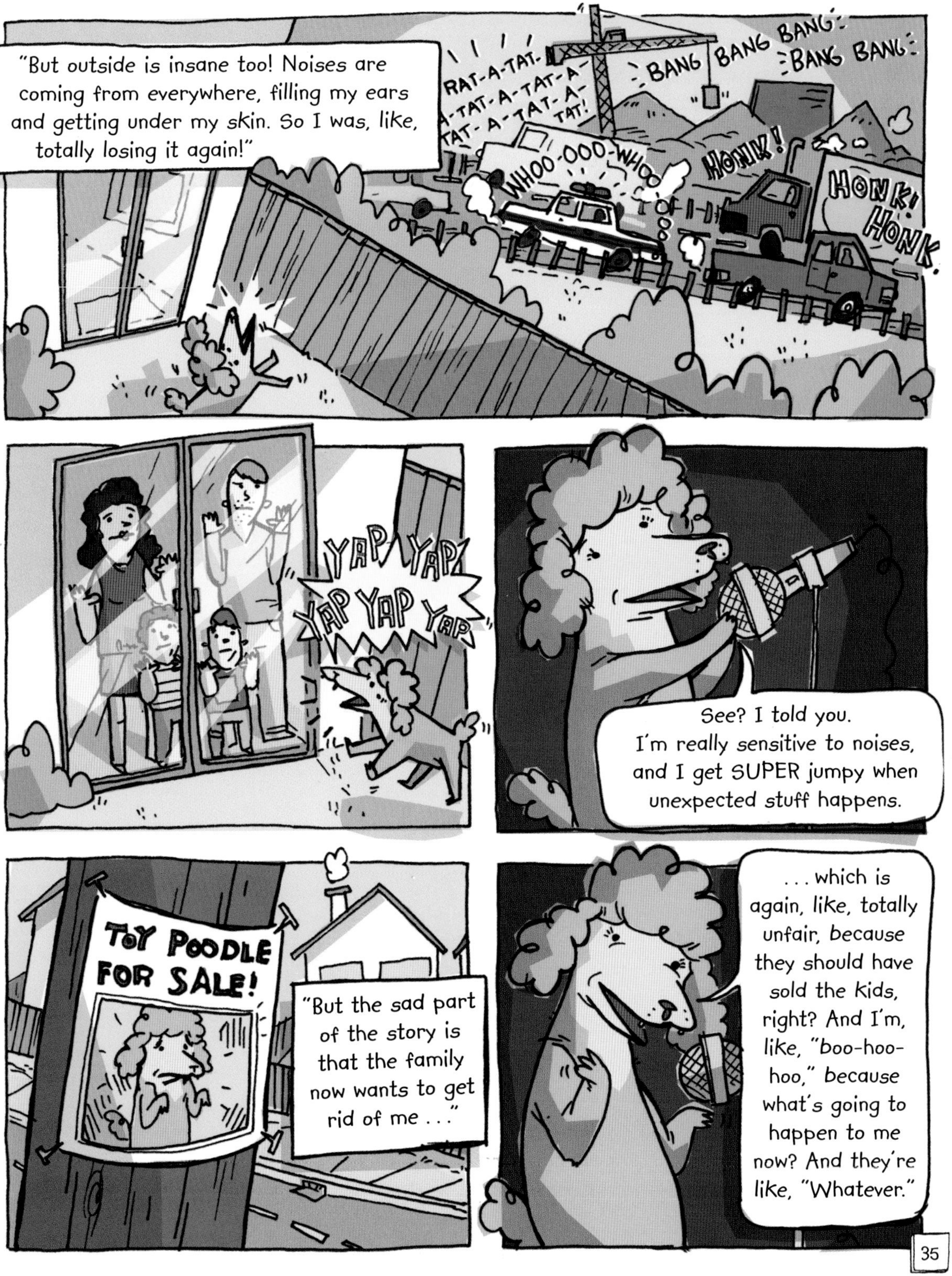
"But outside is insane too! Noises are coming from everywhere, filling my ears and getting under my skin. So I was, like, totally losing it again!"
RAT-A-TAT-A-TAT-A-TAT-A-TAT-A-TAT-A-TAT!
BANG BANG BANG BANG BANG
WHOO-OOO-WHOO
HONK! HONK! HONK!
YAP YAP YAP YAP YAP
See? I told you. I'm really sensitive to noises, and I get SUPER jumpy when unexpected stuff happens.
TOY POODLE FOR SALE!
"But the sad part of the story is that the family now wants to get rid of me . . ."
. . . which is again, like, totally unfair, because they should have sold the kids, right? And I'm, like, "boo-hoo-hoo," because what's going to happen to me now? And they're like, "Whatever."

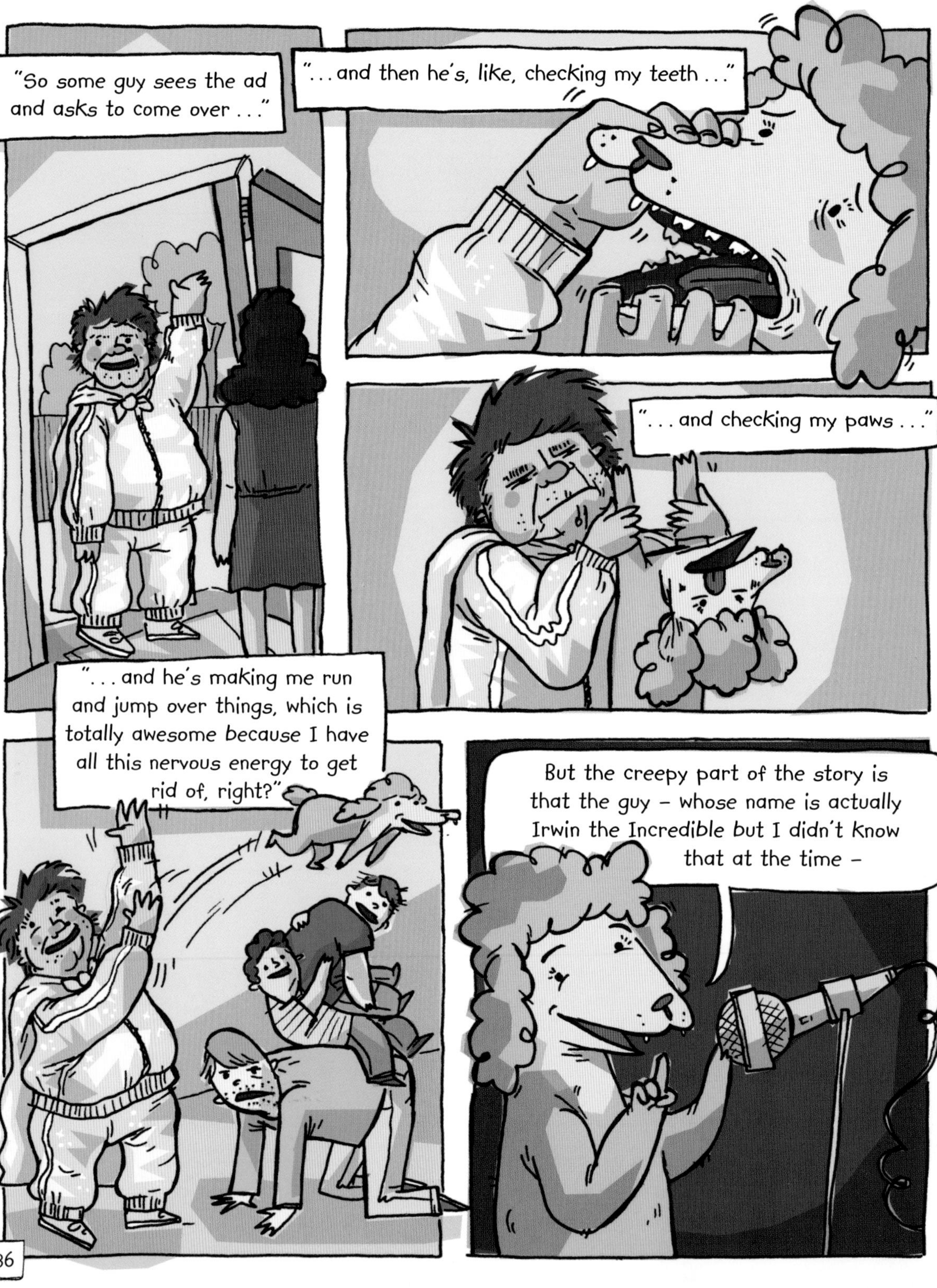
"So some guy sees the ad and asks to come over . . ."
". . . and then he's, like, checking my teeth . . ."
". . . and checking my paws . . ."
". . . and he's making me run and jump over things, which is totally awesome because I have all this nervous energy to get rid of, right?"
But the creepy part of the story is that the guy – whose name is actually Irwin the Incredible but I didn't know that at the time –

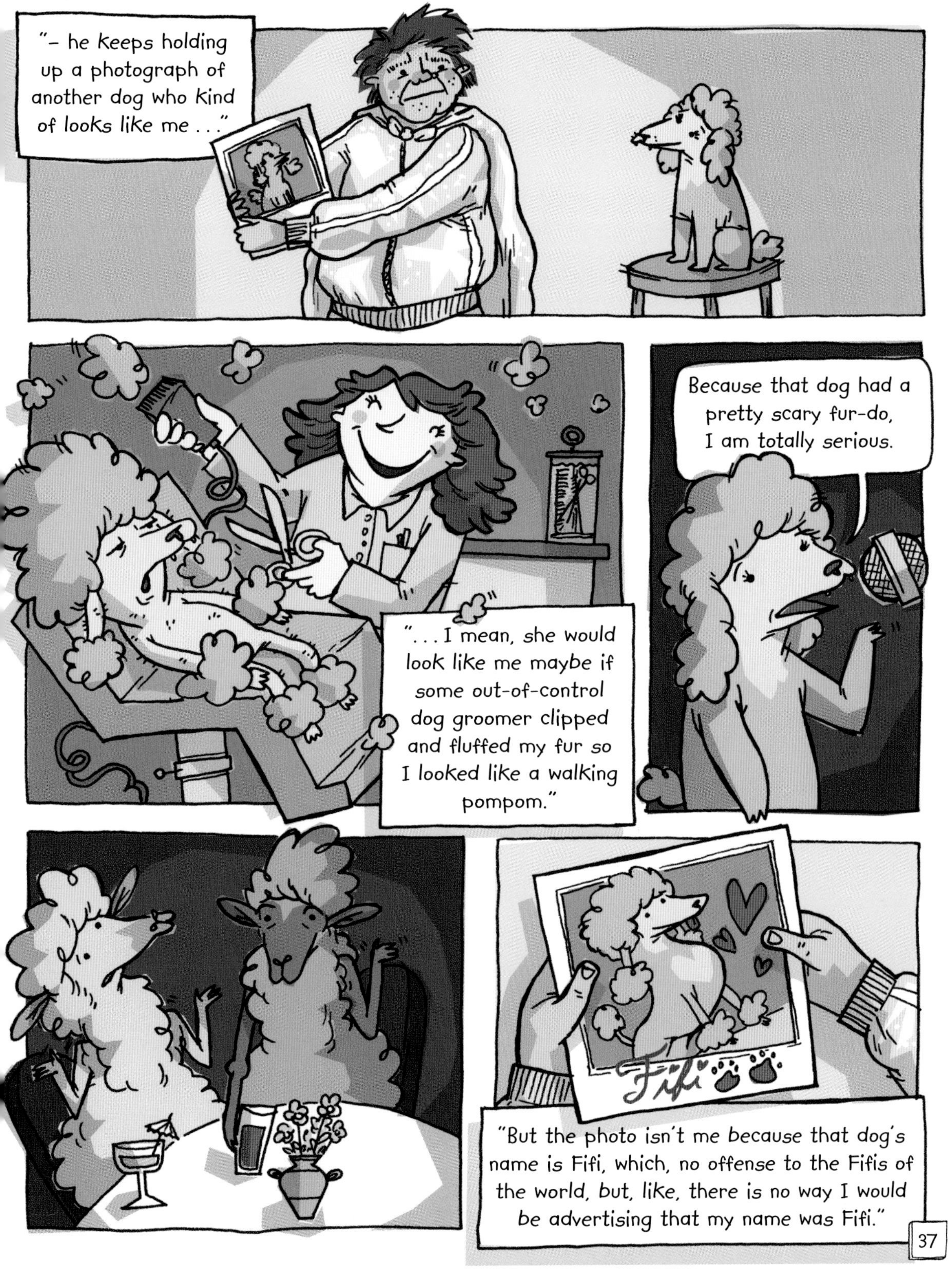
"– he keeps holding up a photograph of another dog who kind of looks like me . . ."
Because that dog had a pretty scary fur-do, I am totally serious.
". . . I mean, she would look like me maybe if some out-of-control dog groomer clipped and fluffed my fur so I looked like a walking pompom."
Fifi
"But the photo isn't me because that dog's name is Fifi, which, no offense to the Fifis of the world, but, like, there is no way I would be advertising that my name was Fifi."

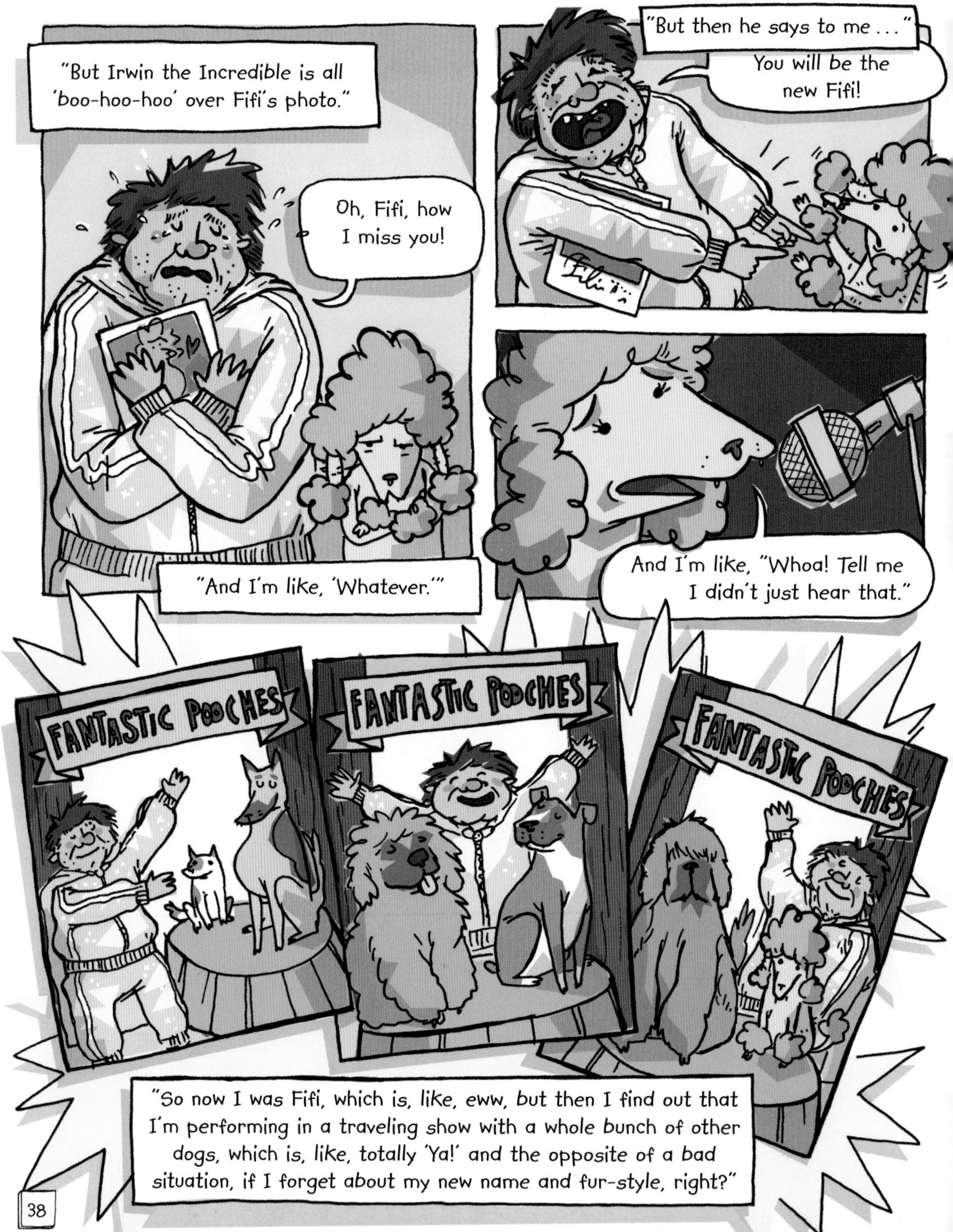
"But Irwin the Incredible is all 'boo-hoo-hoo' over Fifi's photo."
Oh, Fifi, how I miss you!
"And I'm like, 'Whatever.'"
"But then he says to me . . ."
You will be the new Fifi!
And I'm like, "Whoa! Tell me I didn't just hear that."
FANTASTIC POOCHES
FANTASTIC POOCHES
FANTASTIC POOCHES
"So now I was Fifi, which is, like, eww, but then I find out that I'm performing in a traveling show with a whole bunch of other dogs, which is, like, totally 'Ya!' and the opposite of a bad situation, if I forget about my new name and fur-style, right?"

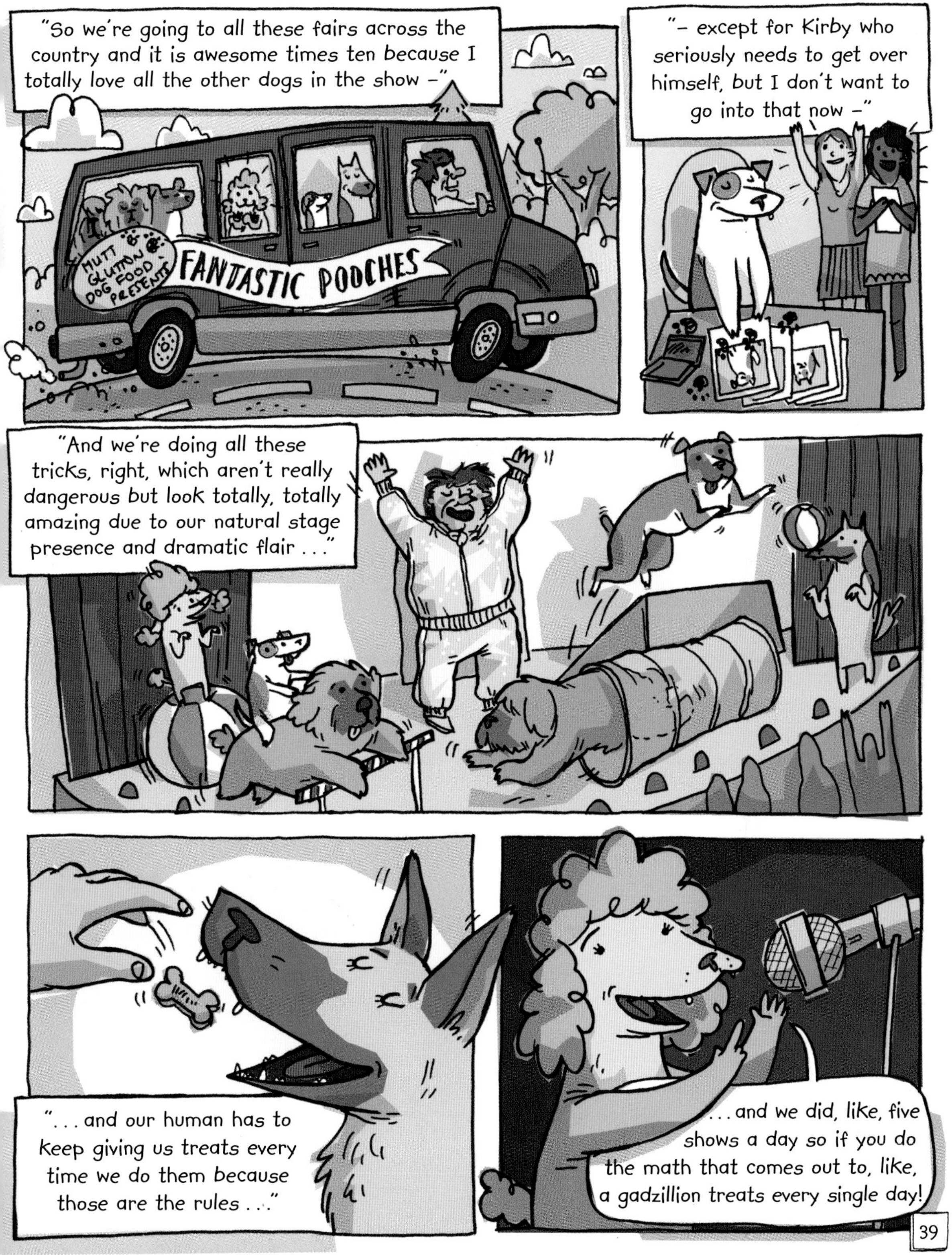
"So we're going to all these fairs across the country and it is awesome times ten because I totally love all the other dogs in the show –"
MUTT & GLUTTON DOG FOOD PRESENTS
FANTASTIC POOCHES
"– except for Kirby who seriously needs to get over himself, but I don't want to go into that now –"
"And we're doing all these tricks, right, which aren't really dangerous but look totally, totally amazing due to our natural stage presence and dramatic flair . . ."
". . . and our human has to keep giving us treats every time we do them because those are the rules . . ."
. . . and we did, like, five shows a day so if you do the math that comes out to, like, a gadzillion treats every single day!

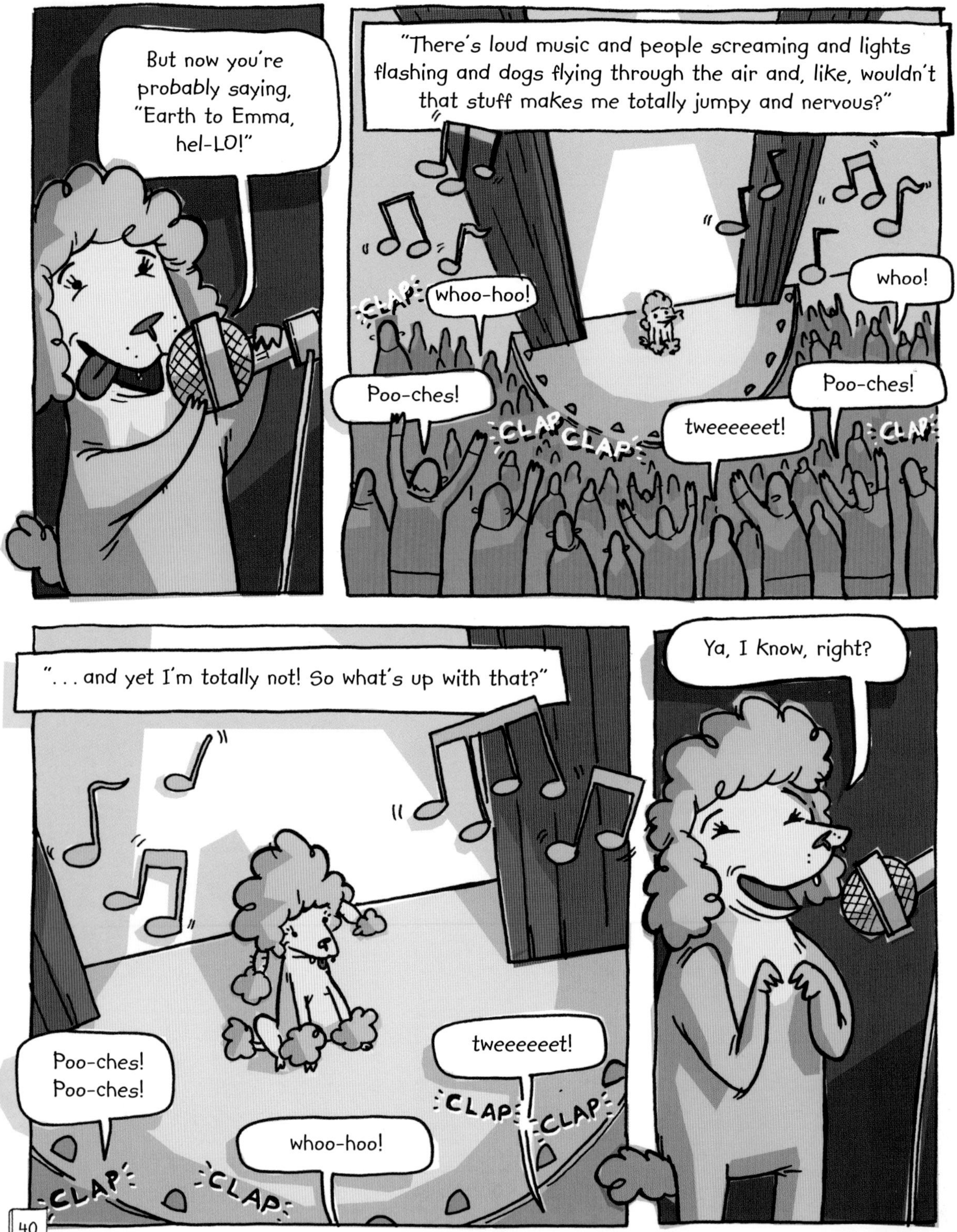

But now you're probably saying, "Earth to Emma, hel-LO!"
"There's loud music and people screaming and lights flashing and dogs flying through the air and, like, wouldn't that stuff makes me totally jumpy and nervous?"
CLAP
whoo-hoo!
whoo!
Poo-ches!
Poo-ches!
CLAP CLAP
tweeeeeet!
CLAP
"... and yet I'm totally not! So what's up with that?"
Poo-ches! Poo-ches!
tweeeeeet!
CLAP
CLAP
whoo-hoo!
CLAP
CLAP
Ya, I know, right?

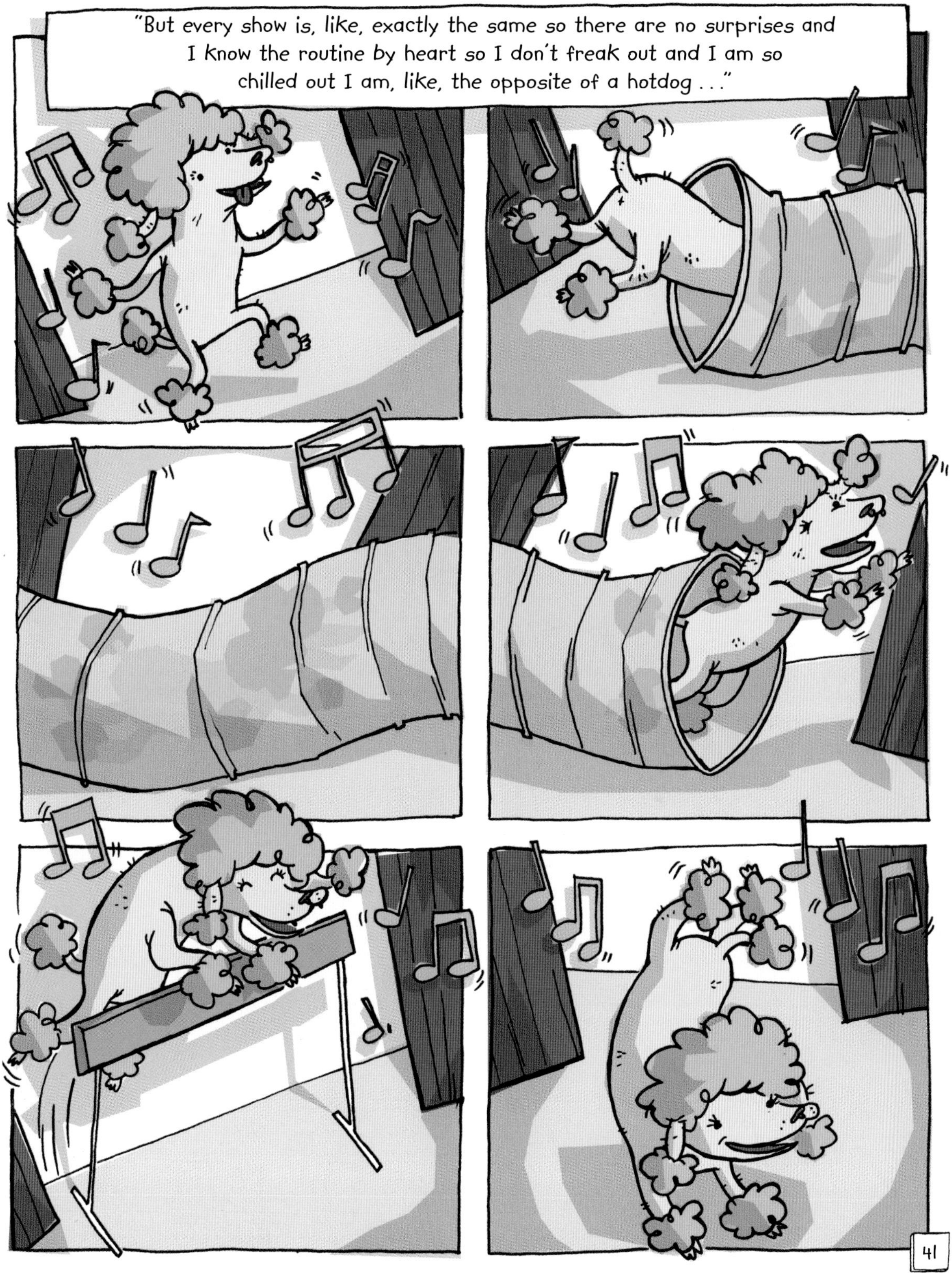
"But every show is, like, exactly the same so there are no surprises and I know the routine by heart so I don't freak out and I am so chilled out I am, like, the opposite of a hotdog . . ."

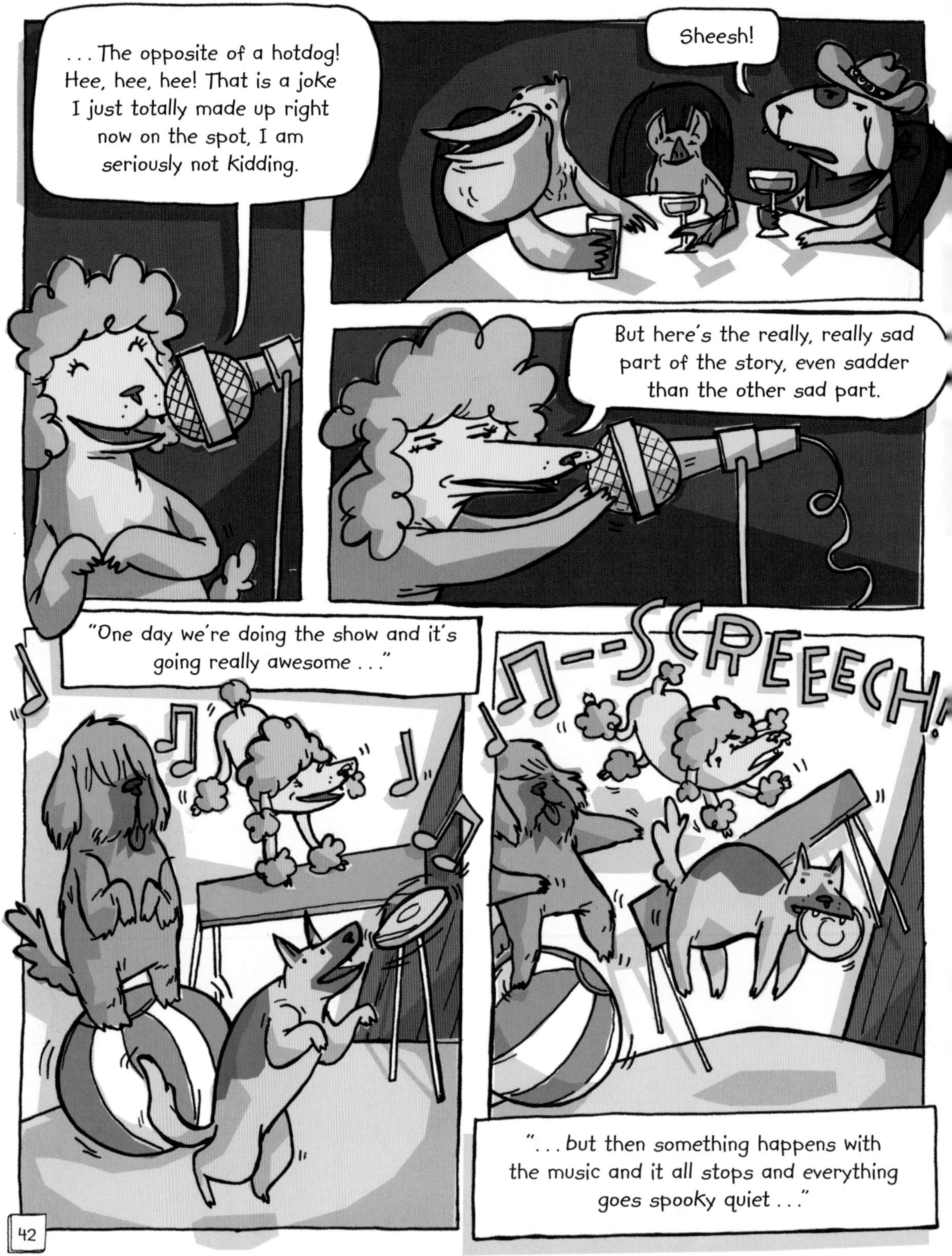
. . . The opposite of a hotdog! Hee, hee, hee! That is a joke I just totally made up right now on the spot, I am seriously not kidding.
Sheesh!
But here's the really, really sad part of the story, even sadder than the other sad part.
"One day we're doing the show and it's going really awesome . . ."
--SCREEECH!
". . . but then something happens with the music and it all stops and everything goes spooky quiet . . ."

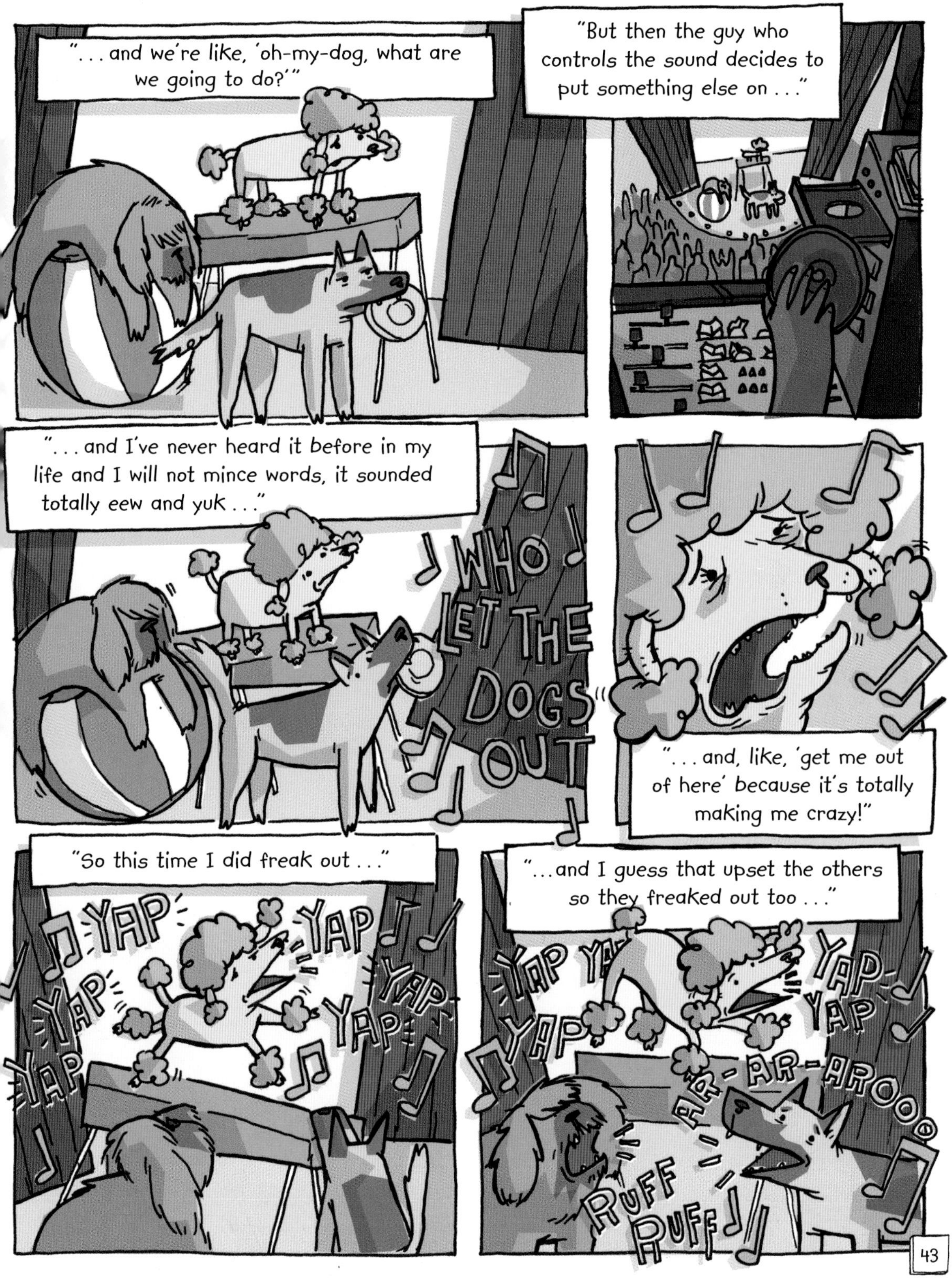
". . . and we're like, 'oh-my-dog, what are we going to do?'"
"But then the guy who controls the sound decides to put something else on . . ."
". . . and I've never heard it before in my life and I will not mince words, it sounded totally eew and yuk . . ."
WHO LET THE DOGS OUT
". . . and, like, 'get me out of here' because it's totally making me crazy!"
"So this time I did freak out . . ."
YAP YAP YAP YAP YAP YAP
"...and I guess that upset the others so they freaked out too . . ."
YAP YAP YAP YAP YAP
AR-AR-AR-AROOOO
RUFF RUFF

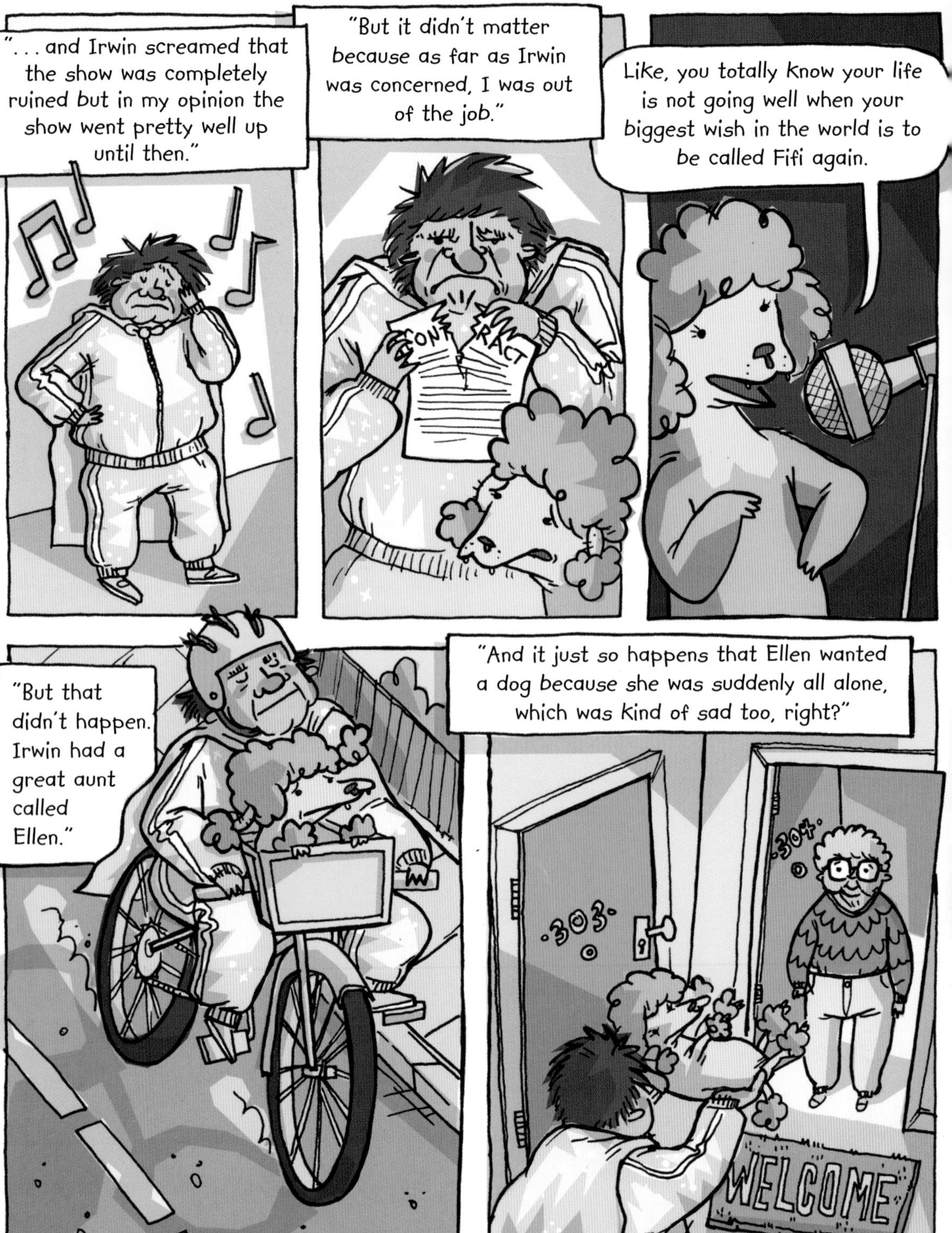
". . . and Irwin screamed that the show was completely ruined but in my opinion the show went pretty well up until then."
"But it didn't matter because as far as Irwin was concerned, I was out of the job."
CONTRACT
Like, you totally know your life is not going well when your biggest wish in the world is to be called Fifi again.
"But that didn't happen. Irwin had a great aunt called Ellen."
"And it just so happens that Ellen wanted a dog because she was suddenly all alone, which was kind of sad too, right?"
303
304
WELCOME

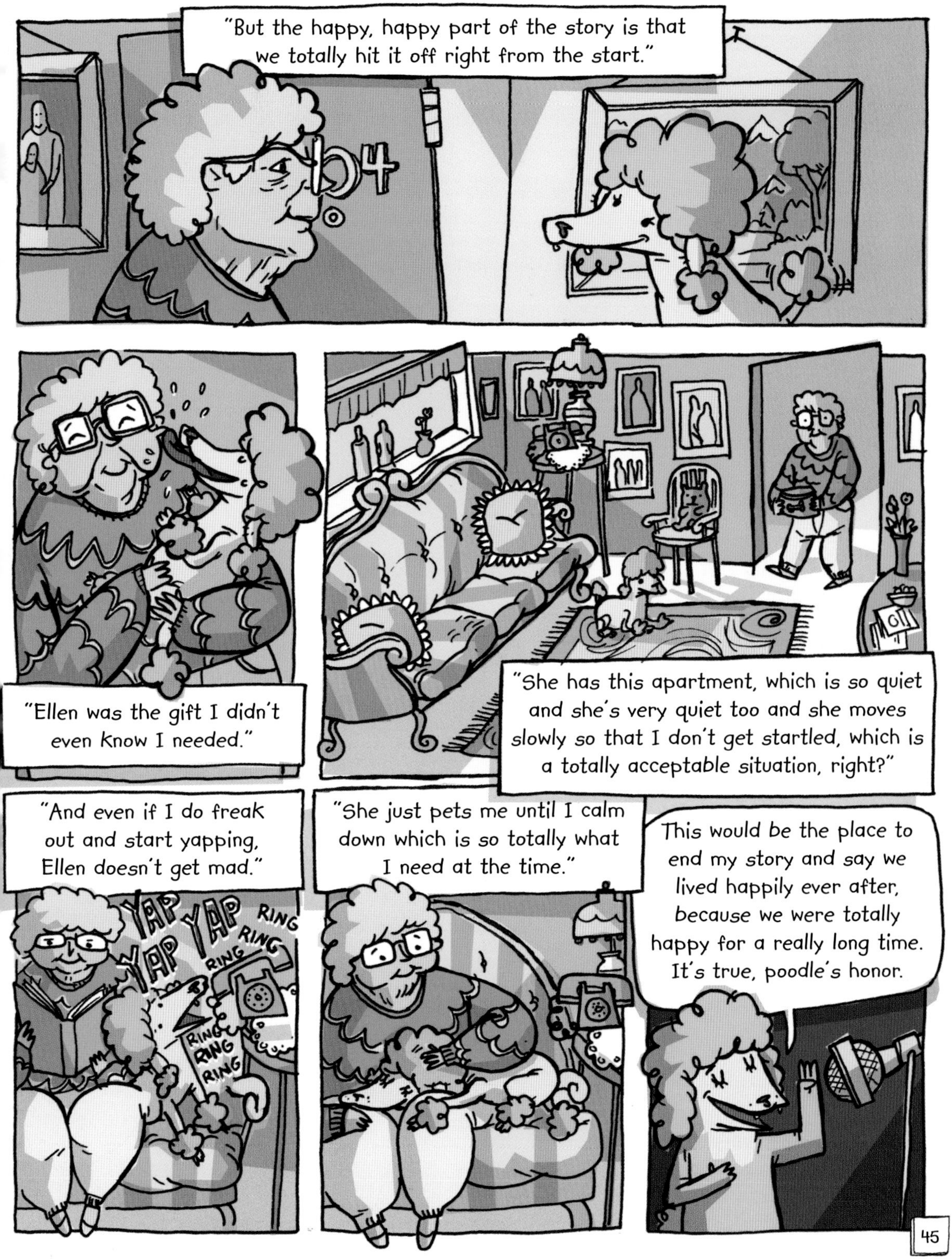
"But the happy, happy part of the story is that we totally hit it off right from the start."
104
"Ellen was the gift I didn't even know I needed."
"She has this apartment, which is so quiet and she's very quiet too and she moves slowly so that I don't get startled, which is a totally acceptable situation, right?"
"And even if I do freak out and start yapping, Ellen doesn't get mad."
YAP YAP YAP
RING RING RING
RING RING RING
"She just pets me until I calm down which is so totally what I need at the time."
This would be the place to end my story and say we lived happily ever after, because we were totally happy for a really long time. It's true, poodle's honor.

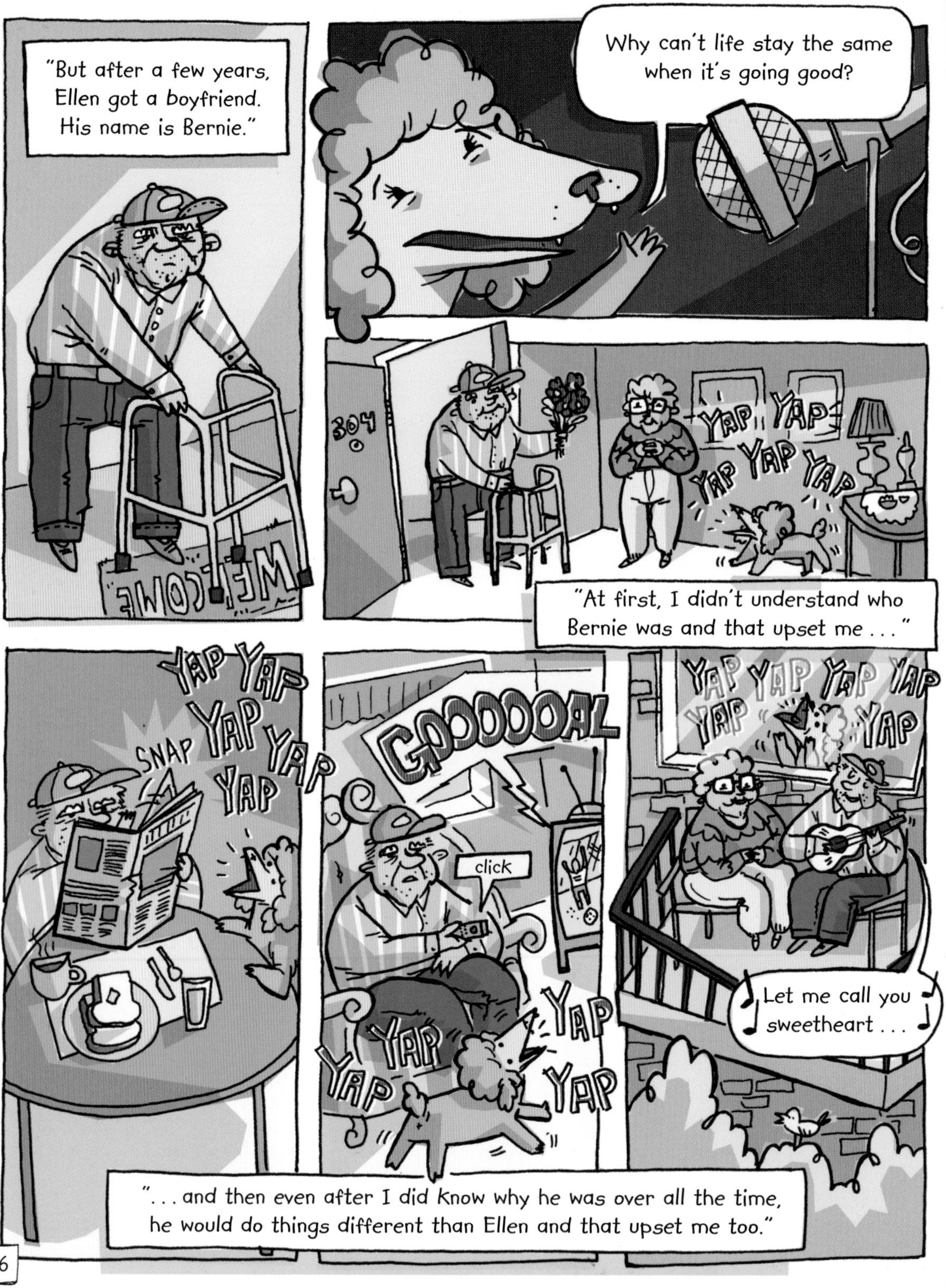
"But after a few years, Ellen got a boyfriend. His name is Bernie."
WELCOME
Why can't life stay the same when it's going good?
304
YAP YAP YAP YAP YAP
"At first, I didn't understand who Bernie was and that upset me . . ."
YAP YAP YAP YAP YAP
SNAP
GOOOOOAL
click
YAP YAP YAP YAP
YAP YAP YAP YAP YAP YAP
Let me call you sweetheart . . .
". . . and then even after I did know why he was over all the time, he would do things different than Ellen and that upset me too."

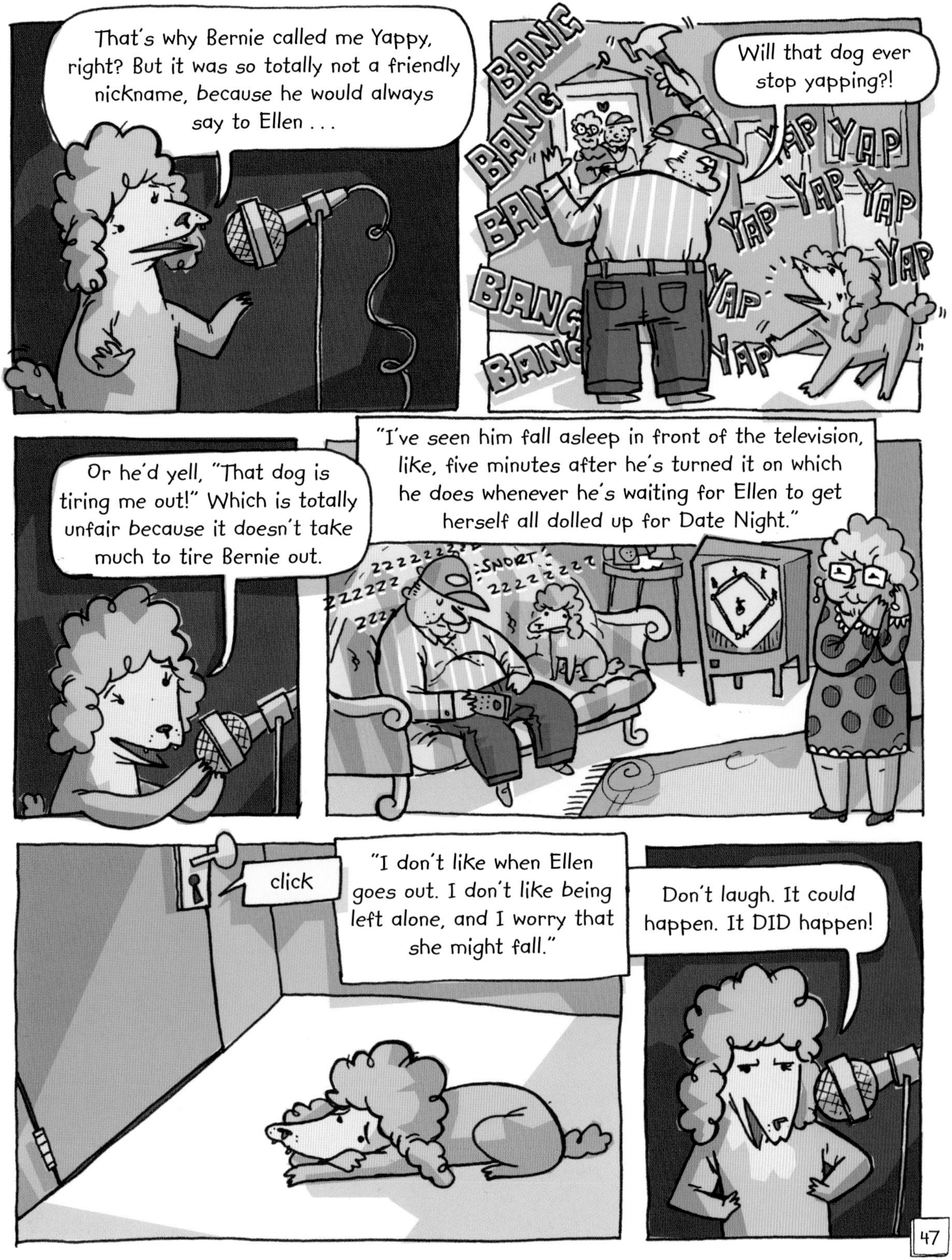
That's why Bernie called me Yappy, right? But it was so totally not a friendly nickname, because he would always say to Ellen . . .
BANG BANG BANG BANG BANG
Will that dog ever stop yapping?!
YAP YAP YAP YAP YAP YAP YAP YAP
Or he'd yell, "That dog is tiring me out!" Which is totally unfair because it doesn't take much to tire Bernie out.
"I've seen him fall asleep in front of the television, like, five minutes after he's turned it on which he does whenever he's waiting for Ellen to get herself all dolled up for Date Night."
SNORT
click
"I don't like when Ellen goes out. I don't like being left alone, and I worry that she might fall."
Don't laugh. It could happen. It DID happen!

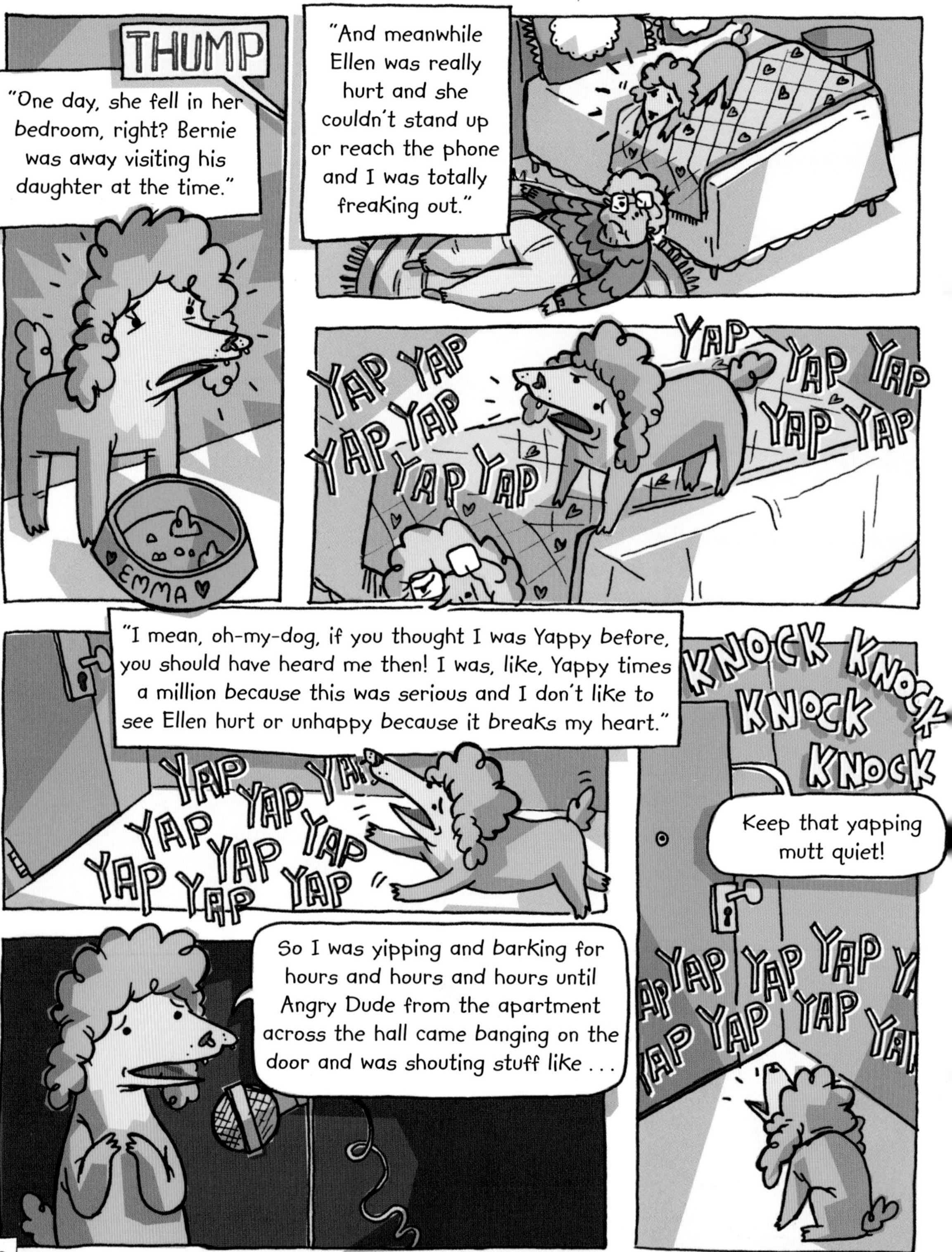

THUMP
"One day, she fell in her bedroom, right? Bernie was away visiting his daughter at the time."
EMMA
"And meanwhile Ellen was really hurt and she couldn't stand up or reach the phone and I was totally freaking out."
YAP YAP YAP YAP YAP YAP
YAP YAP YAP YAP YAP
"I mean, oh-my-dog, if you thought I was Yappy before, you should have heard me then! I was, like, Yappy times a million because this was serious and I don't like to see Ellen hurt or unhappy because it breaks my heart."
YAP YAP YAP YAP YAP YAP YAP YAP
KNOCK KNOCK KNOCK KNOCK
Keep that yapping mutt quiet!
So I was yipping and barking for hours and hours and hours until Angry Dude from the apartment across the hall came banging on the door and was shouting stuff like . . .
YAP YAP YAP YAP YAP YAP

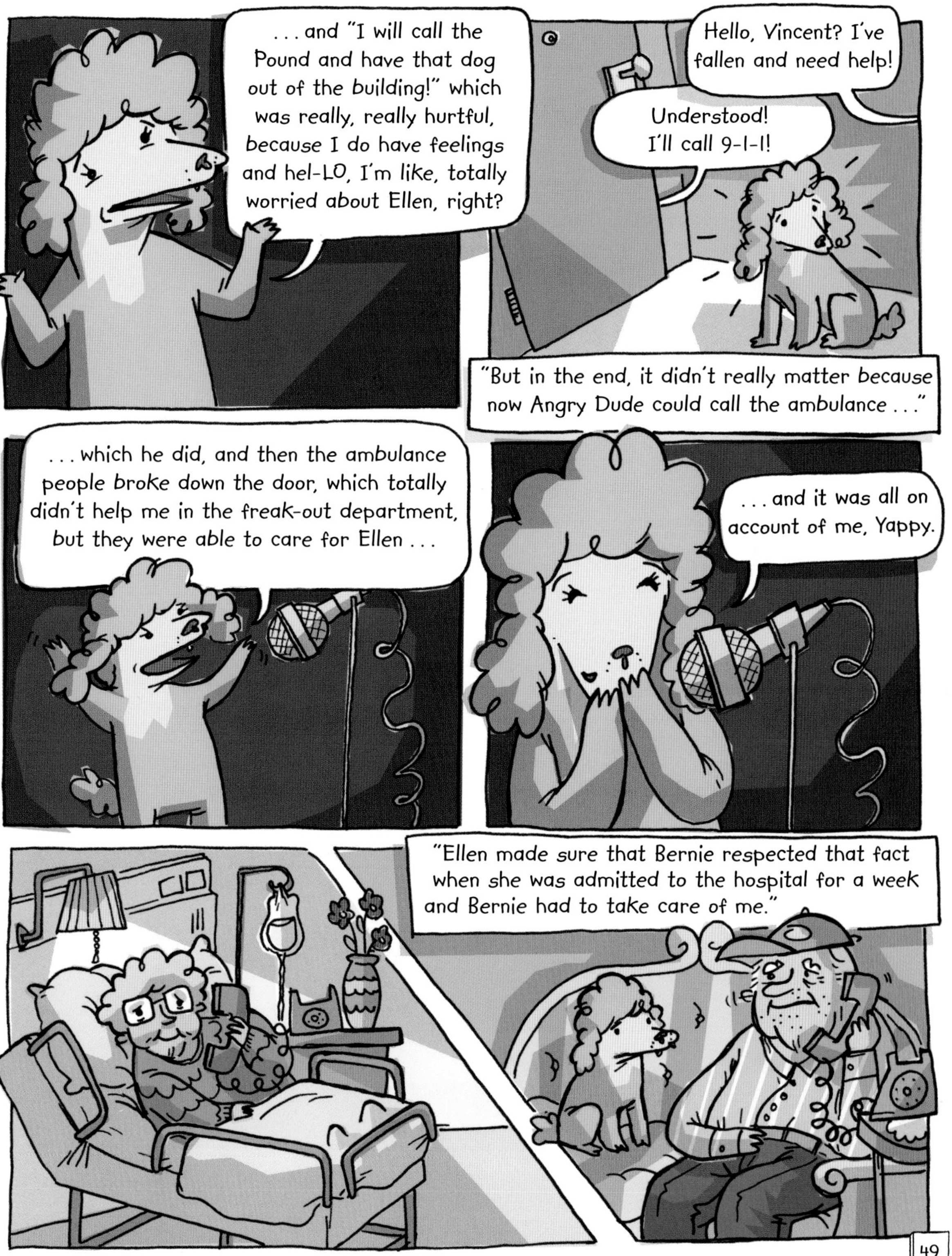
. . . and "I will call the Pound and have that dog out of the building!" which was really, really hurtful, because I do have feelings and hel-LO, I'm like, totally worried about Ellen, right?
Hello, Vincent? I've fallen and need help!
Understood! I'll call 9-1-1!
"But in the end, it didn't really matter because now Angry Dude could call the ambulance . . ."
. . . which he did, and then the ambulance people broke down the door, which totally didn't help me in the freak-out department, but they were able to care for Ellen . . .
. . . and it was all on account of me, Yappy.
"Ellen made sure that Bernie respected that fact when she was admitted to the hospital for a week and Bernie had to take care of me."

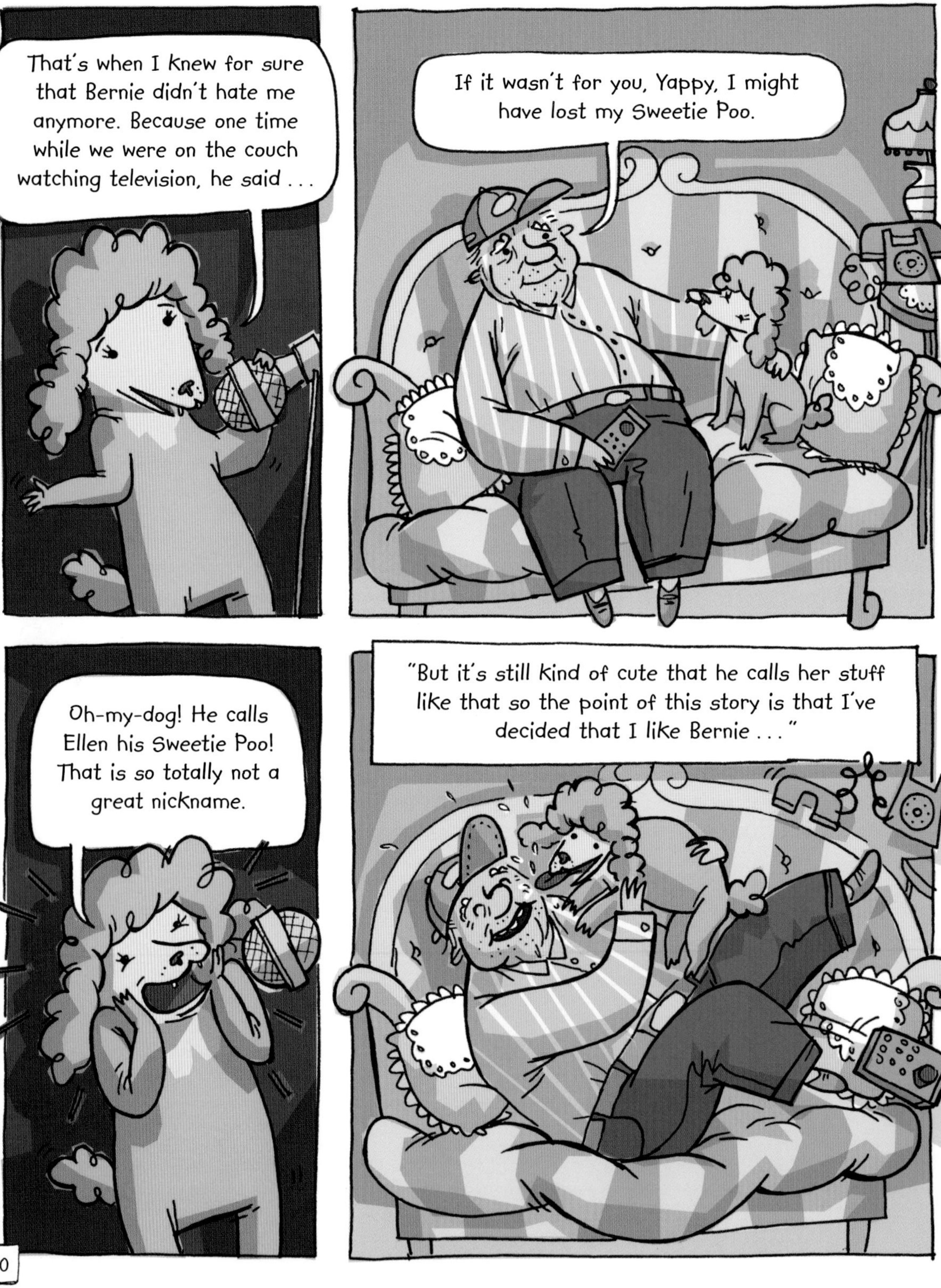
That's when I knew for sure that Bernie didn't hate me anymore. Because one time while we were on the couch watching television, he said . . .
If it wasn't for you, Yappy, I might have lost my Sweetie Poo.
Oh-my-dog! He calls Ellen his Sweetie Poo! That is so totally not a great nickname.
"But it's still kind of cute that he calls her stuff like that so the point of this story is that I've decided that I like Bernie . . ."

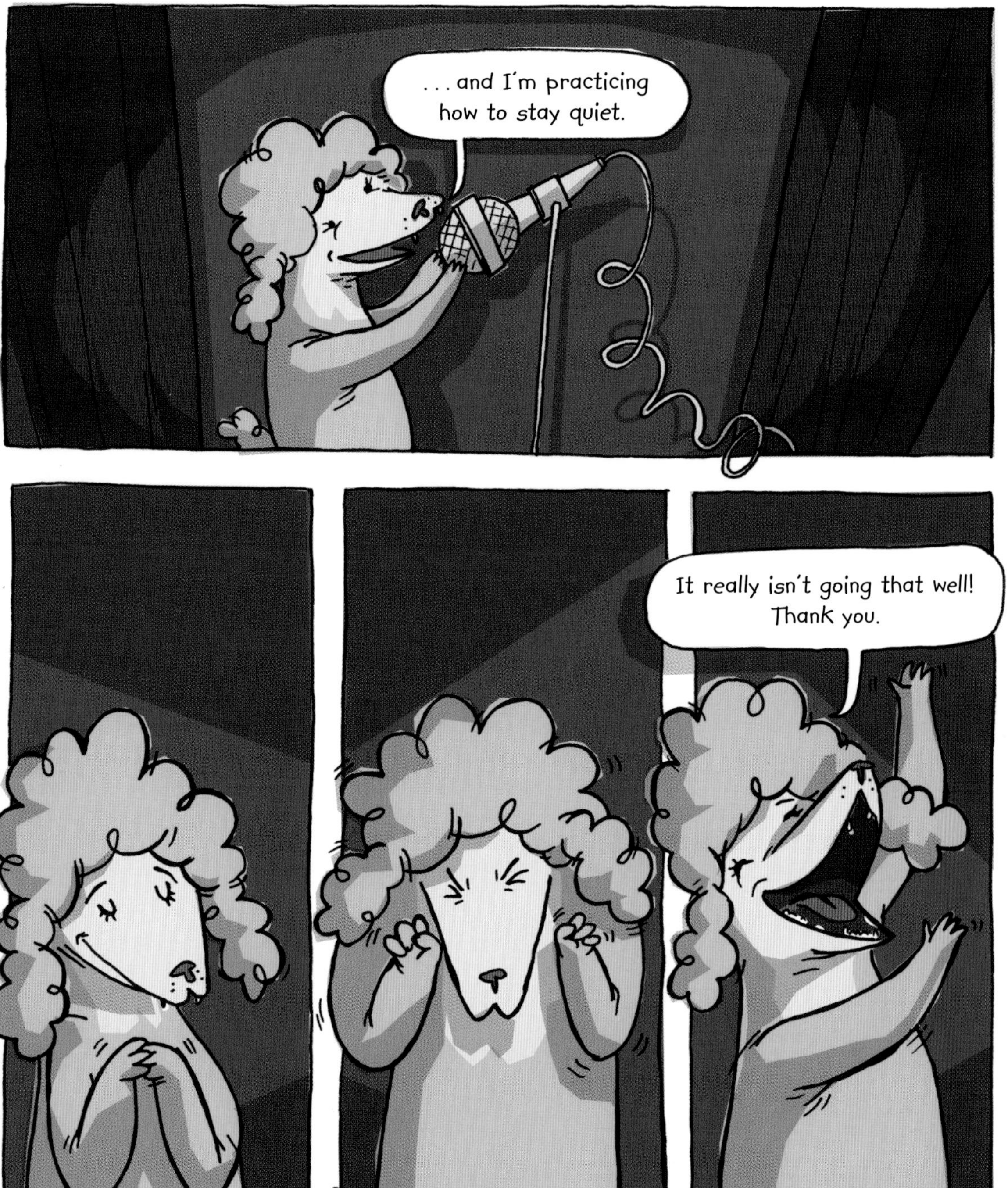
. . . and I'm practicing how to stay quiet.
It really isn't going that well! Thank you.

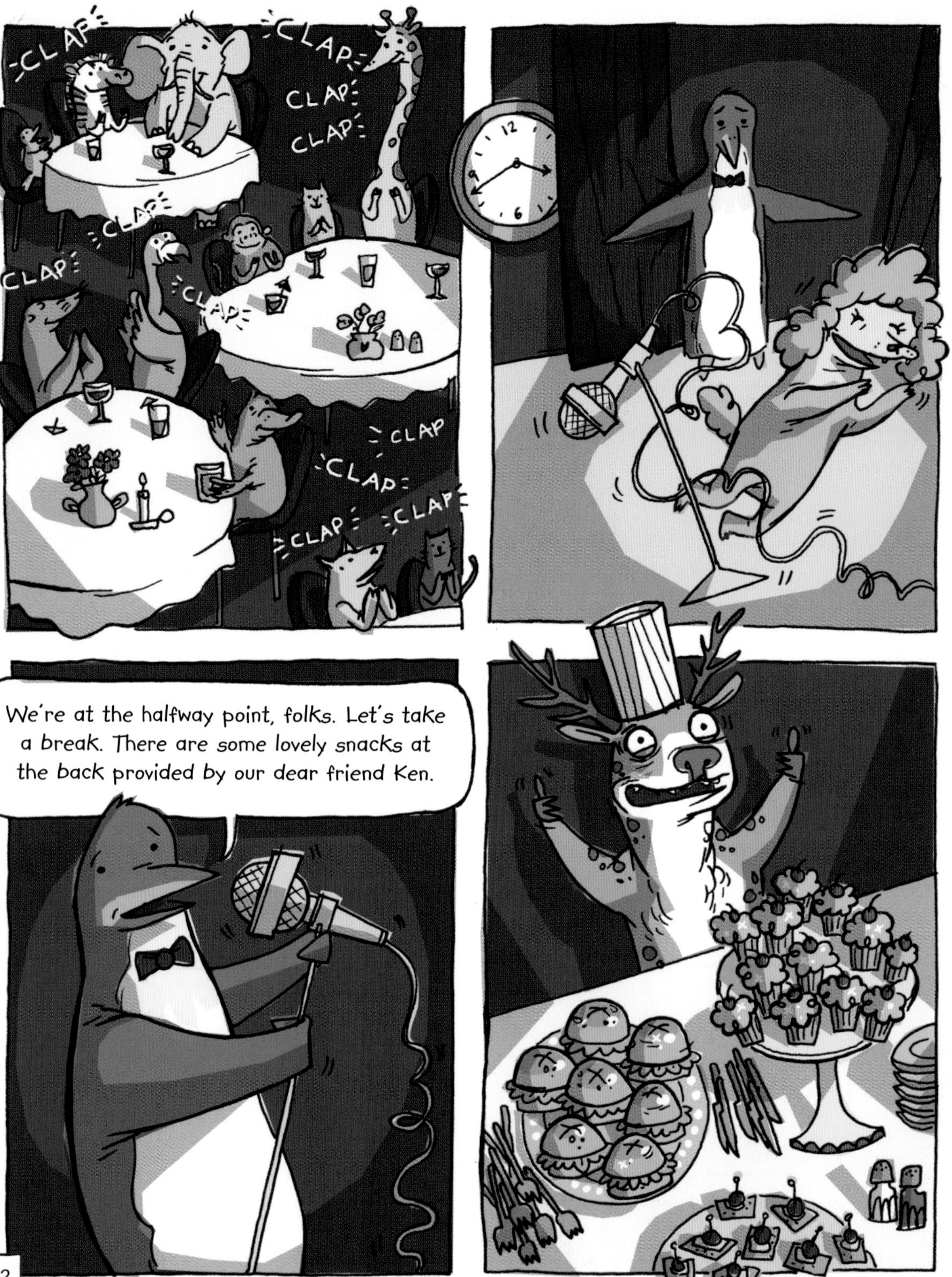
CLAP
CLAP
CLAP
CLAP
CLAP
CLAP
CLAP
CLAP
CLAP
CLAP
CLAP
CLAP
We're at the halfway point, folks. Let's take a break. There are some lovely snacks at the back provided by our dear friend Ken.

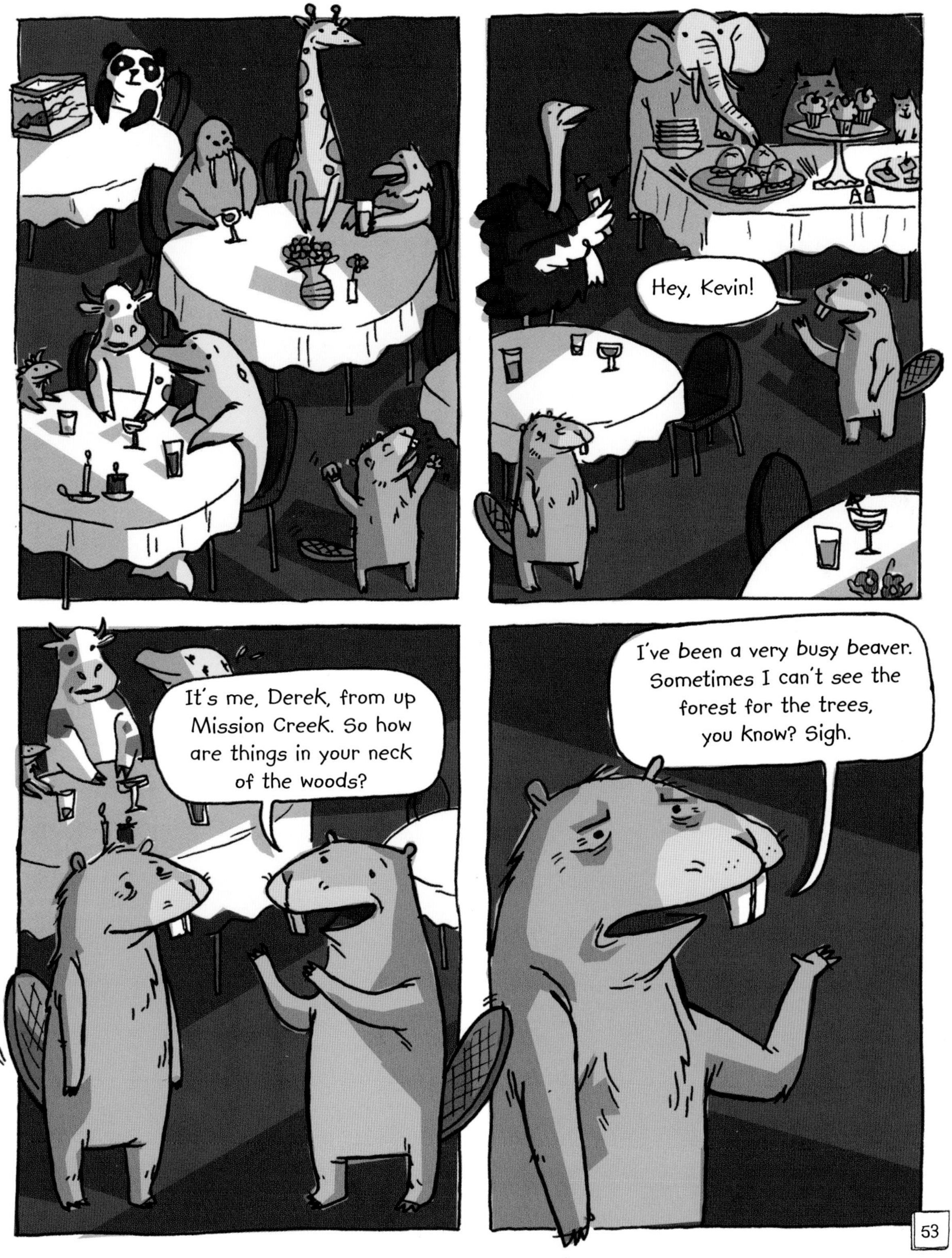
Hey, Kevin!
It's me, Derek, from up Mission Creek. So how are things in your neck of the woods?
I've been a very busy beaver. Sometimes I can't see the forest for the trees, you know? Sigh.

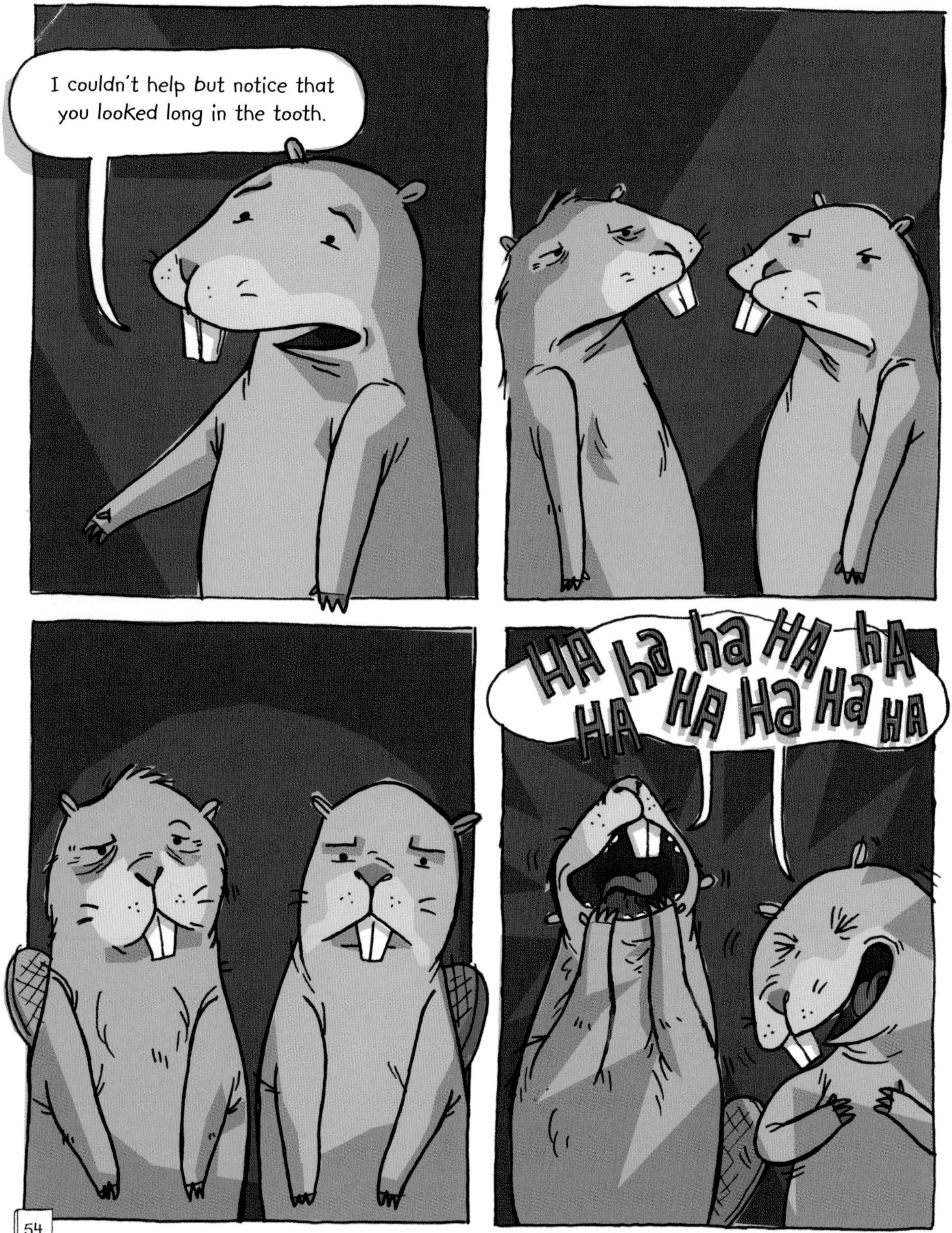
I couldn't help but notice that you looked long in the tooth.
HA ha ha HA hA HA HA Ha Ha HA

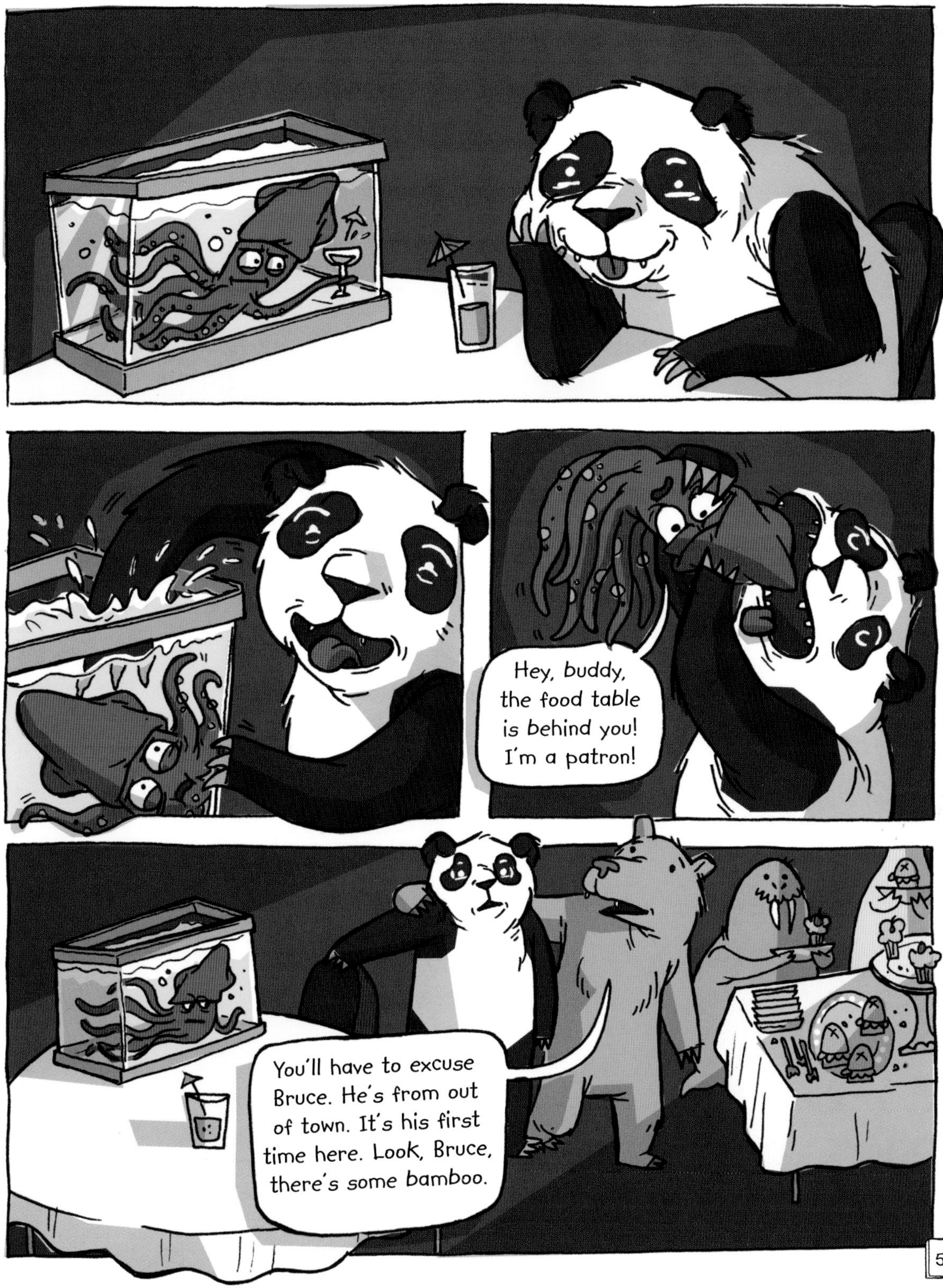
Hey, buddy, the food table is behind you! I'm a patron!
You'll have to excuse Bruce. He's from out of town. It's his first time here. Look, Bruce, there's some bamboo.

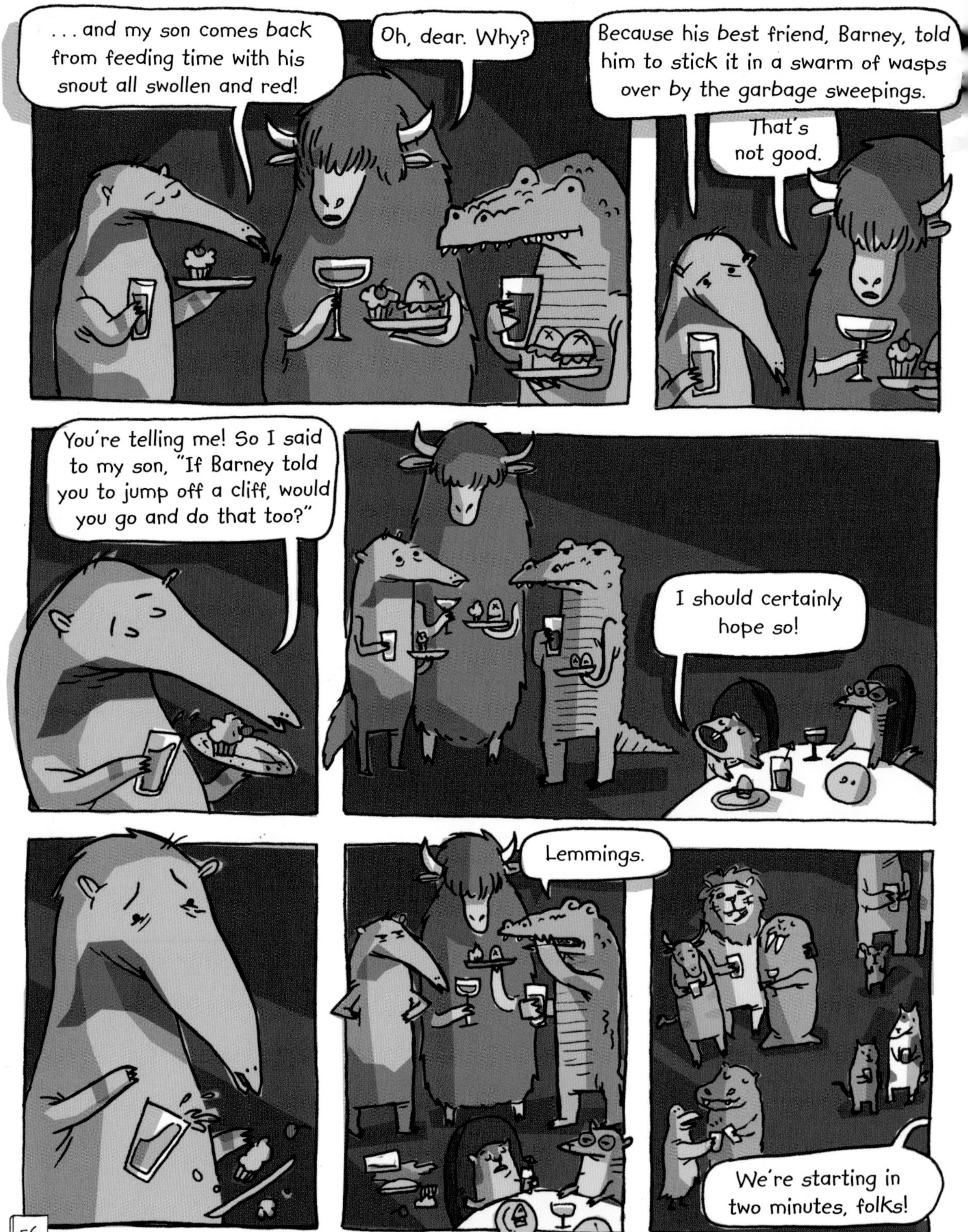

. . . and my son comes back from feeding time with his snout all swollen and red!
Oh, dear. Why?
Because his best friend, Barney, told him to stick it in a swarm of wasps over by the garbage sweepings.
That's not good.
You're telling me! So I said to my son, "If Barney told you to jump off a cliff, would you go and do that too?"
I should certainly hope so!
Lemmings.
We're starting in two minutes, folks!

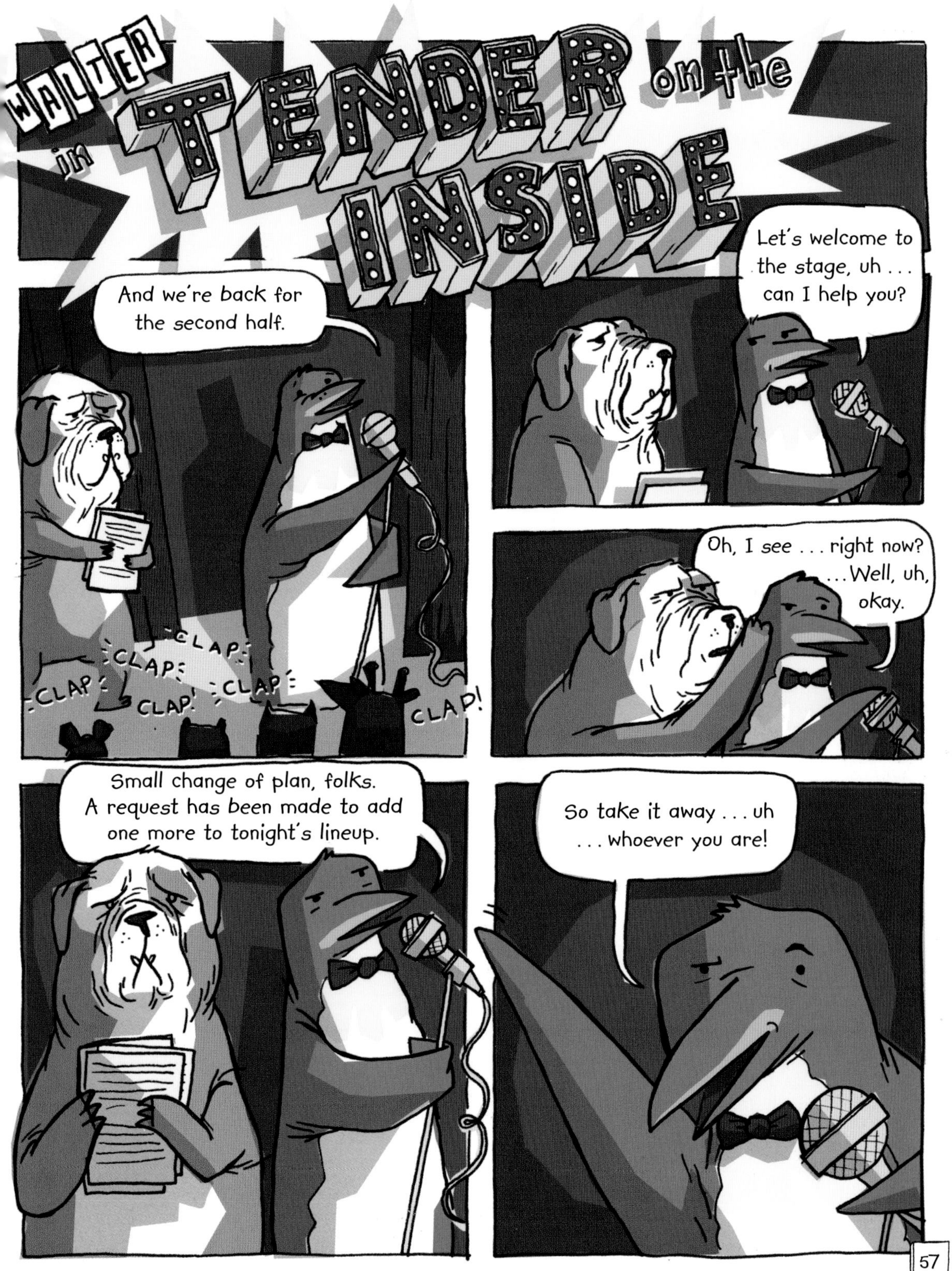
WALTER
in
TENDER on the INSIDE
And we're back for the second half.
CLAP CLAP CLAP CLAP CLAP CLAP!
Let's welcome to the stage, uh . . . can I help you?
Oh, I see . . . right now? . . . Well, uh, okay.
Small change of plan, folks. A request has been made to add one more to tonight's lineup.
So take it away . . . uh . . . whoever you are!

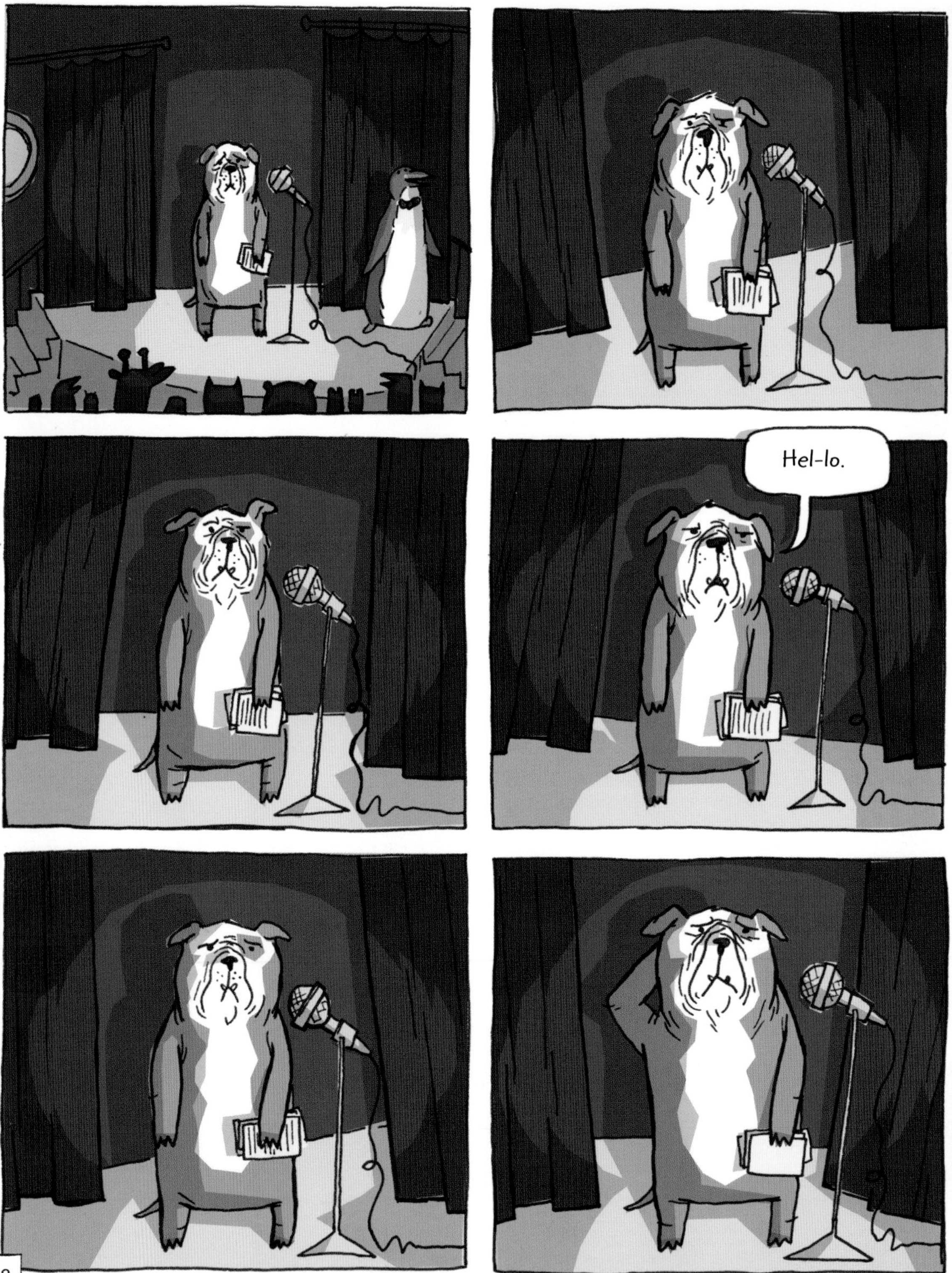
Hel-lo.

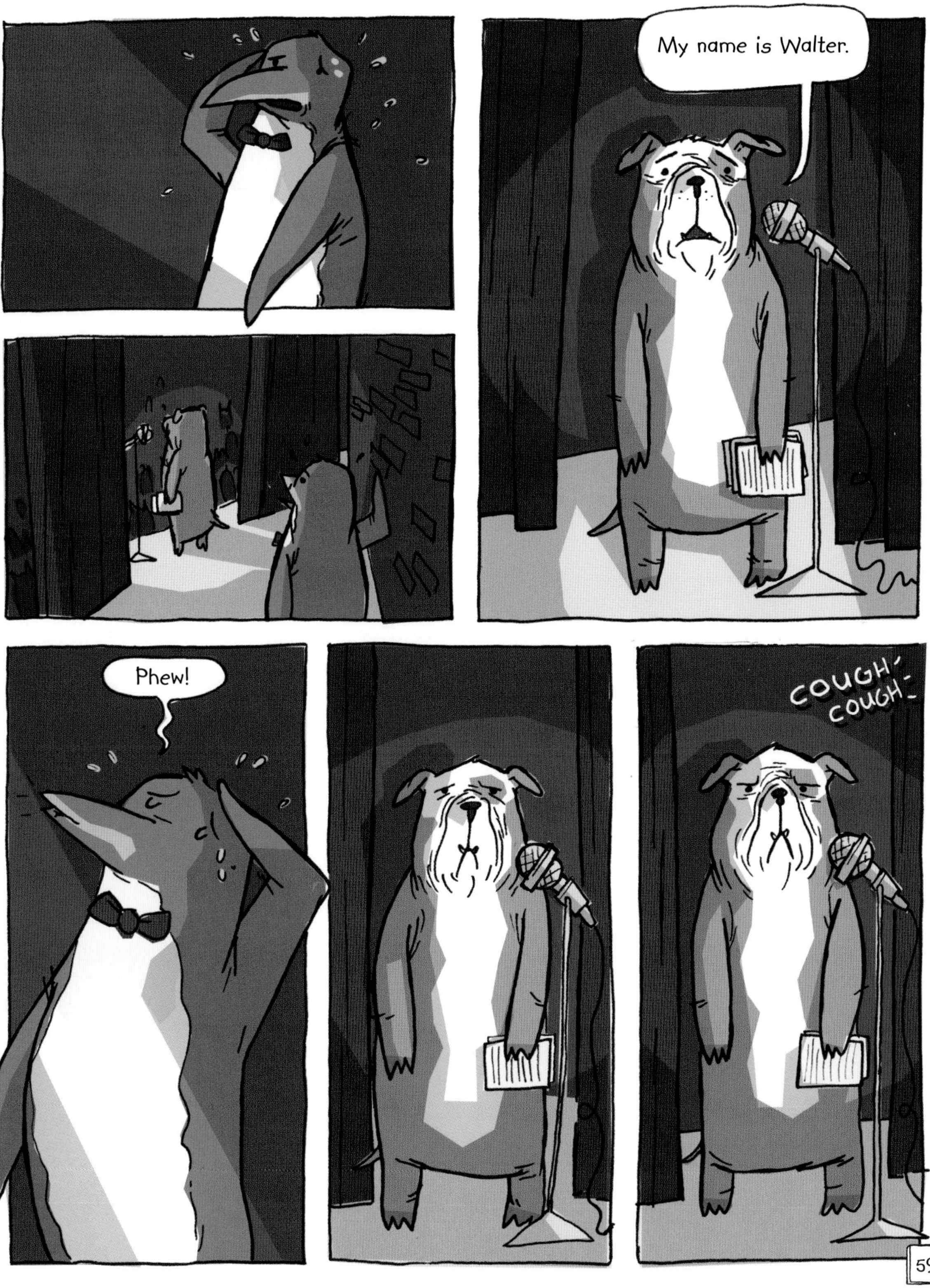
My name is Walter.
Phew!
COUGH-
COUGH-

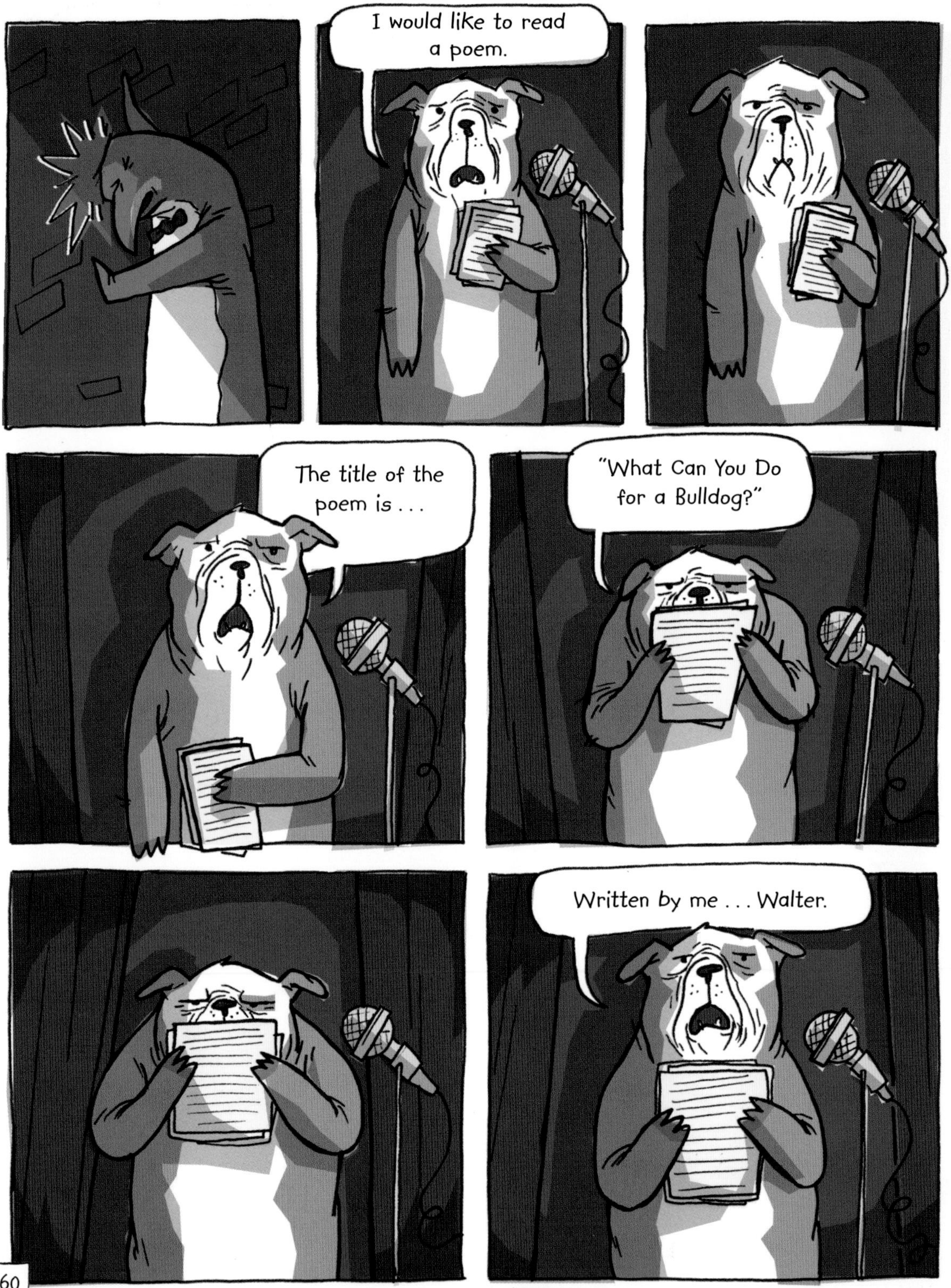
I would like to read a poem.
The title of the poem is . . .
"What Can You Do for a Bulldog?"
Written by me . . . Walter.

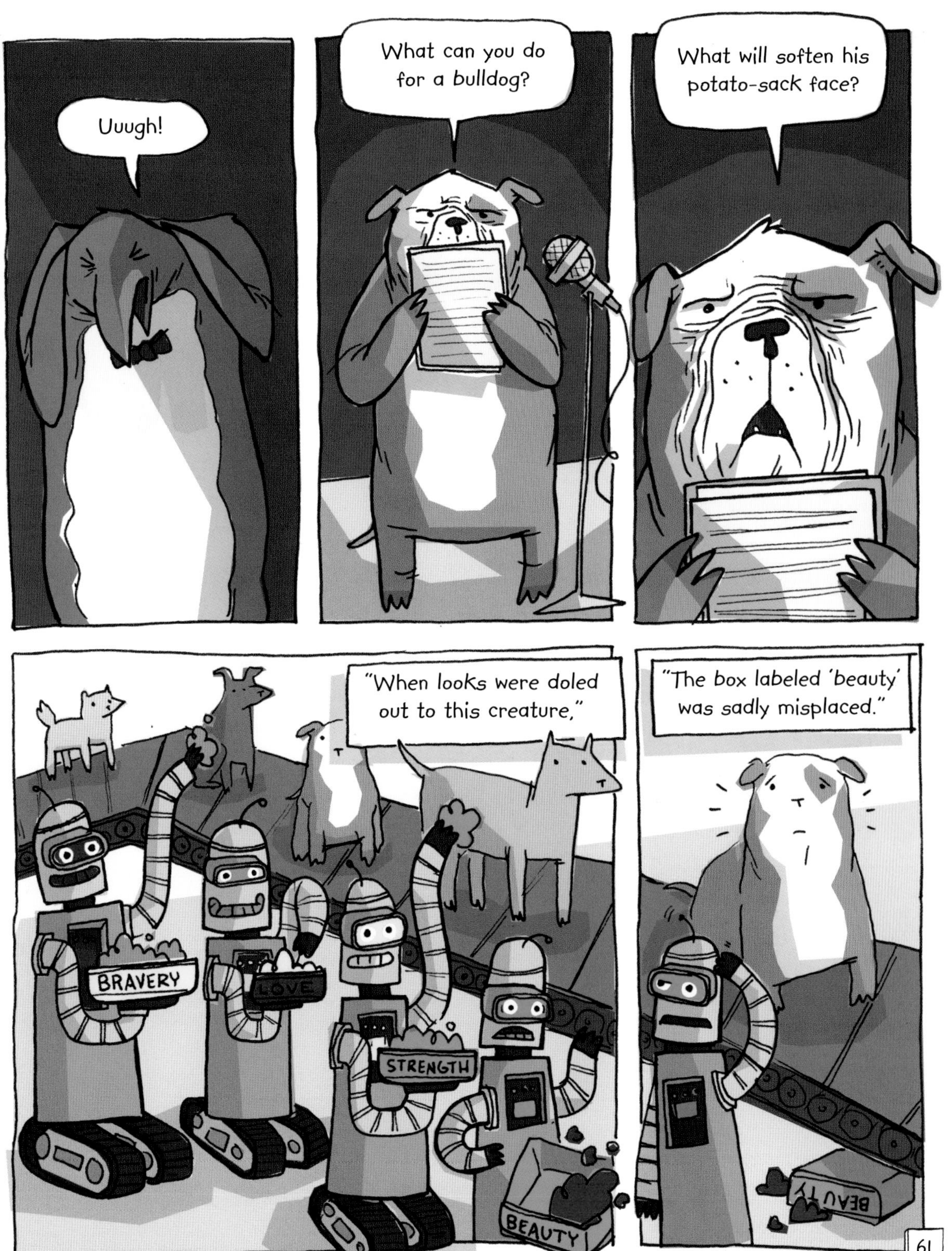
Uuugh!
What can you do for a bulldog?
What will soften his potato-sack face?
"When looks were doled out to this creature,"
BRAVERY
LOVE
STRENGTH
BEAUTY
"The box labeled 'beauty' was sadly misplaced."
BEAUTY

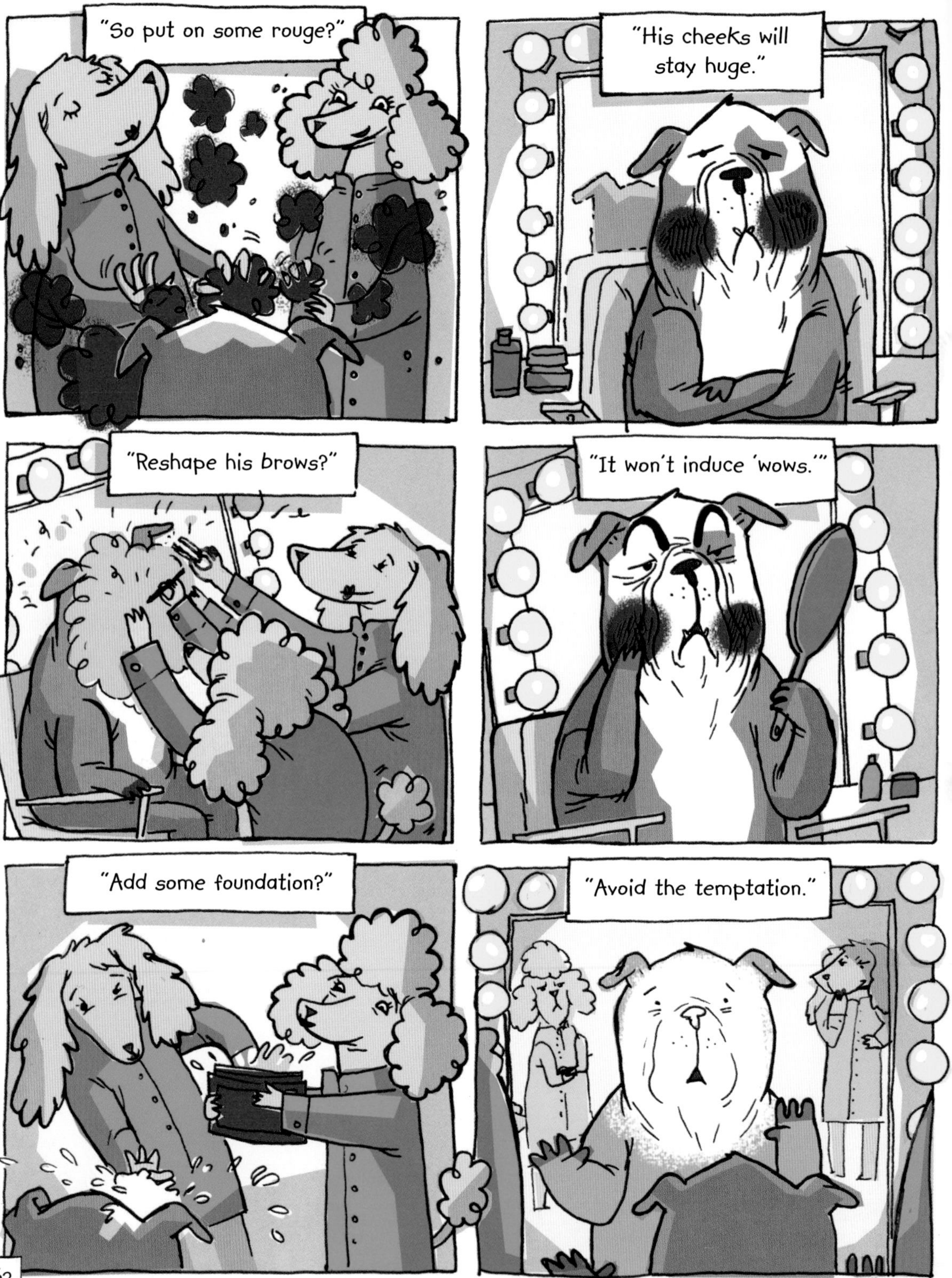
"So put on some rouge?"
"His cheeks will stay huge."
"Reshape his brows?"
"It won't induce 'wows.'"
"Add some foundation?"
"Avoid the temptation."

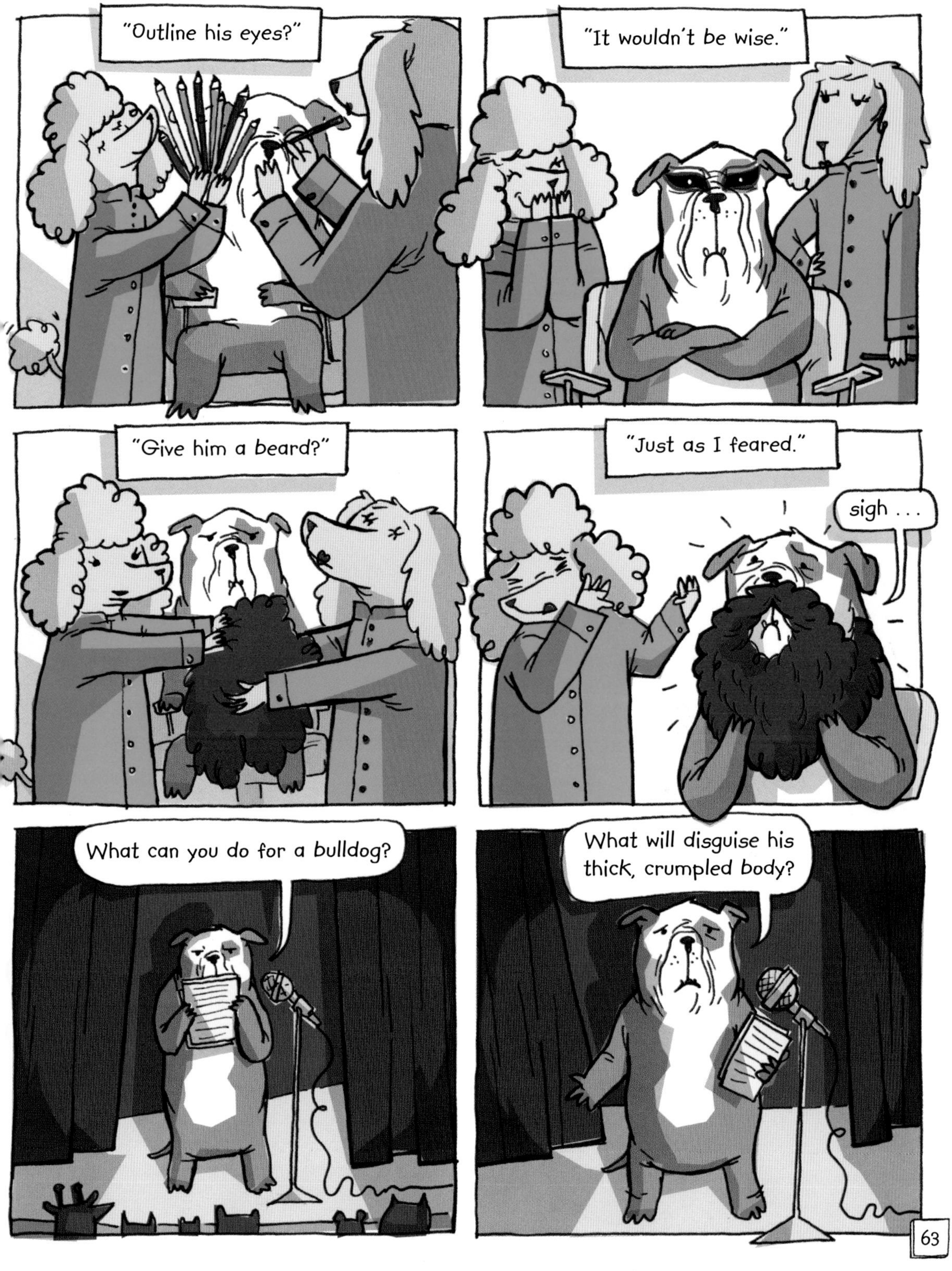
"Outline his eyes?"
"It wouldn't be wise."
"Give him a beard?"
"Just as I feared."
sigh . . .
What can you do for a bulldog?
What will disguise his thick, crumpled body?

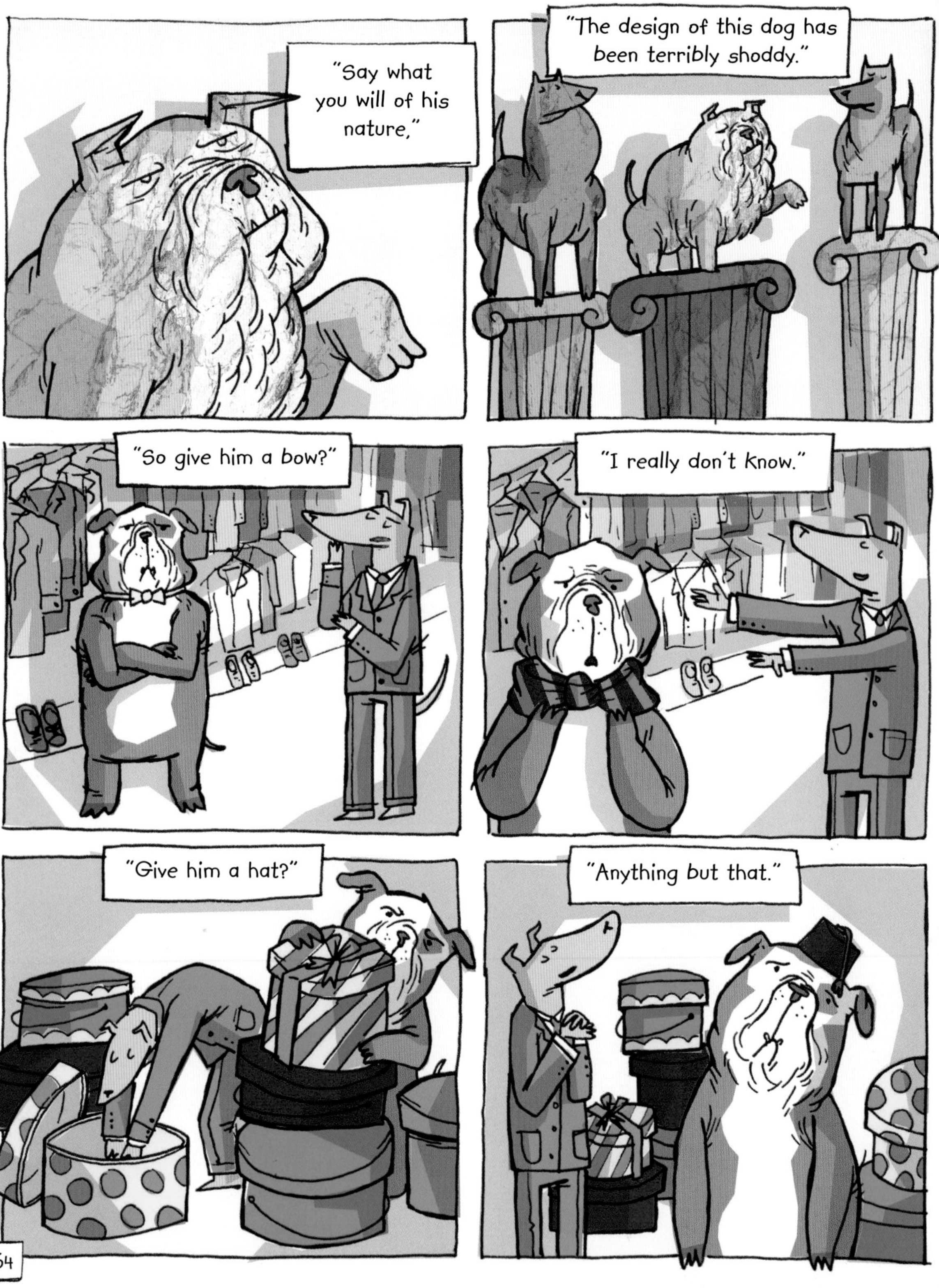
"Say what you will of his nature,"
"The design of this dog has been terribly shoddy."
"So give him a bow?"
"I really don't know."
"Give him a hat?"
"Anything but that."

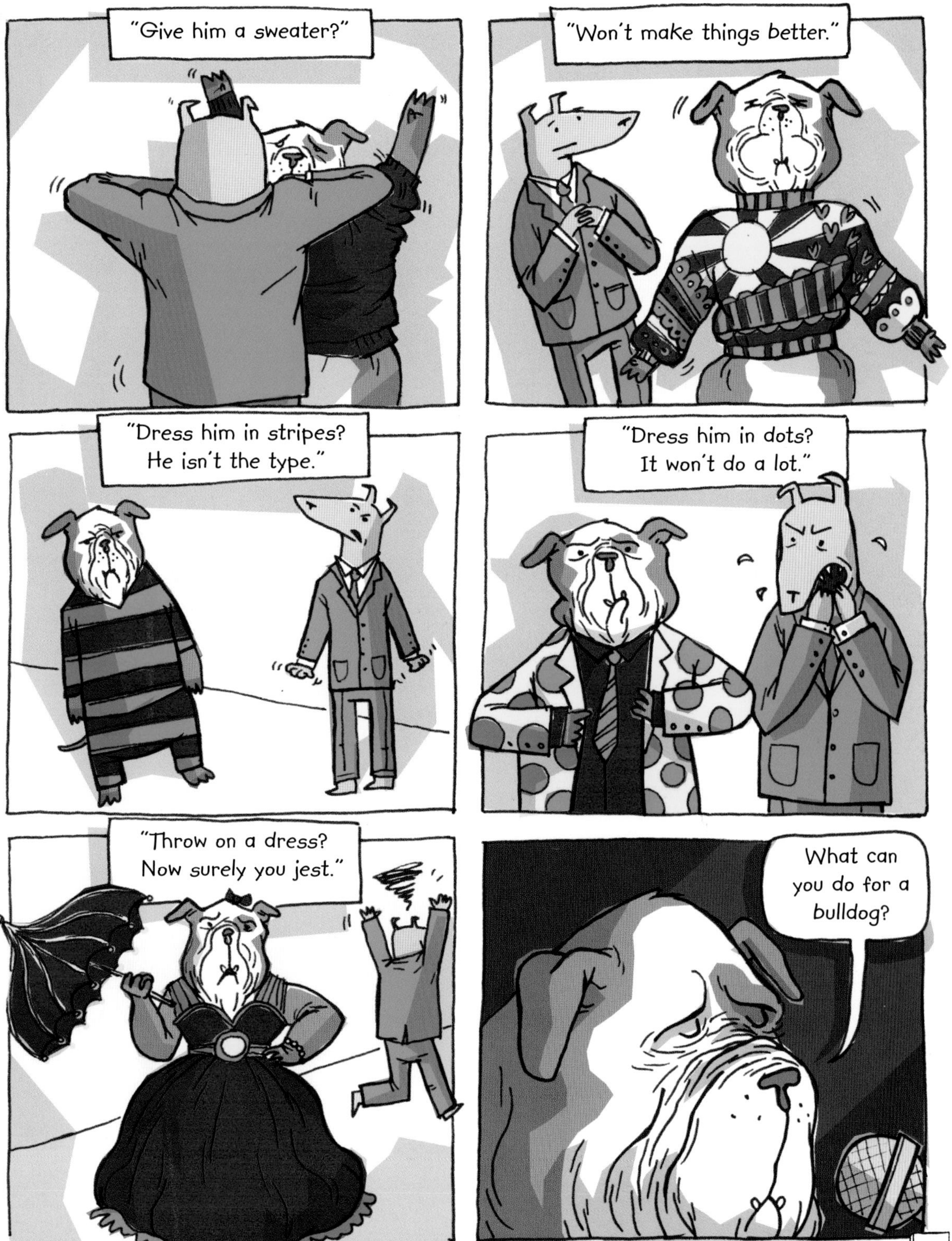
"Give him a sweater?"
"Won't make things better."
"Dress him in stripes? He isn't the type."
"Dress him in dots? It won't do a lot."
"Throw on a dress? Now surely you jest."
What can you do for a bulldog?

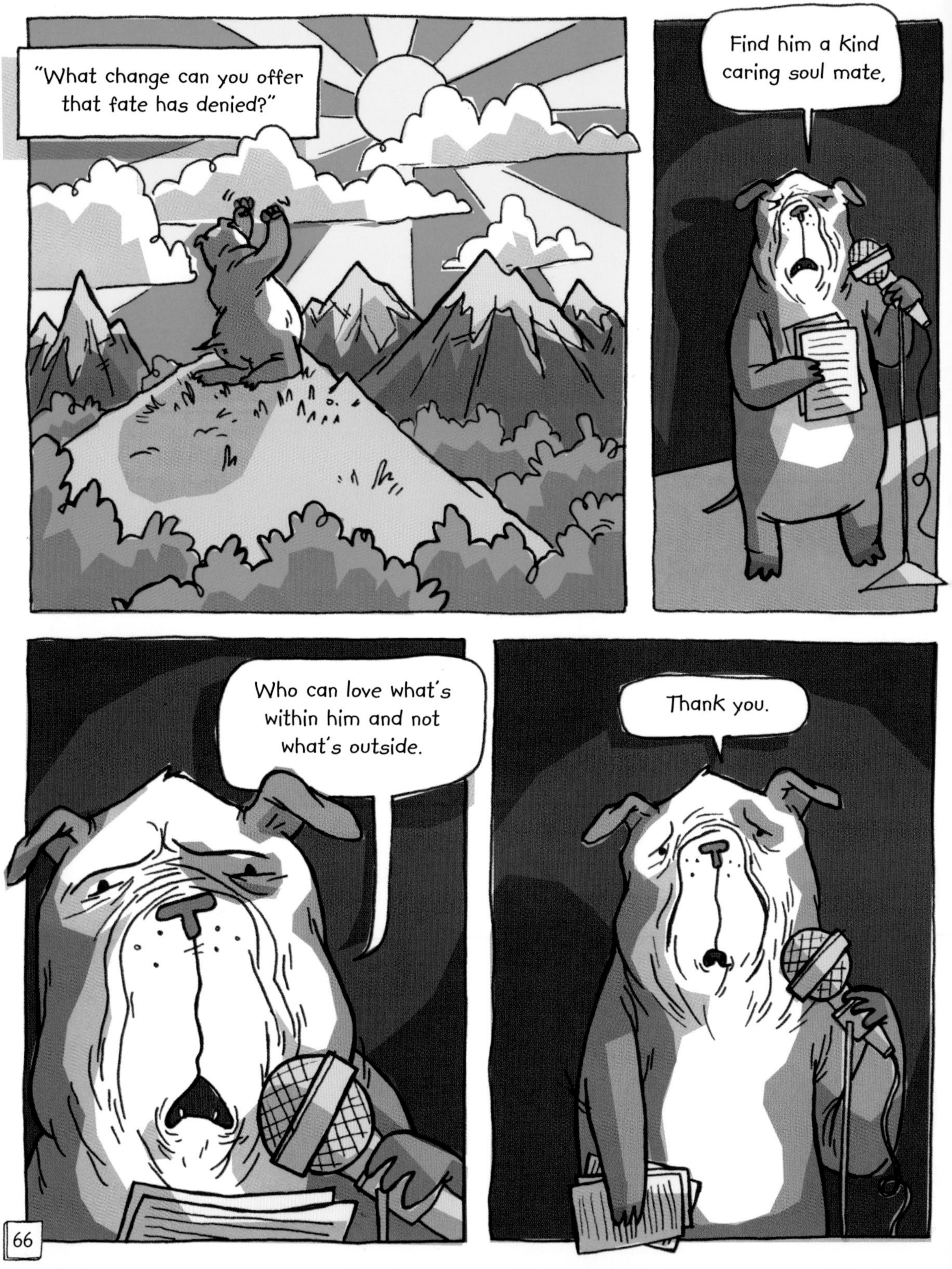
"What change can you offer that fate has denied?"
Find him a kind caring soul mate,
Who can love what's within him and not what's outside.
Thank you.

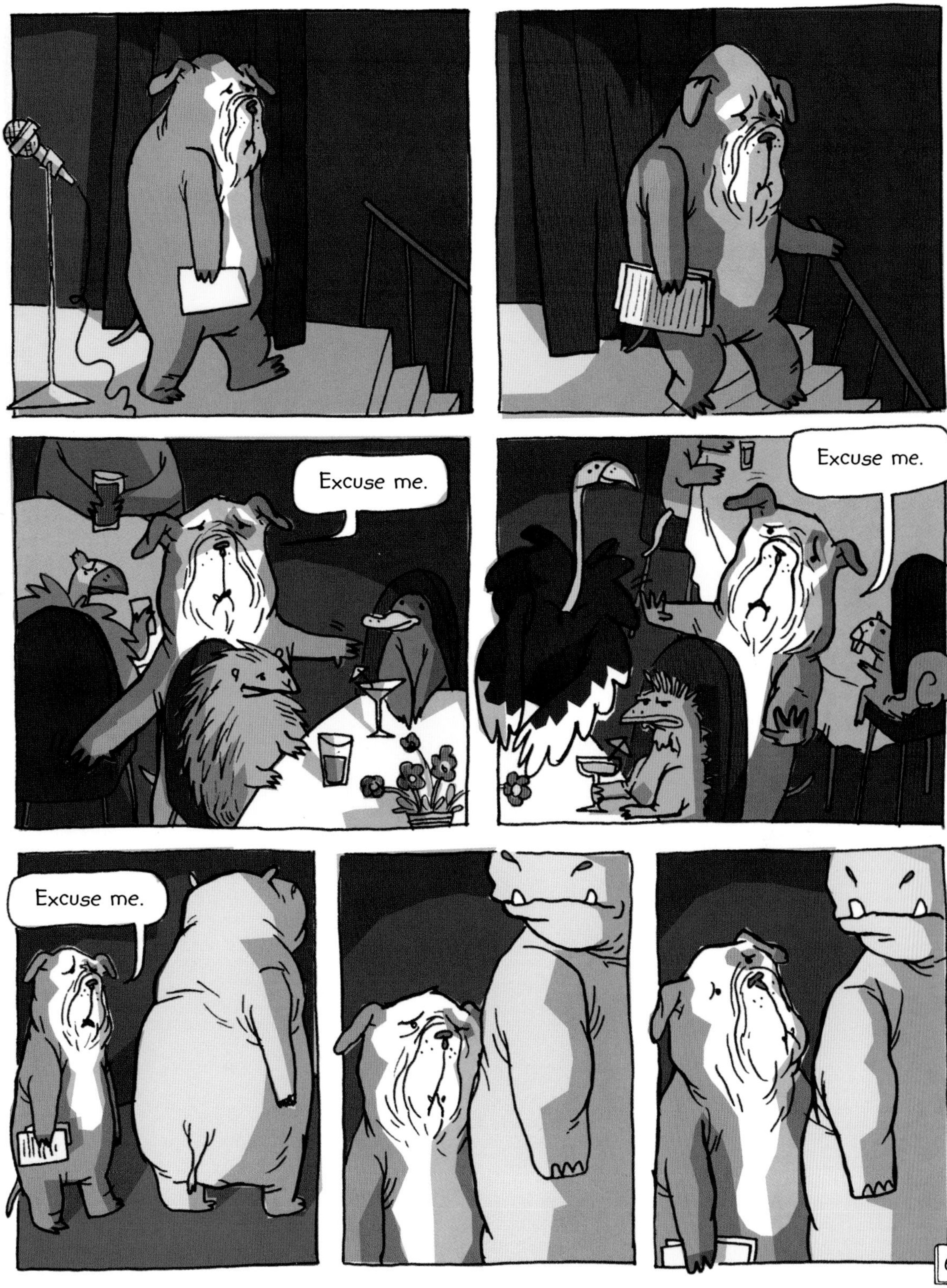
Excuse me.
Excuse me.
Excuse me.

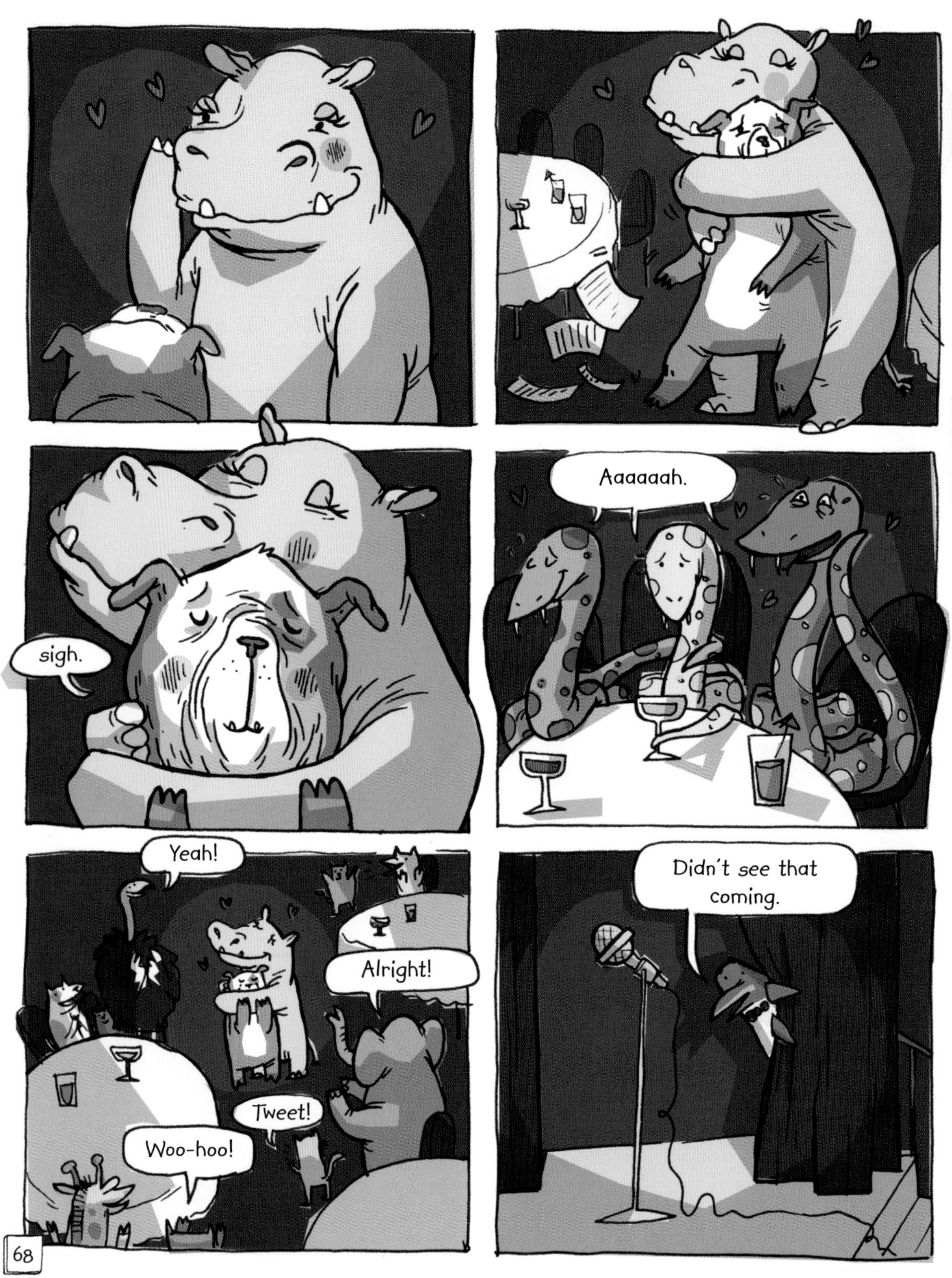
sigh.
Aaaaaah.
Yeah!
Alright!
Tweet!
Woo-hoo!
Didn't see that coming.

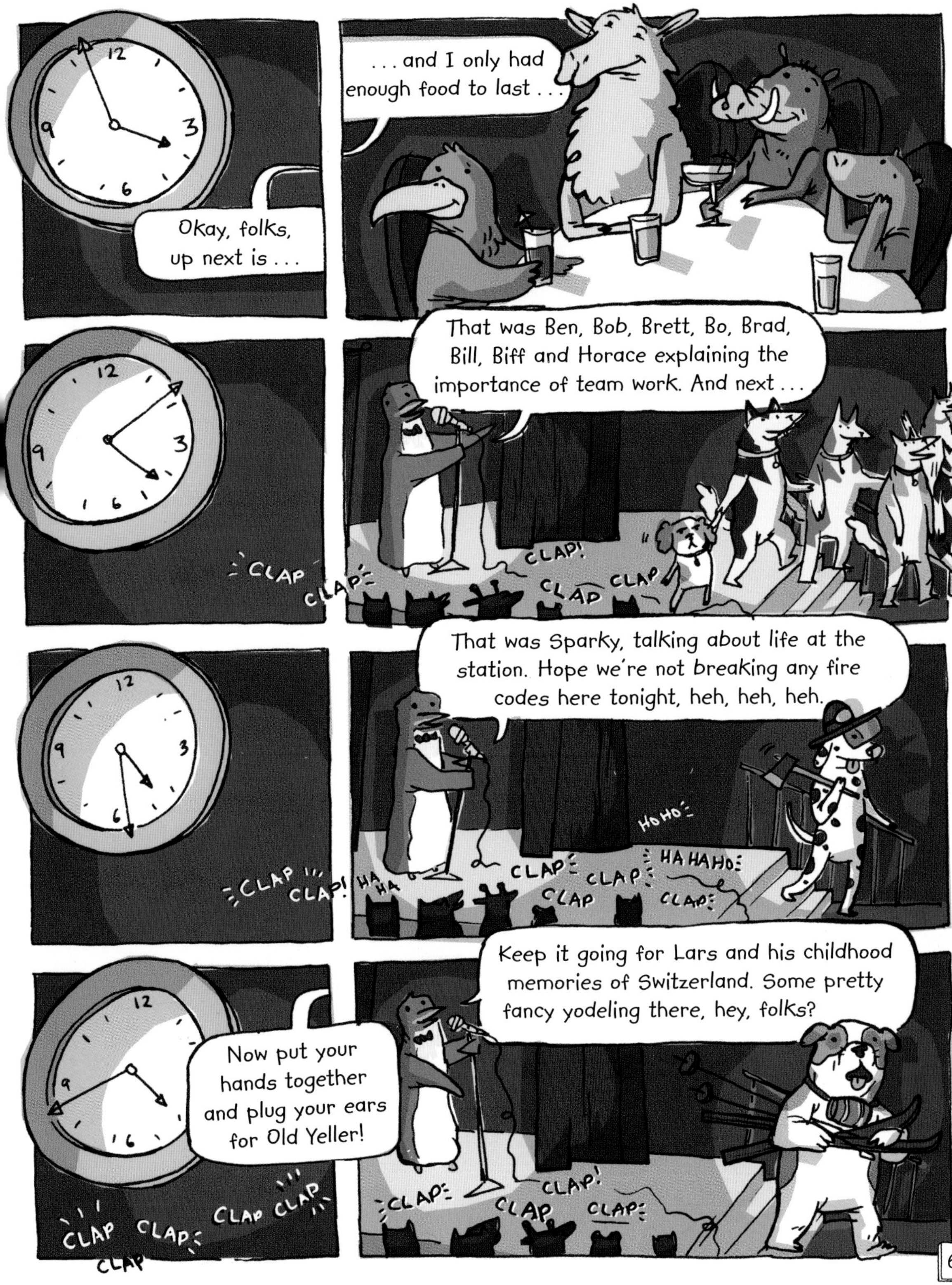
Okay, folks, up next is . . .
. . . and I only had enough food to last . . .
That was Ben, Bob, Brett, Bo, Brad, Bill, Biff and Horace explaining the importance of team work. And next . . .
CLAP
CLAP
CLAP!
CLAP
CLAP
That was Sparky, talking about life at the station. Hope we're not breaking any fire codes here tonight, heh, heh, heh.
HO HO
CLAP
CLAP!
HA HA
CLAP
CLAP
CLAP
HA HA HO
CLAP
Keep it going for Lars and his childhood memories of Switzerland. Some pretty fancy yodeling there, hey, folks?
Now put your hands together and plug your ears for Old Yeller!
CLAP CLAP
CLAP CLAP
CLAP
CLAP
CLAP!
CLAP
CLAP

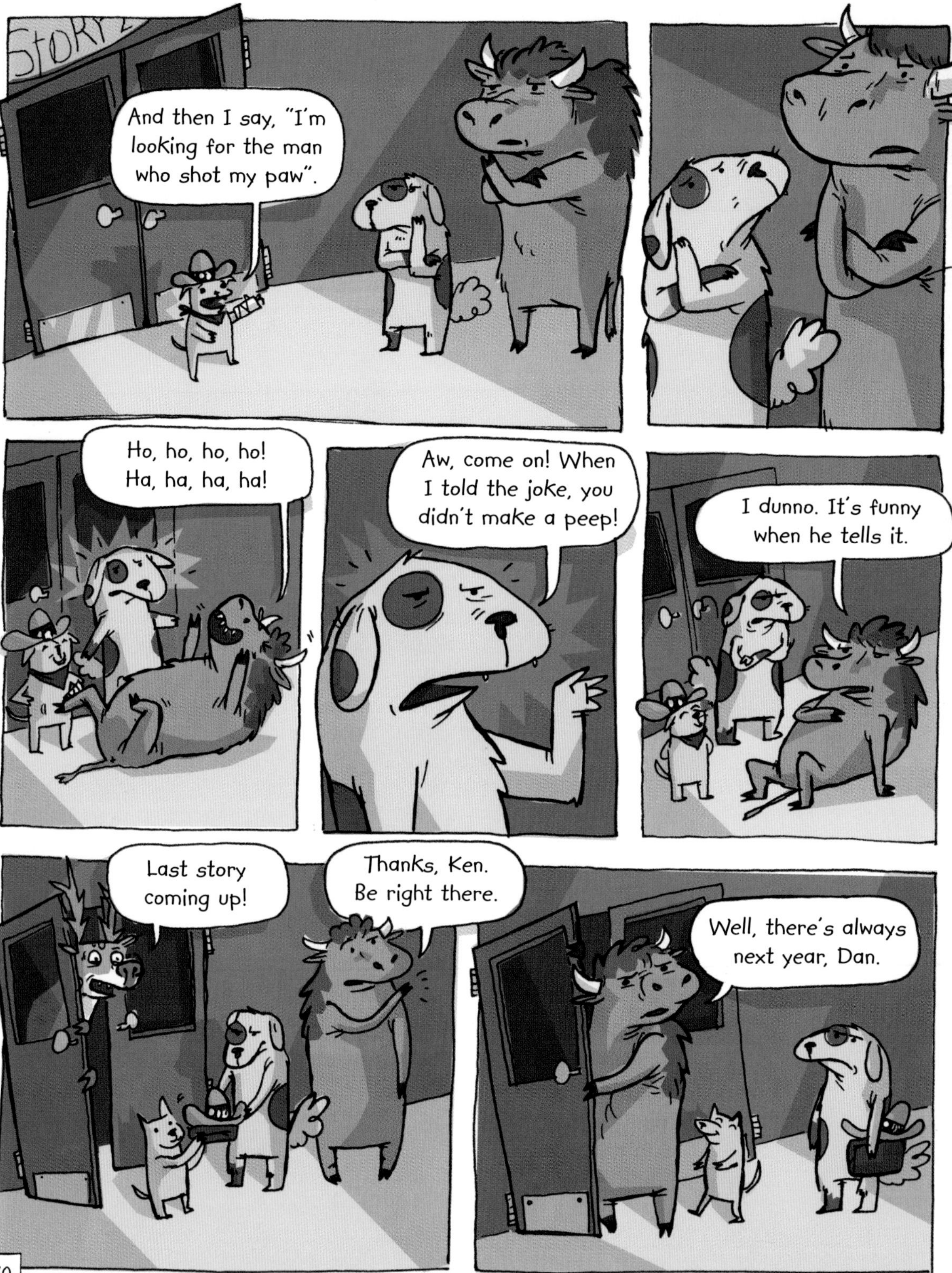
STORY 2
And then I say, "I'm looking for the man who shot my paw".
Ho, ho, ho, ho! Ha, ha, ha, ha!
Aw, come on! When I told the joke, you didn't make a peep!
I dunno. It's funny when he tells it.
Last story coming up!
Thanks, Ken. Be right there.
Well, there's always next year, Dan.

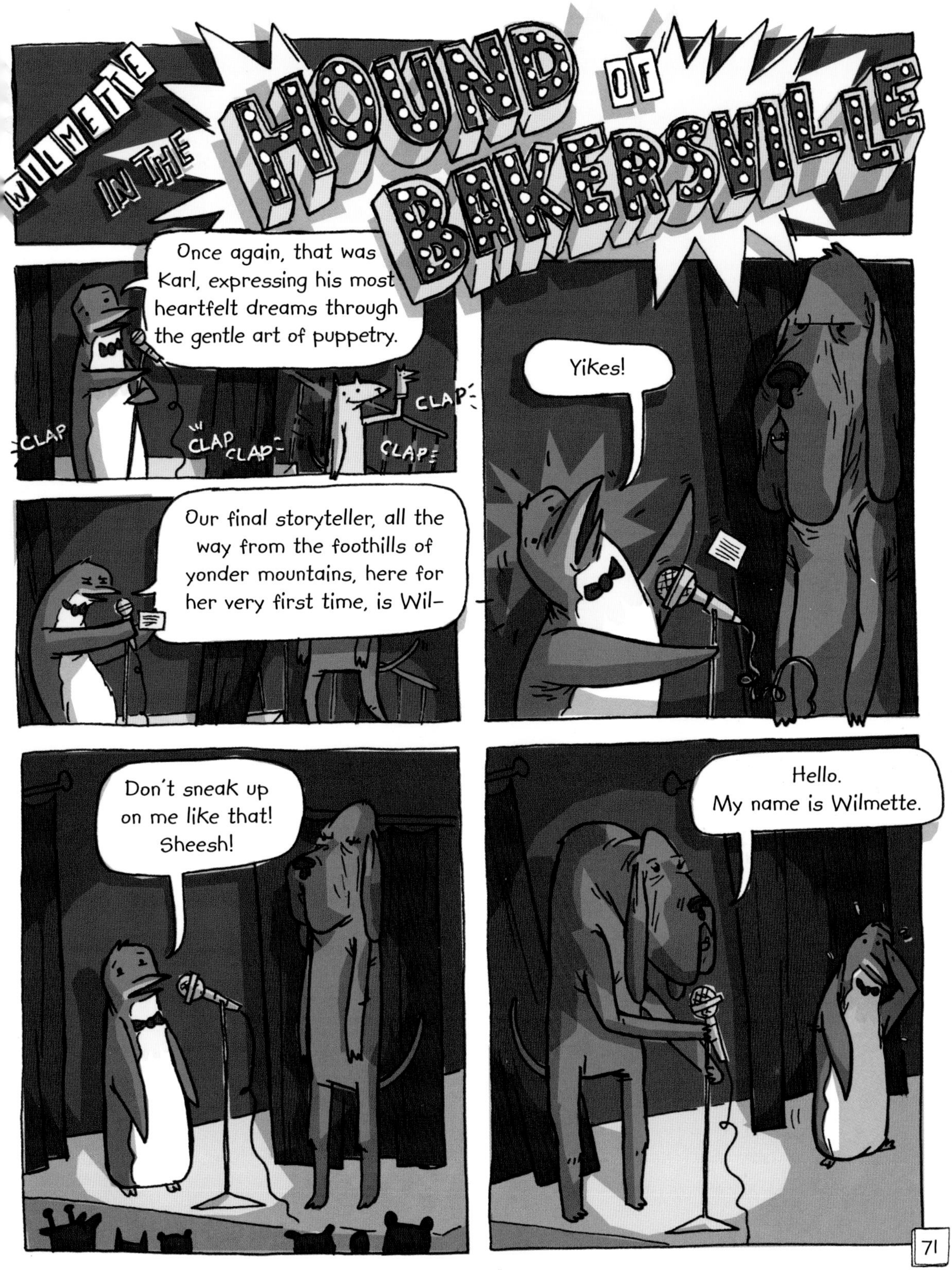
WILMETTE IN THE HOUND OF BAKERSVILLE
Once again, that was Karl, expressing his most heartfelt dreams through the gentle art of puppetry.
CLAP
CLAP CLAP
CLAP
CLAP
Our final storyteller, all the way from the foothills of yonder mountains, here for her very first time, is Wil-
Yikes!
Don't sneak up on me like that! Sheesh!
Hello. My name is Wilmette.

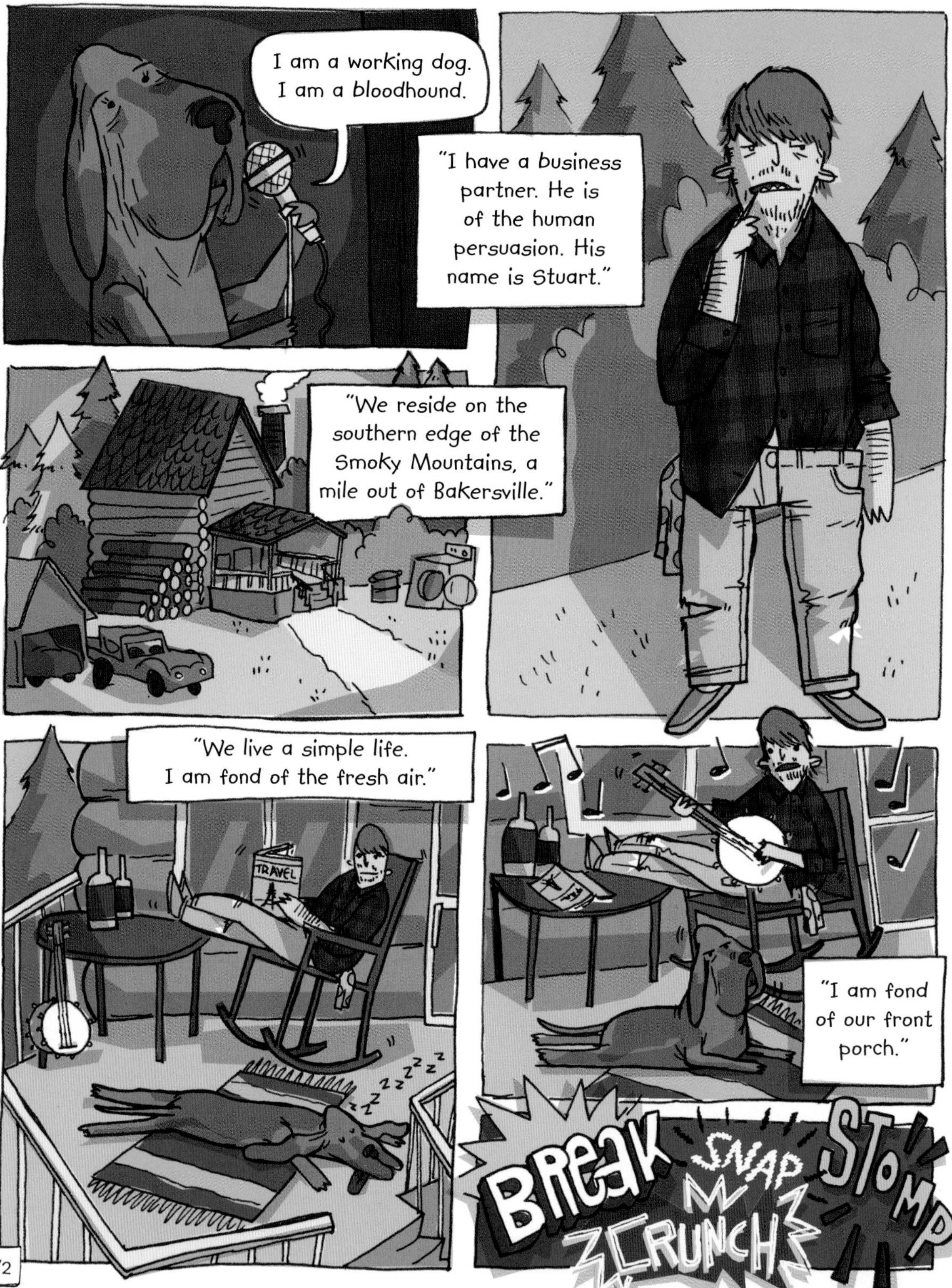
I am a working dog. I am a bloodhound.
"I have a business partner. He is of the human persuasion. His name is Stuart."
"We reside on the southern edge of the Smoky Mountains, a mile out of Bakersville."
"We live a simple life. I am fond of the fresh air."
TRAVEL
"I am fond of our front porch."
BREAK
SNAP
STOMP
CRUNCH

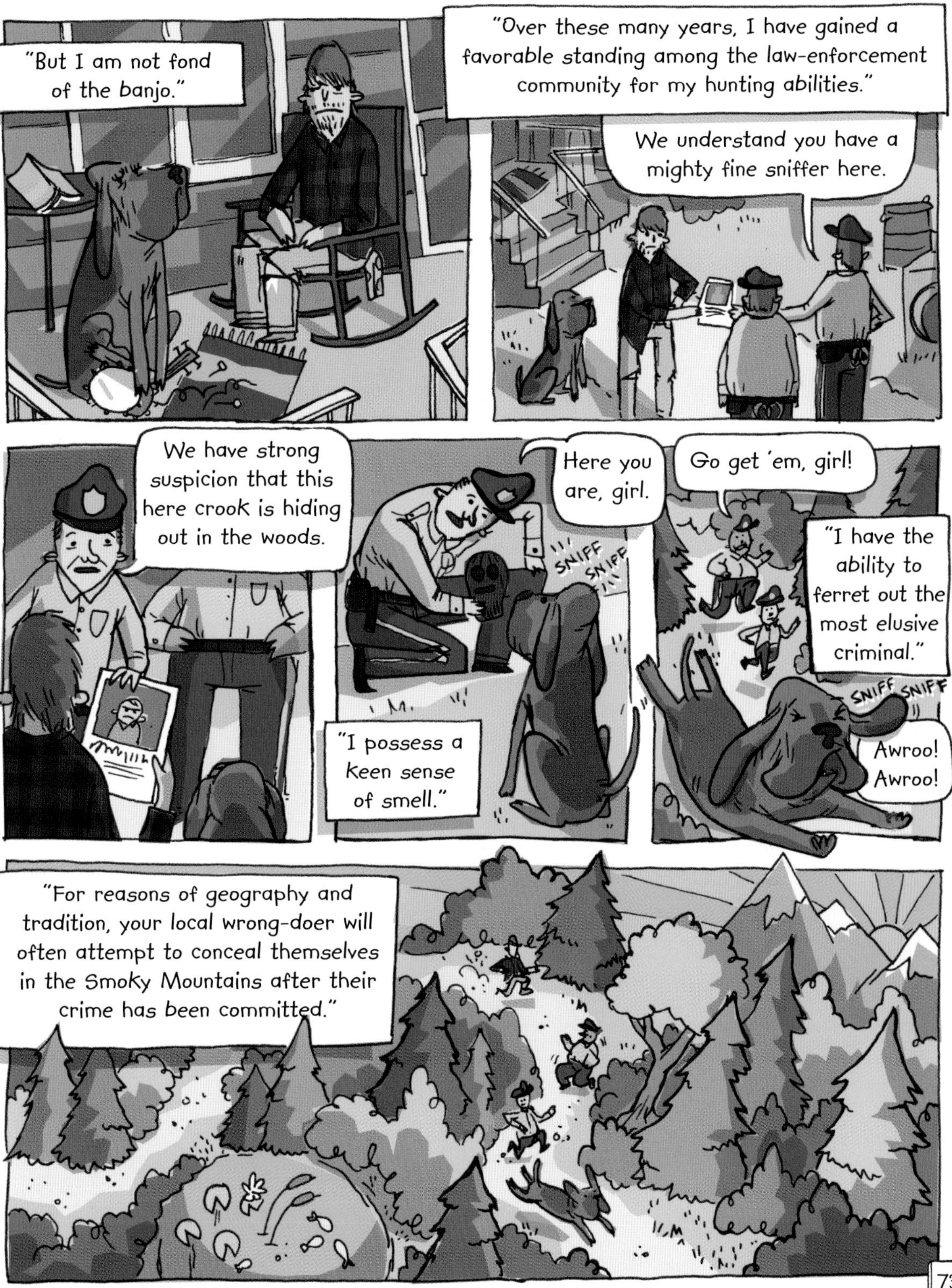
"But I am not fond of the banjo."
"Over these many years, I have gained a favorable standing among the law-enforcement community for my hunting abilities."
We understand you have a mighty fine sniffer here.
We have strong suspicion that this here crook is hiding out in the woods.
Here you are, girl.
SNIFF SNIFF
"I possess a keen sense of smell."
Go get 'em, girl!
"I have the ability to ferret out the most elusive criminal."
SNIFF SNIFF
Awroo! Awroo!
"For reasons of geography and tradition, your local wrong-doer will often attempt to conceal themselves in the Smoky Mountains after their crime has been committed."

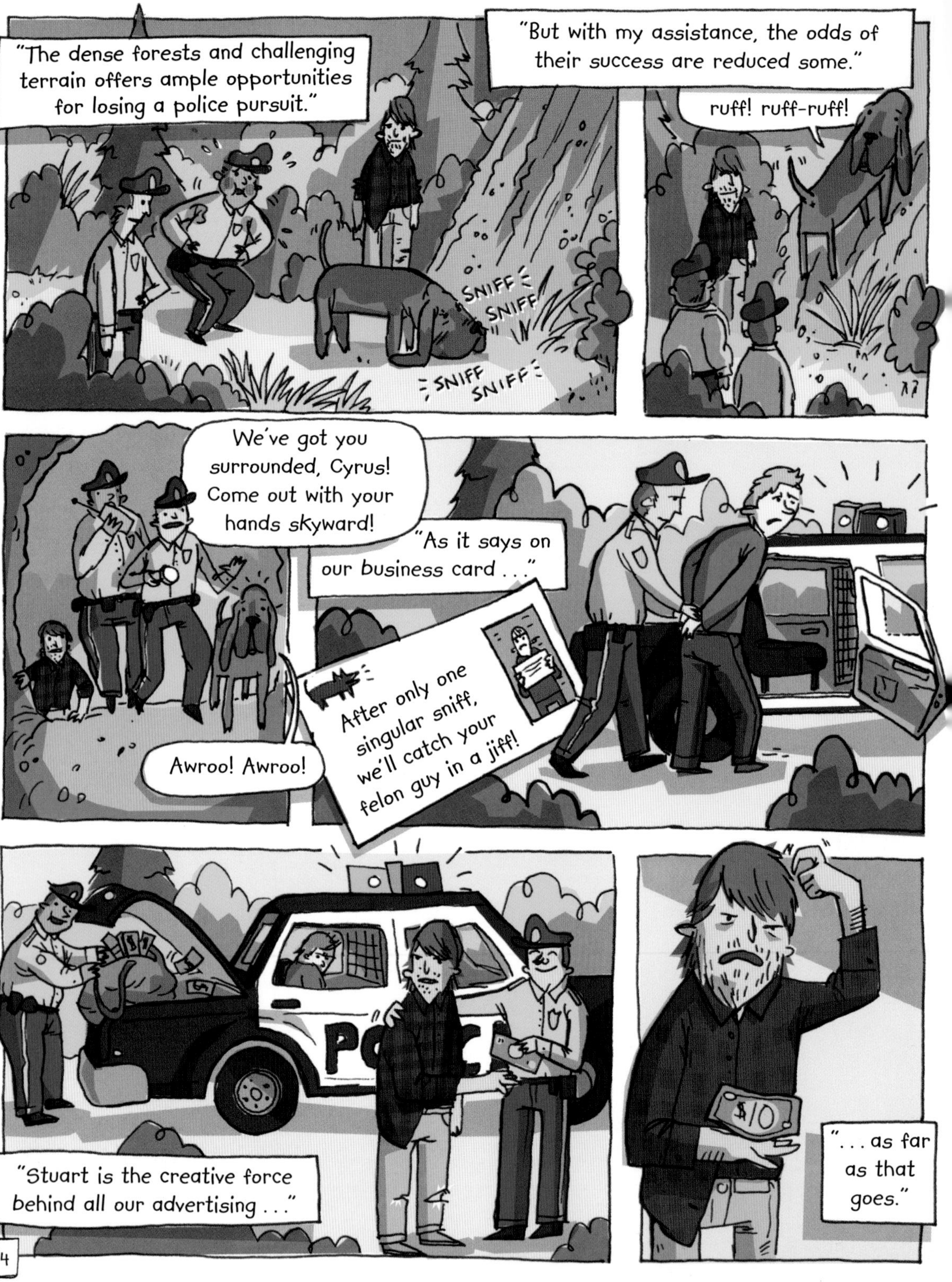
"The dense forests and challenging terrain offers ample opportunities for losing a police pursuit."
SNIFF SNIFF
SNIFF SNIFF
"But with my assistance, the odds of their success are reduced some."
ruff! ruff-ruff!
We've got you surrounded, Cyrus! Come out with your hands skyward!
Awroo! Awroo!
"As it says on our business card . . ."
After only one singular sniff, we'll catch your felon guy in a jiff!
"Stuart is the creative force behind all our advertising . . ."
$10
". . . as far as that goes."

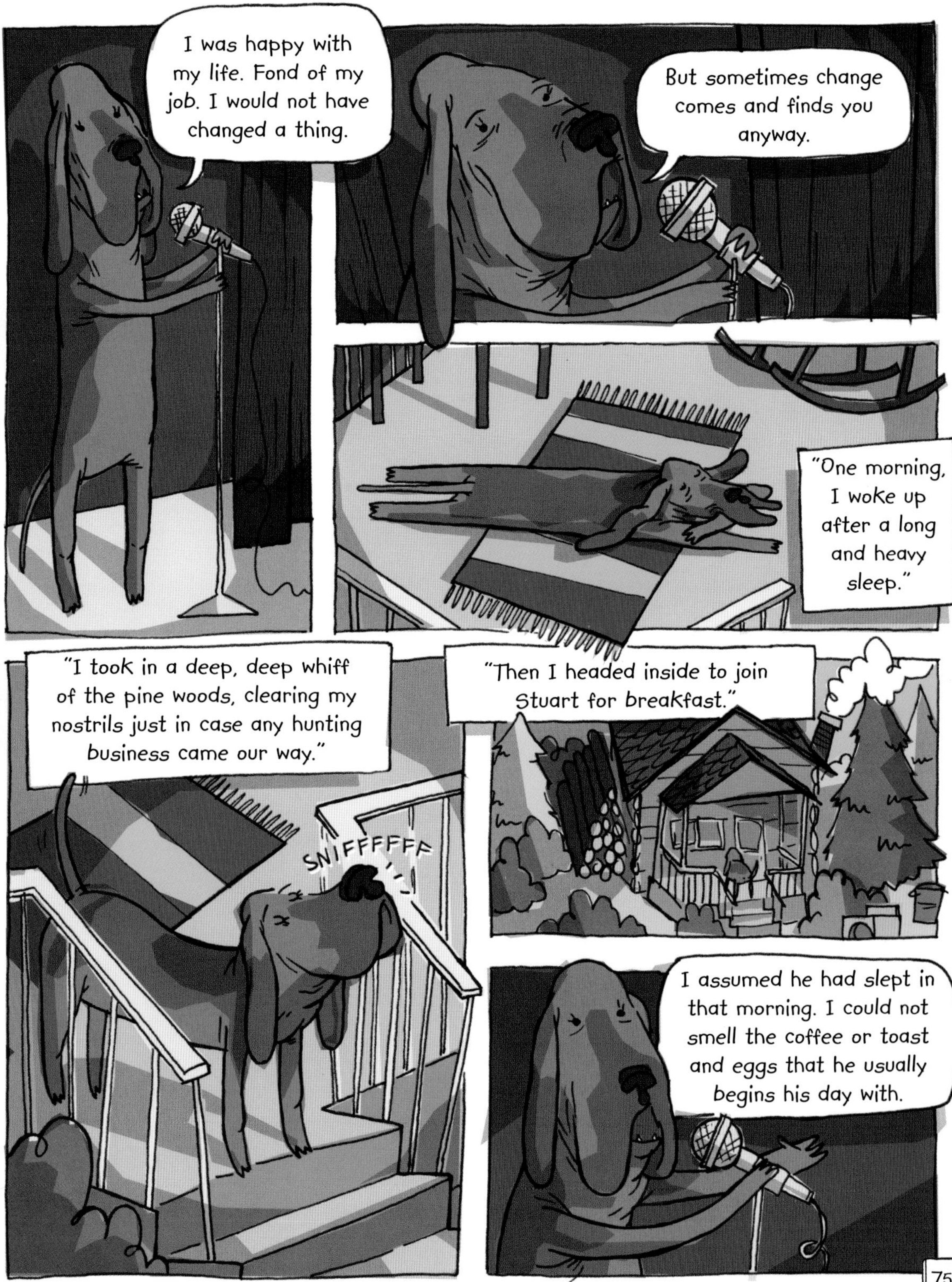
I was happy with my life. Fond of my job. I would not have changed a thing.
But sometimes change comes and finds you anyway.
"One morning, I woke up after a long and heavy sleep."
"I took in a deep, deep whiff of the pine woods, clearing my nostrils just in case any hunting business came our way."
SNIFFFFFF
"Then I headed inside to join Stuart for breakfast."
I assumed he had slept in that morning. I could not smell the coffee or toast and eggs that he usually begins his day with.

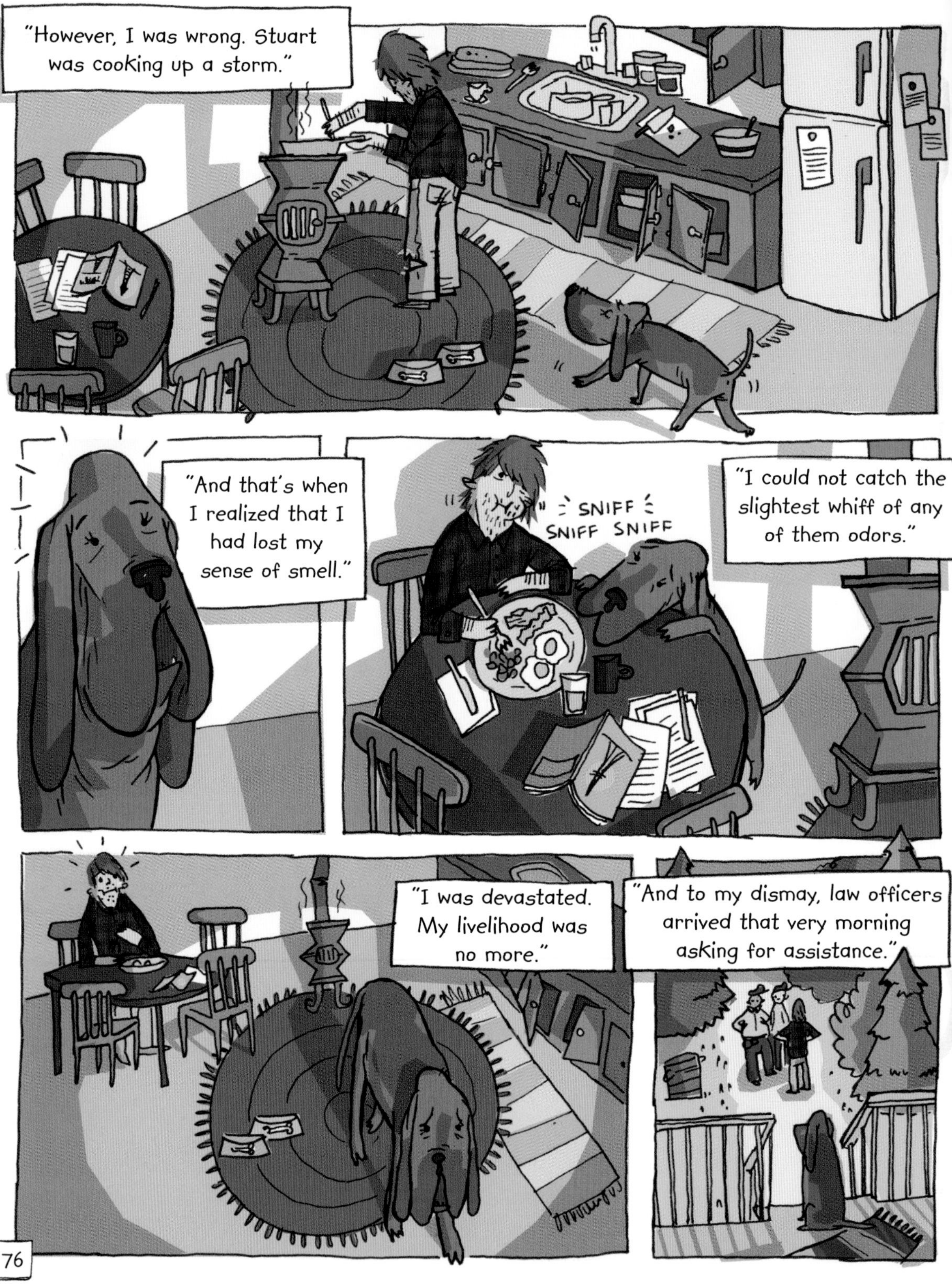
"However, I was wrong. Stuart was cooking up a storm."
"And that's when I realized that I had lost my sense of smell."
SNIFF
SNIFF SNIFF
"I could not catch the slightest whiff of any of them odors."
"I was devastated. My livelihood was no more."
"And to my dismay, law officers arrived that very morning asking for assistance."

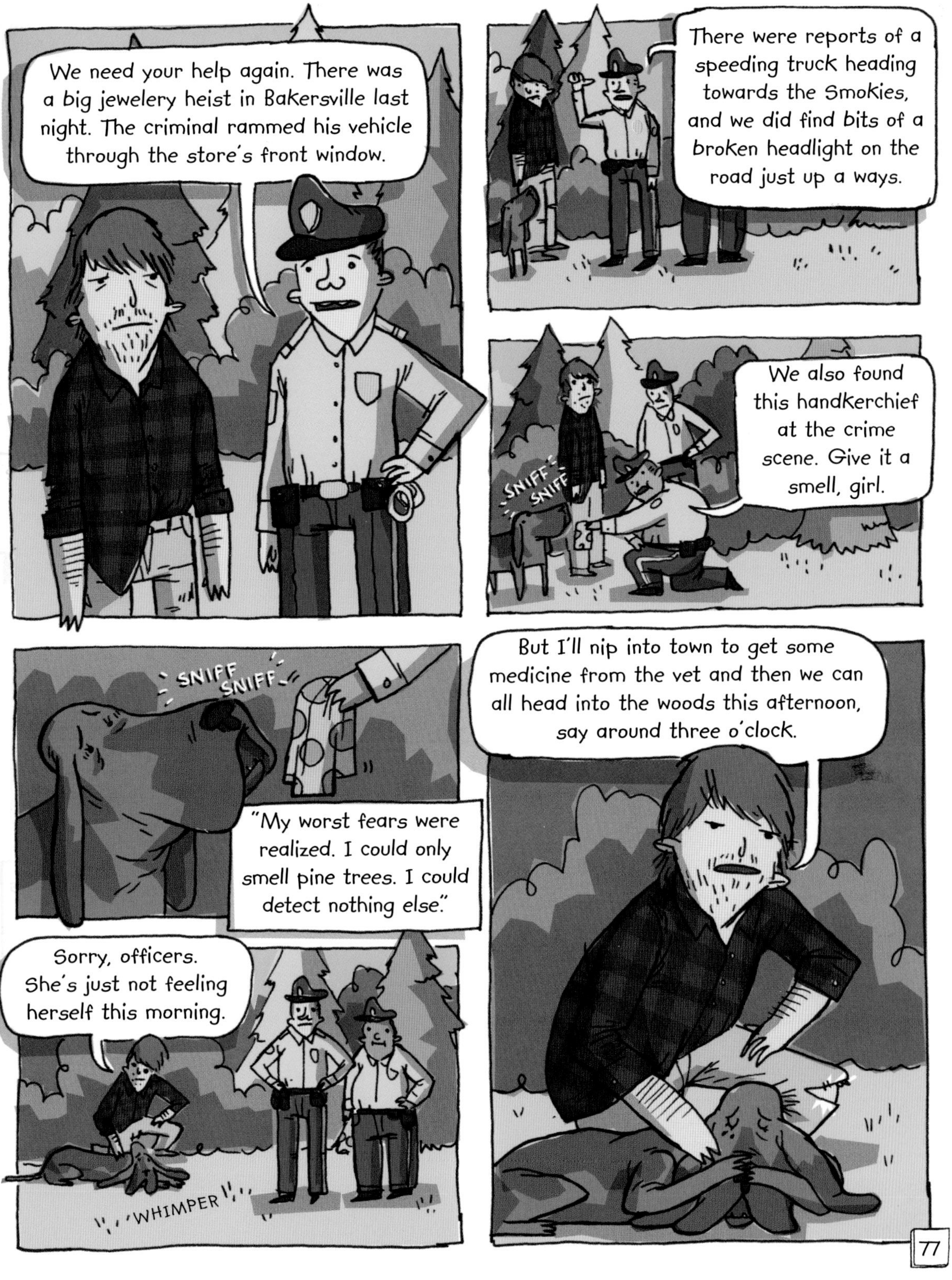

We need your help again. There was a big jewelery heist in Bakersville last night. The criminal rammed his vehicle through the store's front window.
There were reports of a speeding truck heading towards the Smokies, and we did find bits of a broken headlight on the road just up a ways.
SNIFF SNIFF
We also found this handkerchief at the crime scene. Give it a smell, girl.
SNIFF SNIFF
"My worst fears were realized. I could only smell pine trees. I could detect nothing else."
Sorry, officers. She's just not feeling herself this morning.
WHIMPER
But I'll nip into town to get some medicine from the vet and then we can all head into the woods this afternoon, say around three o'clock.

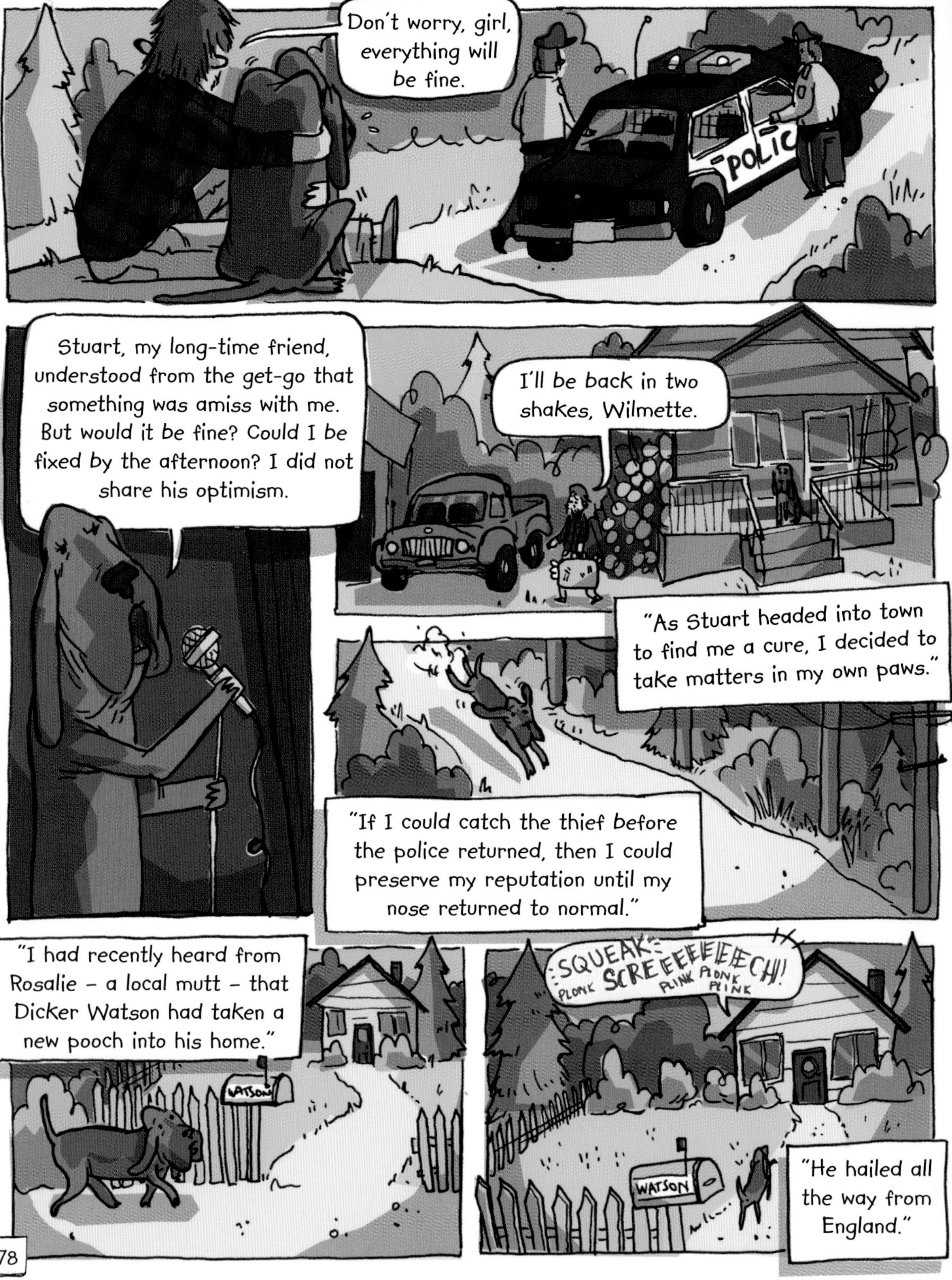
Don't worry, girl, everything will be fine.
Stuart, my long-time friend, understood from the get-go that something was amiss with me. But would it be fine? Could I be fixed by the afternoon? I did not share his optimism.
I'll be back in two shakes, Wilmette.
POLIC
"As Stuart headed into town to find me a cure, I decided to take matters in my own paws."
"If I could catch the thief before the police returned, then I could preserve my reputation until my nose returned to normal."
"I had recently heard from Rosalie – a local mutt – that Dicker Watson had taken a new pooch into his home."
WATSON
SQUEAK SCREEEEEEECH! PLONK PLINK PLONK PLINK
WATSON
"He hailed all the way from England."

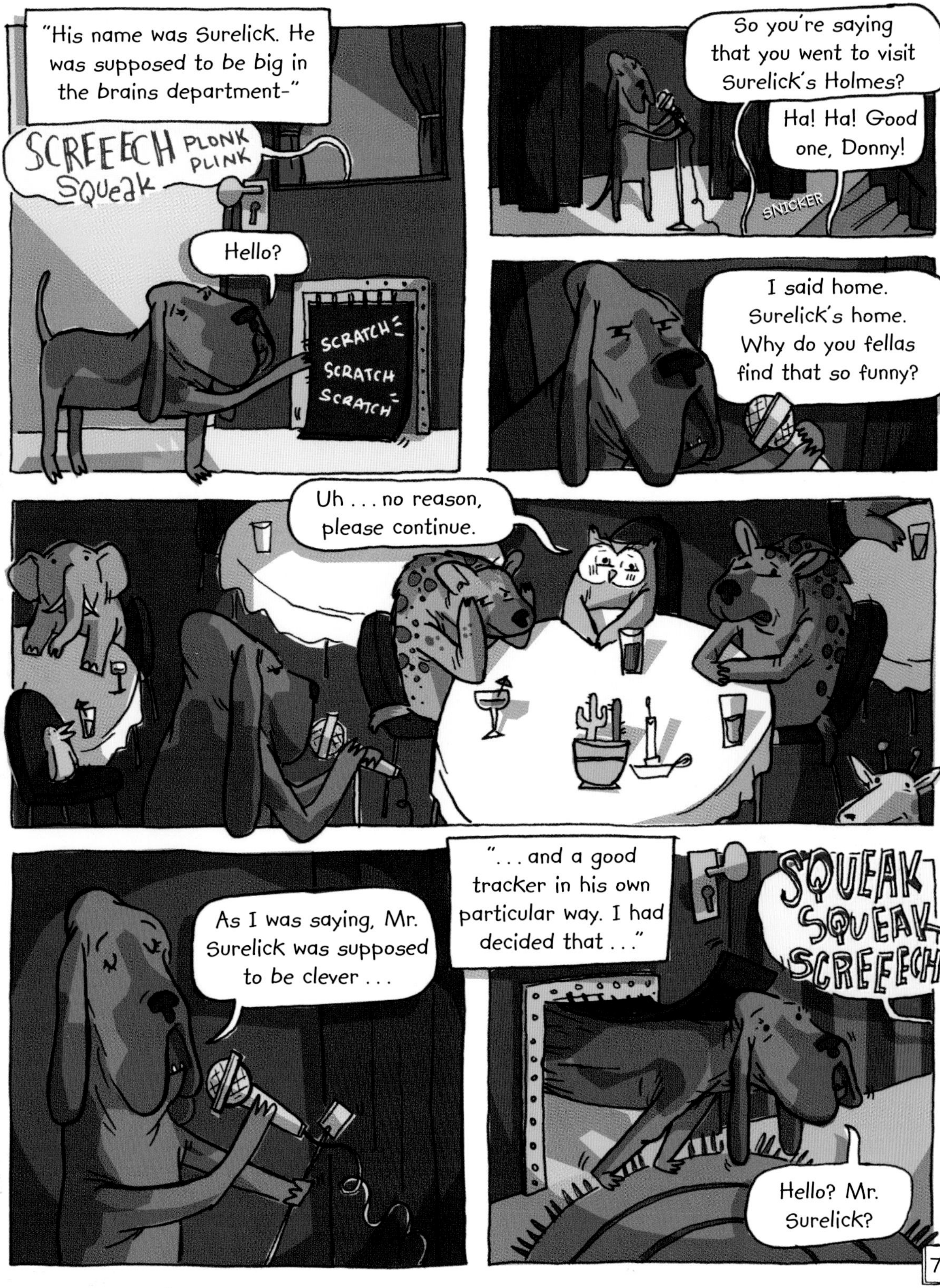
"His name was Surelick. He was supposed to be big in the brains department-"
SCREEECH PLONK PLINK SQUEAK
Hello?
SCRATCH SCRATCH SCRATCH
So you're saying that you went to visit Surelick's Holmes?
Ha! Ha! Good one, Donny!
SNICKER
I said home. Surelick's home. Why do you fellas find that so funny?
Uh . . . no reason, please continue.
As I was saying, Mr. Surelick was supposed to be clever . . .
". . . and a good tracker in his own particular way. I had decided that . . ."
SQUEAK SQUEAK SCREEECH
Hello? Mr. Surelick?

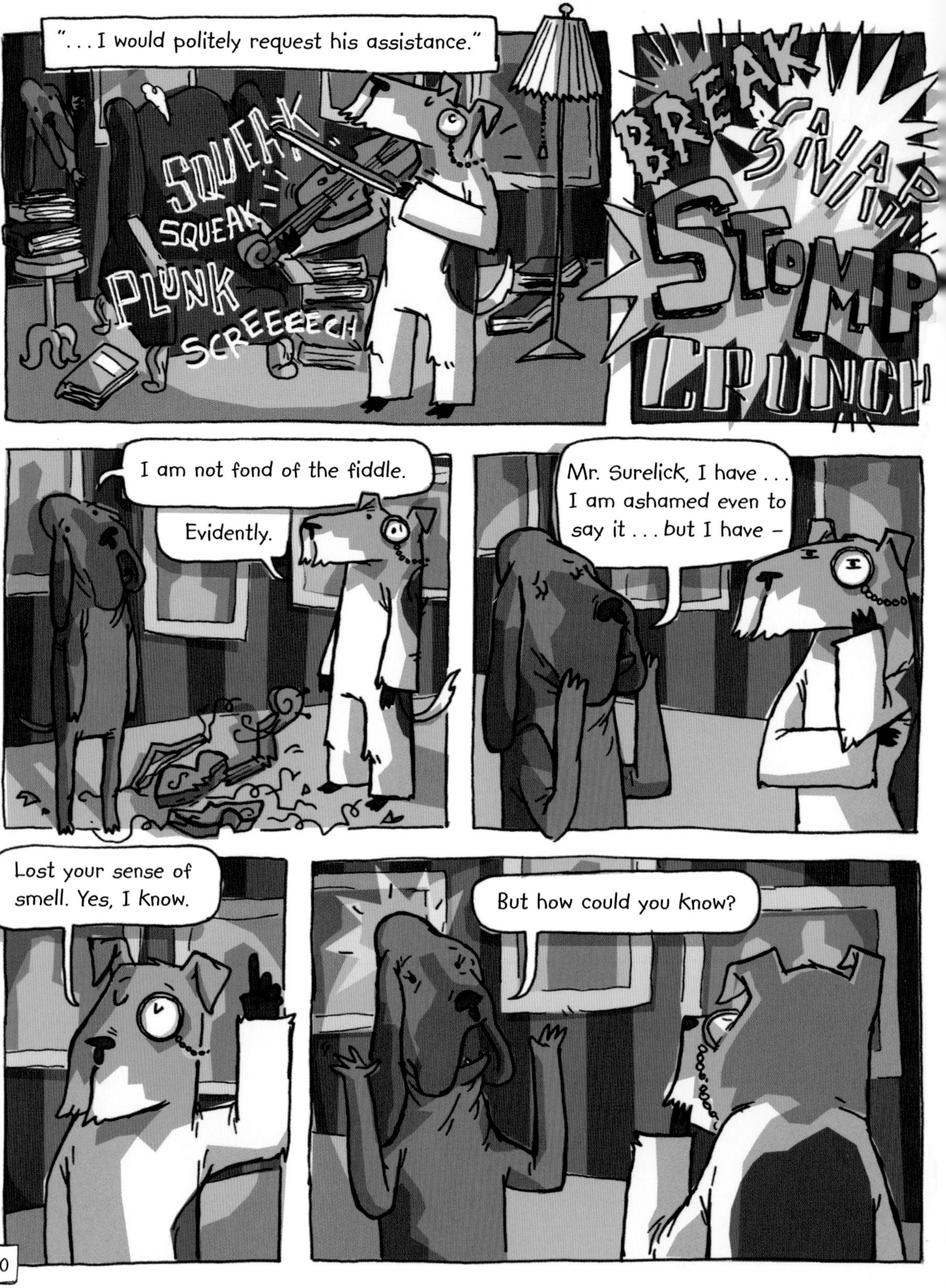

"... I would politely request his assistance."
SQUEAK
SQUEAK
PLUNK
SCREEEEECH
BREAK
SNAP
STOMP
CRUNCH
I am not fond of the fiddle.
Evidently.
Mr. Surelick, I have ... I am ashamed even to say it ... but I have –
Lost your sense of smell. Yes, I know.
But how could you know?

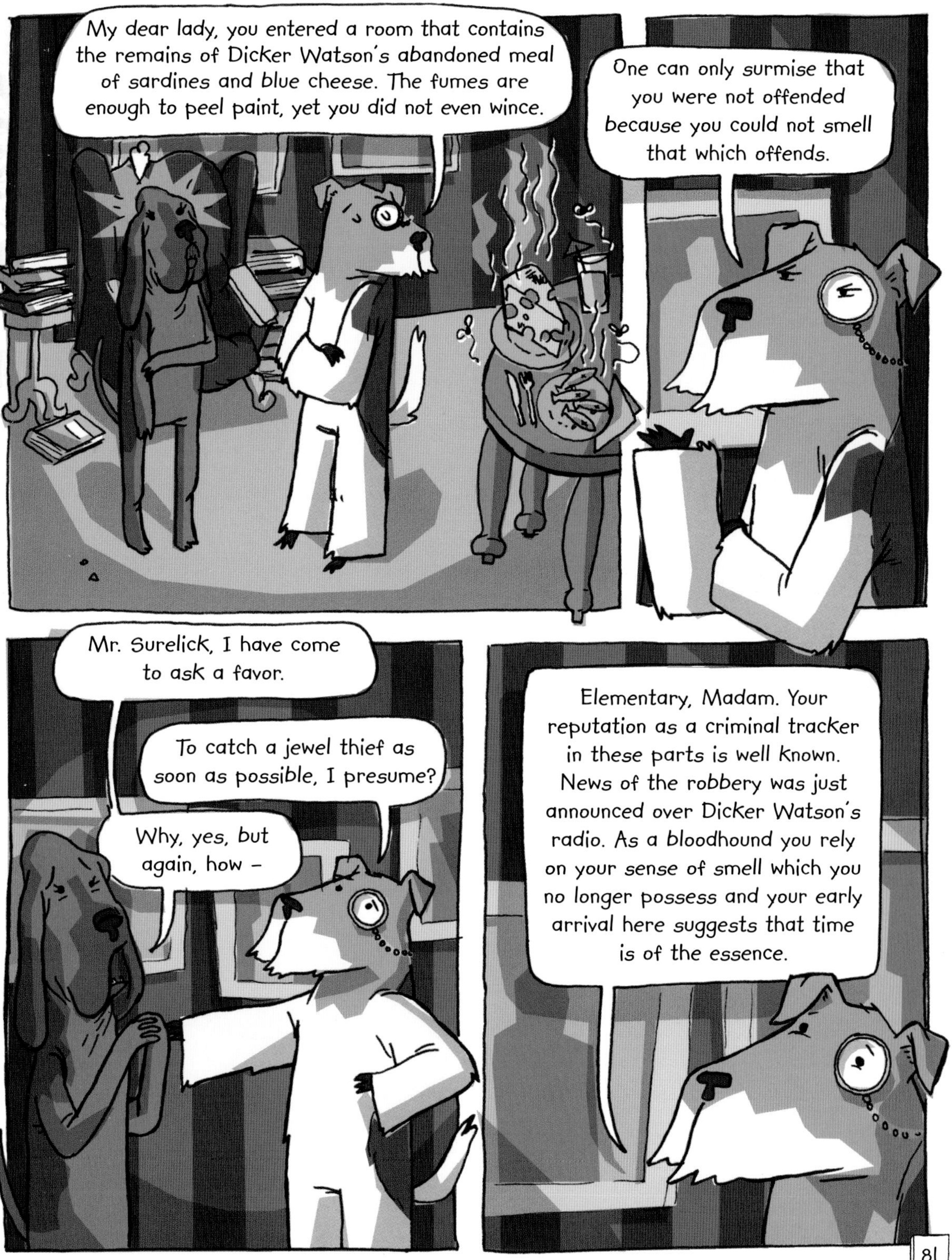

My dear lady, you entered a room that contains the remains of Dicker Watson's abandoned meal of sardines and blue cheese. The fumes are enough to peel paint, yet you did not even wince.
One can only surmise that you were not offended because you could not smell that which offends.
Mr. Surelick, I have come to ask a favor.
To catch a jewel thief as soon as possible, I presume?
Why, yes, but again, how –
Elementary, Madam. Your reputation as a criminal tracker in these parts is well known. News of the robbery was just announced over Dicker Watson's radio. As a bloodhound you rely on your sense of smell which you no longer possess and your early arrival here suggests that time is of the essence.

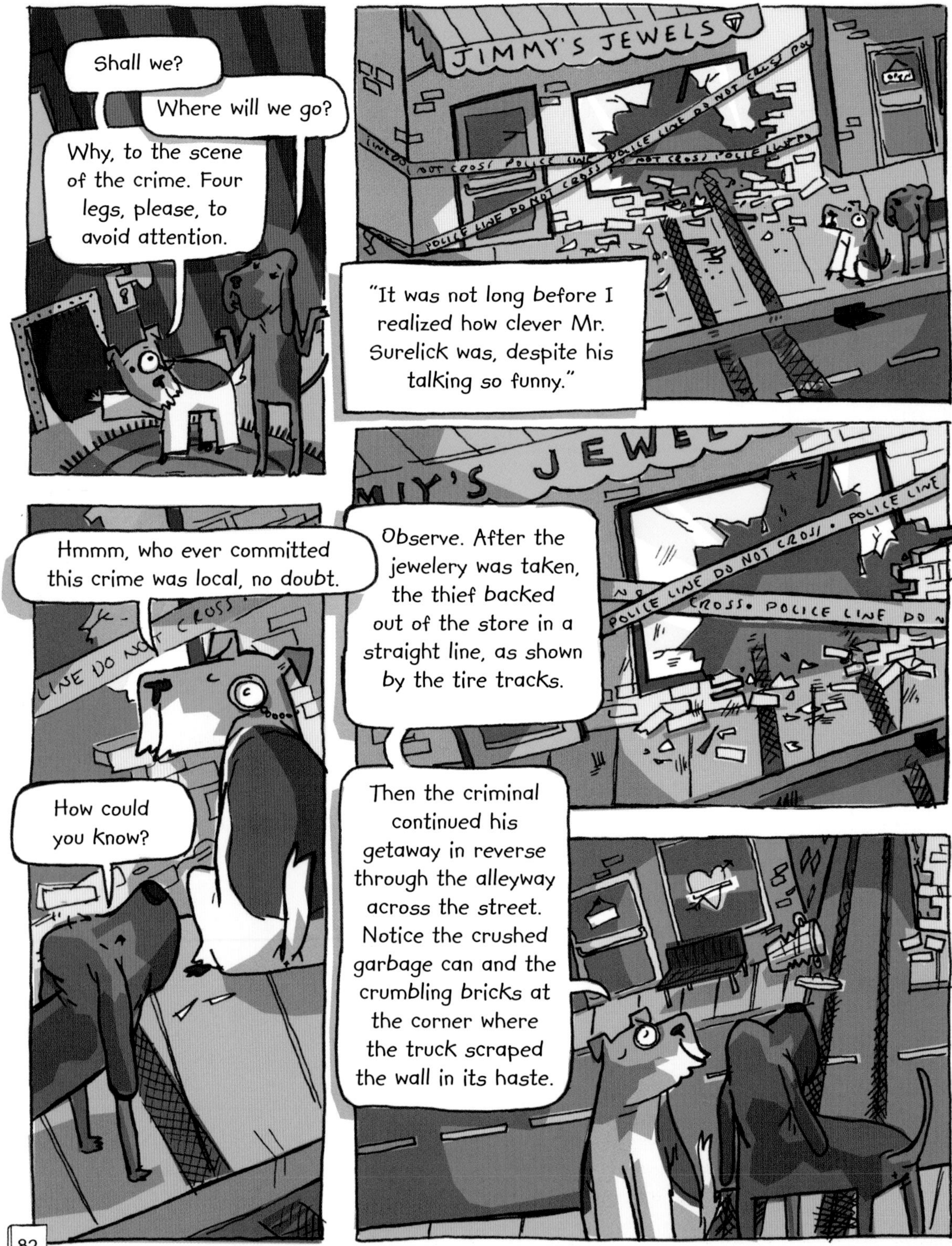

Shall we?
Where will we go?
Why, to the scene of the crime. Four legs, please, to avoid attention.
JIMMY'S JEWELS
"It was not long before I realized how clever Mr. Surelick was, despite his talking so funny."
Hmmm, who ever committed this crime was local, no doubt.
How could you know?
Observe. After the jewelery was taken, the thief backed out of the store in a straight line, as shown by the tire tracks.
POLICE LINE DO NOT CROSS
Then the criminal continued his getaway in reverse through the alleyway across the street. Notice the crushed garbage can and the crumbling bricks at the corner where the truck scraped the wall in its haste.

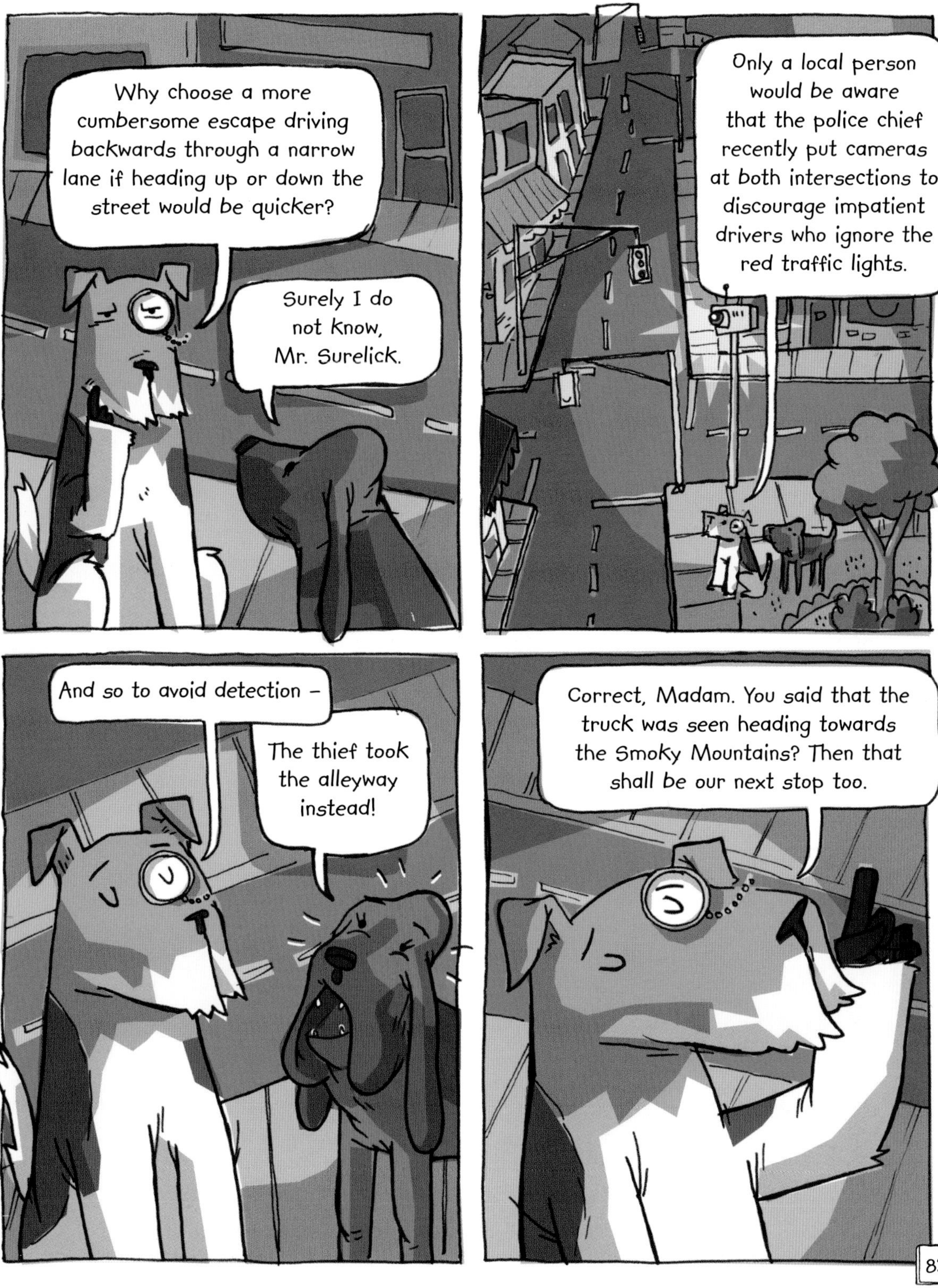
Why choose a more cumbersome escape driving backwards through a narrow lane if heading up or down the street would be quicker?
Surely I do not know, Mr. Surelick.
Only a local person would be aware that the police chief recently put cameras at both intersections to discourage impatient drivers who ignore the red traffic lights.
And so to avoid detection –
The thief took the alleyway instead!
Correct, Madam. You said that the truck was seen heading towards the Smoky Mountains? Then that shall be our next stop too.

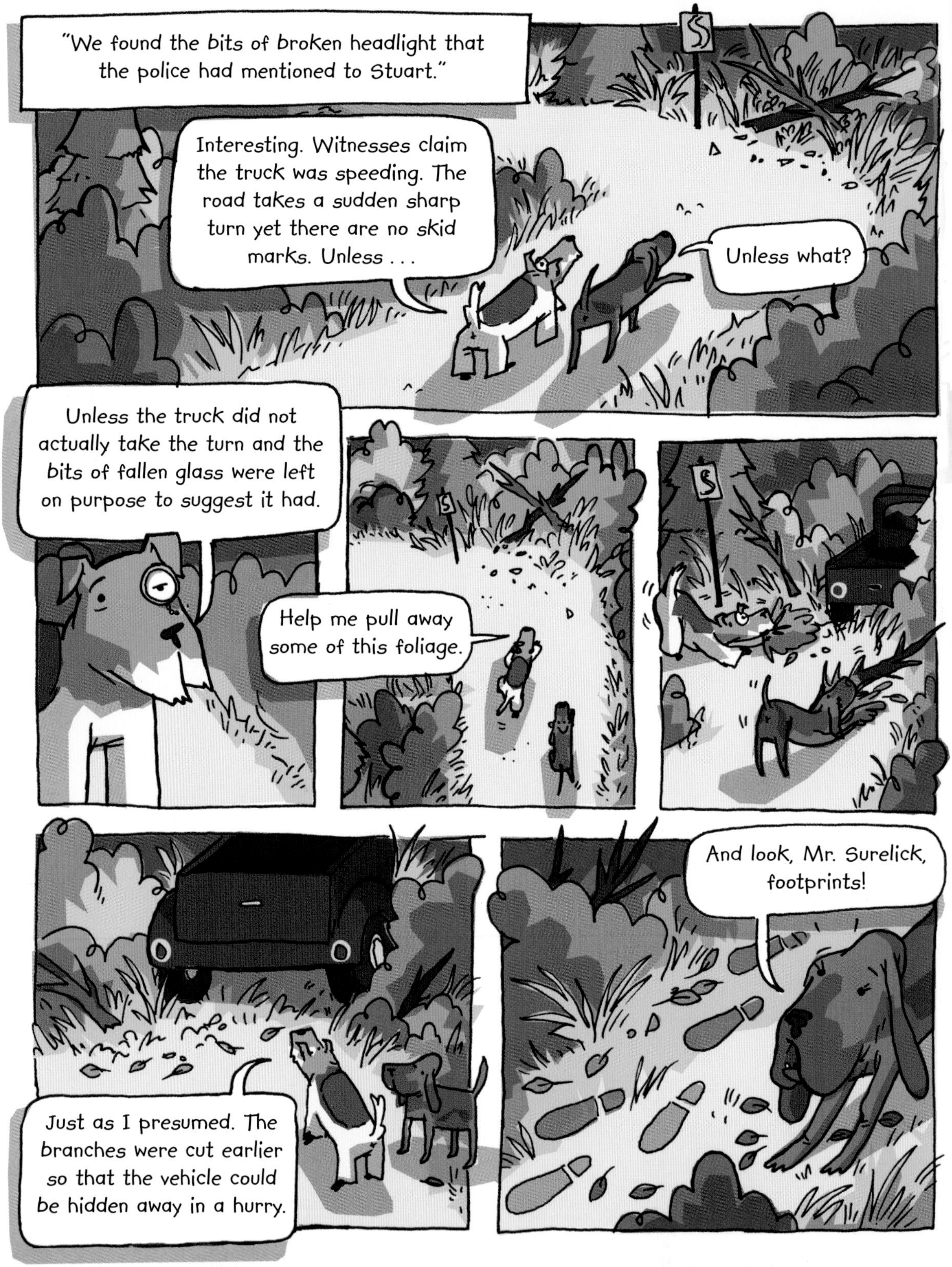
"We found the bits of broken headlight that the police had mentioned to Stuart."
Interesting. Witnesses claim the truck was speeding. The road takes a sudden sharp turn yet there are no skid marks. Unless . . .
Unless what?
Unless the truck did not actually take the turn and the bits of fallen glass were left on purpose to suggest it had.
Help me pull away some of this foliage.
Just as I presumed. The branches were cut earlier so that the vehicle could be hidden away in a hurry.
And look, Mr. Surelick, footprints!

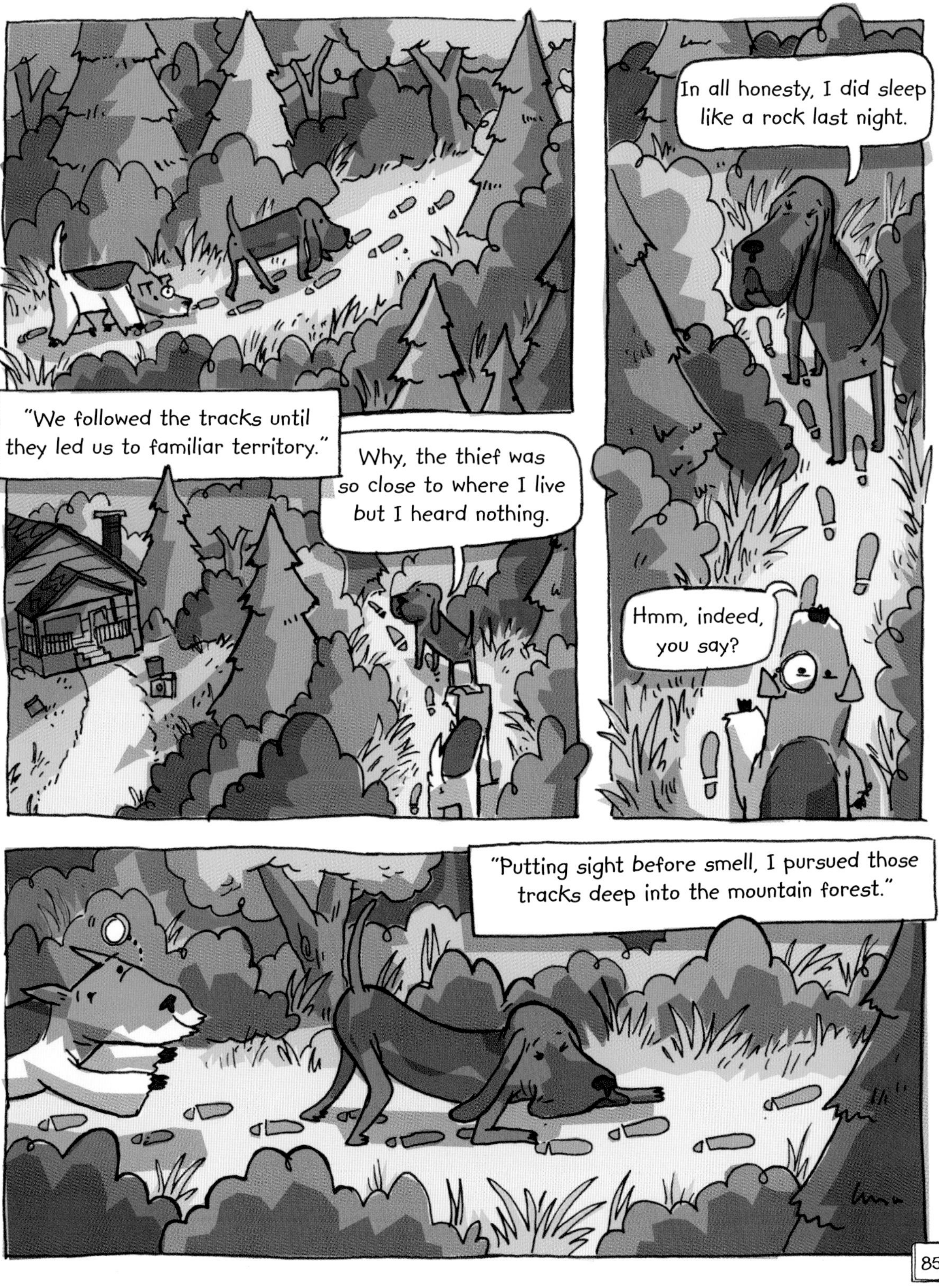

"We followed the tracks until they led us to familiar territory."
Why, the thief was so close to where I live but I heard nothing.
In all honesty, I did sleep like a rock last night.
Hmm, indeed, you say?
"Putting sight before smell, I pursued those tracks deep into the mountain forest."

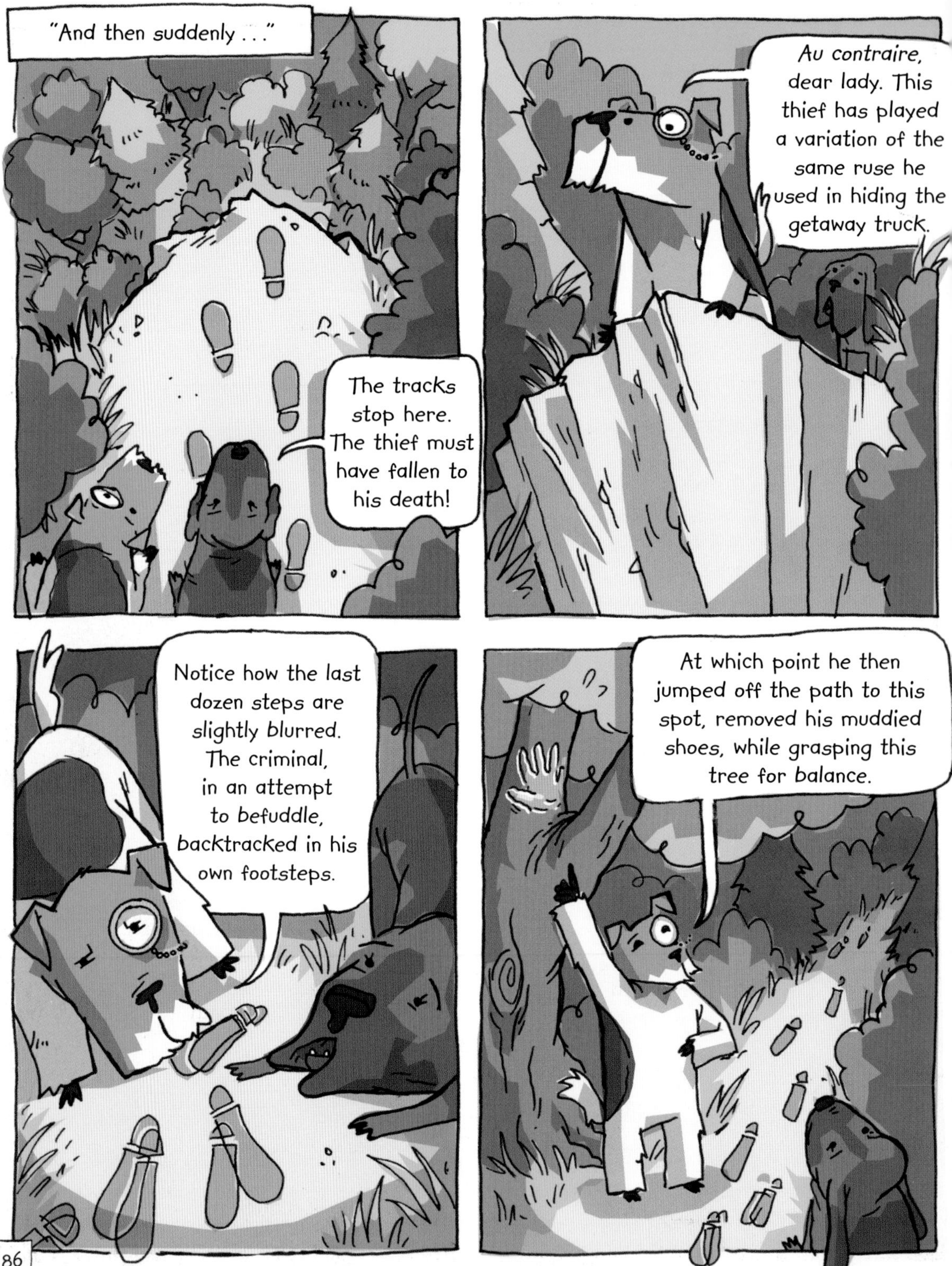
"And then suddenly . . ."
The tracks stop here. The thief must have fallen to his death!
Au contraire, dear lady. This thief has played a variation of the same ruse he used in hiding the getaway truck.
Notice how the last dozen steps are slightly blurred. The criminal, in an attempt to befuddle, backtracked in his own footsteps.
At which point he then jumped off the path to this spot, removed his muddied shoes, while grasping this tree for balance.

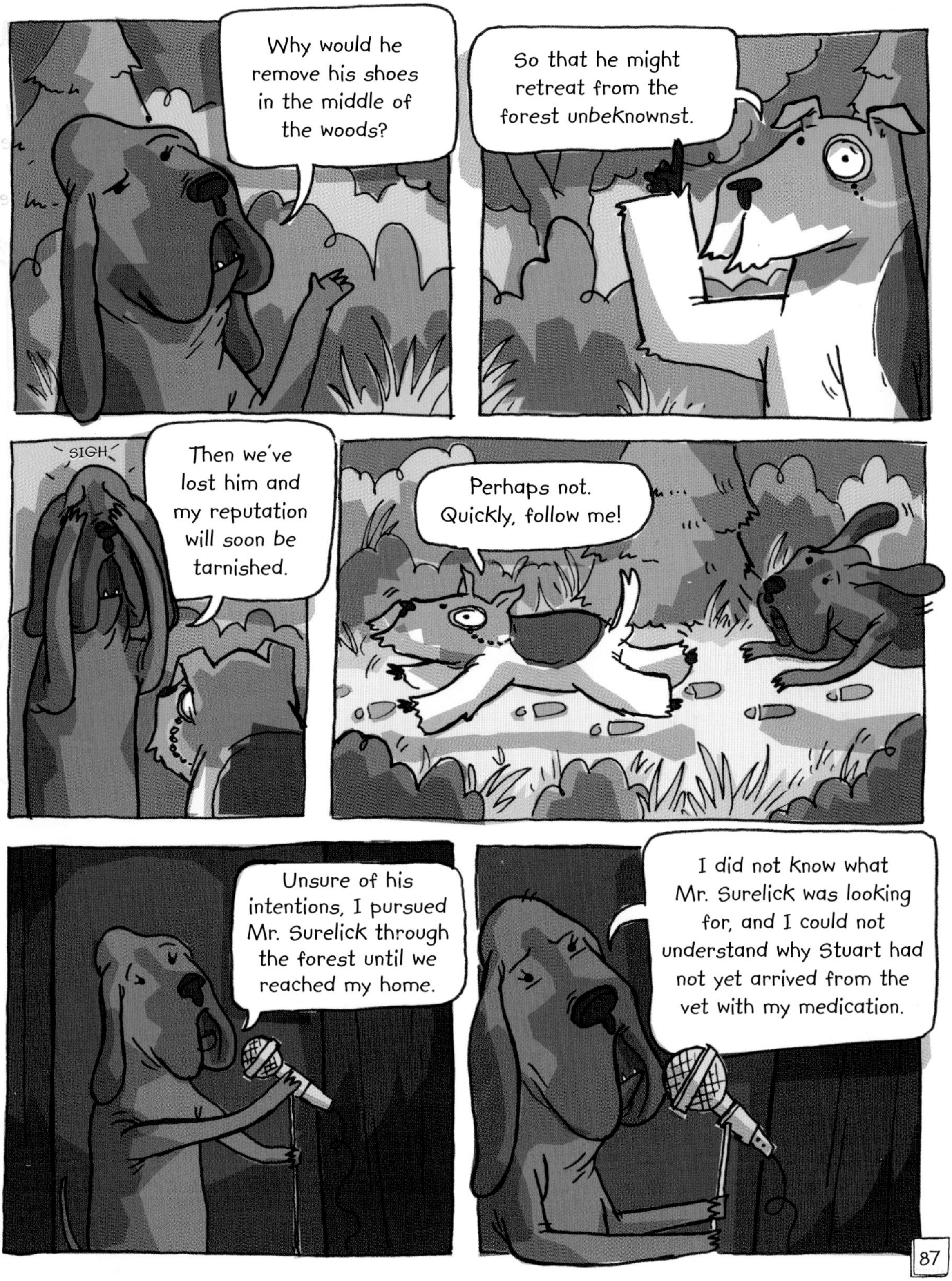
Why would he remove his shoes in the middle of the woods?
So that he might retreat from the forest unbeknownst.
SIGH
Then we've lost him and my reputation will soon be tarnished.
Perhaps not. Quickly, follow me!
Unsure of his intentions, I pursued Mr. Surelick through the forest until we reached my home.
I did not know what Mr. Surelick was looking for, and I could not understand why Stuart had not yet arrived from the vet with my medication.

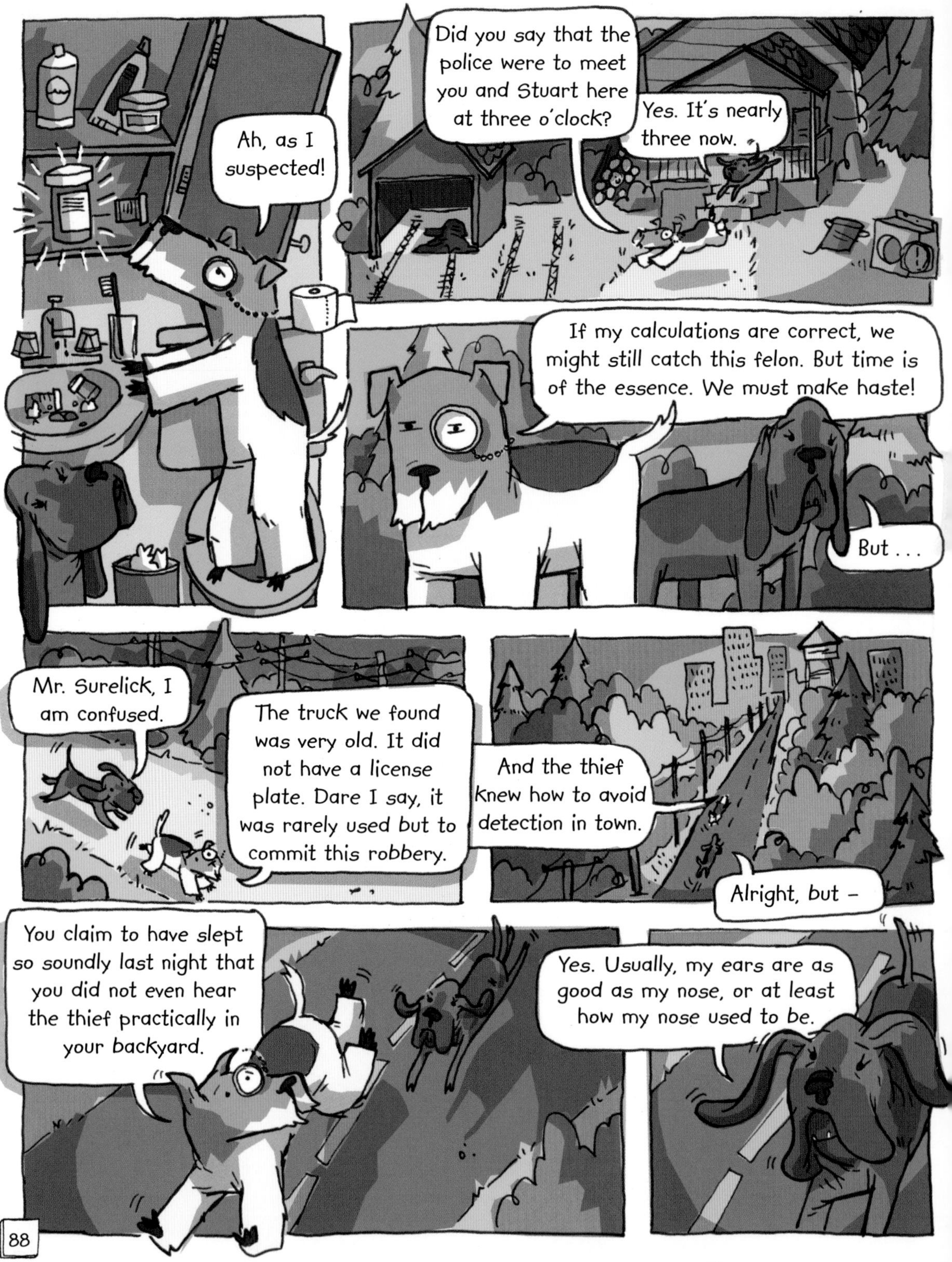
Ah, as I suspected!
Did you say that the police were to meet you and Stuart here at three o'clock?
Yes. It's nearly three now.
If my calculations are correct, we might still catch this felon. But time is of the essence. We must make haste!
But . . .
Mr. Surelick, I am confused.
The truck we found was very old. It did not have a license plate. Dare I say, it was rarely used but to commit this robbery.
And the thief knew how to avoid detection in town.
Alright, but –
You claim to have slept so soundly last night that you did not even hear the thief practically in your backyard.
Yes. Usually, my ears are as good as my nose, or at least how my nose used to be.

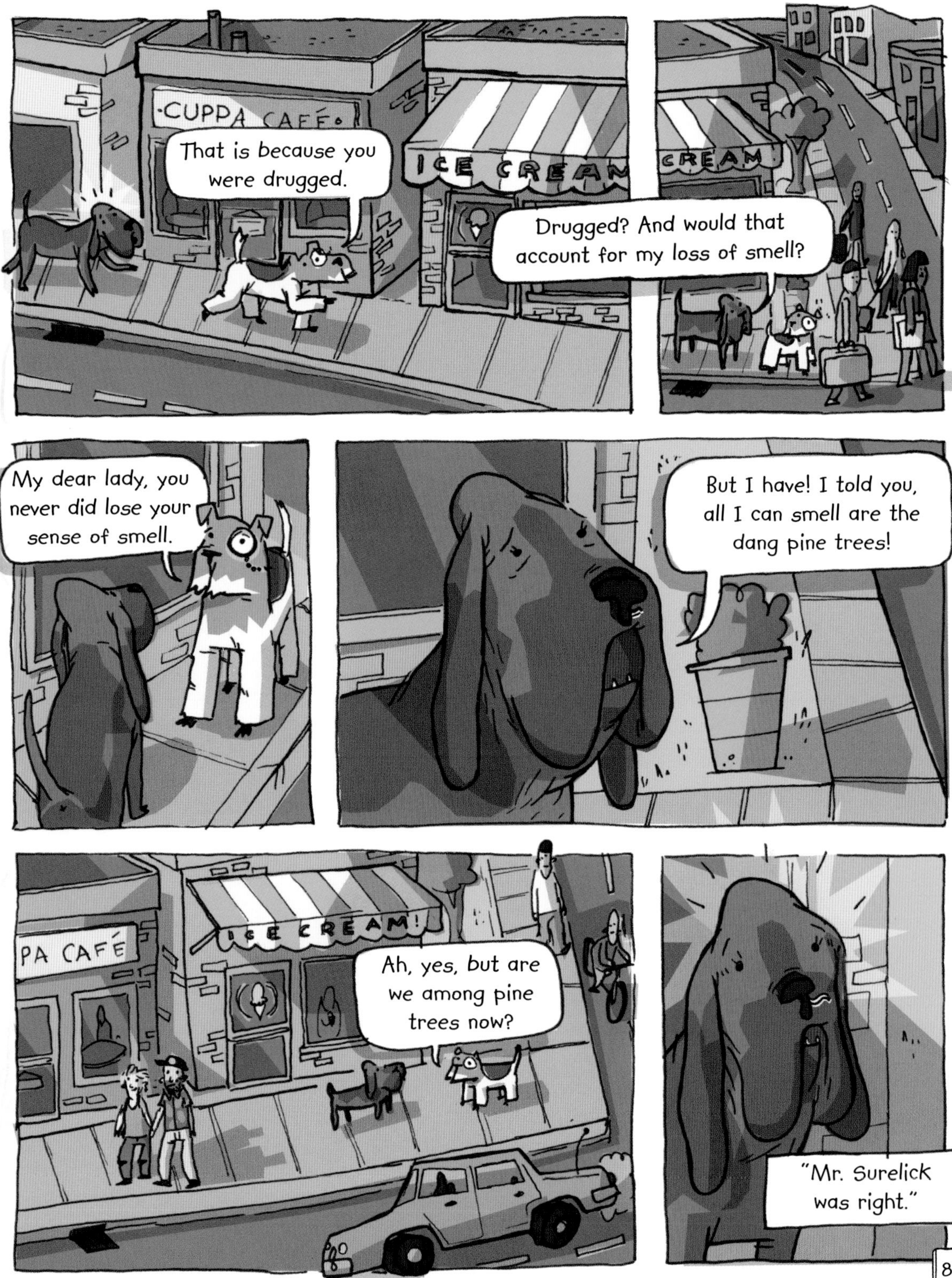
CUPPA CAFÉ
That is because you were drugged.
ICE CREAM
CREAM
Drugged? And would that account for my loss of smell?
My dear lady, you never did lose your sense of smell.
But I have! I told you, all I can smell are the dang pine trees!
PA CAFÉ
ICE CREAM!
Ah, yes, but are we among pine trees now?
"Mr. Surelick was right."

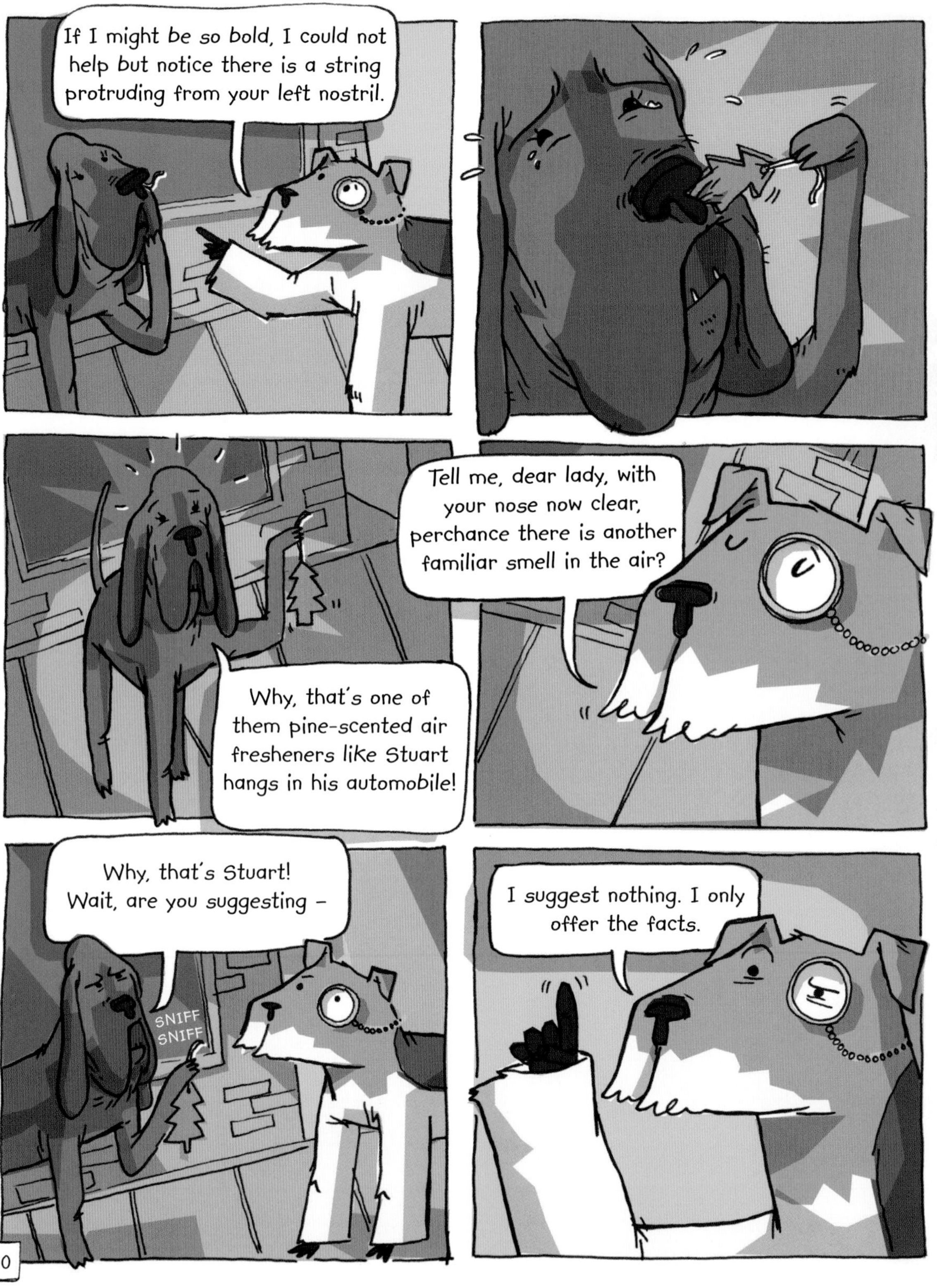
If I might be so bold, I could not help but notice there is a string protruding from your left nostril.
Why, that's one of them pine-scented air fresheners like Stuart hangs in his automobile!
Tell me, dear lady, with your nose now clear, perchance there is another familiar smell in the air?
Why, that's Stuart! Wait, are you suggesting –
SNIFF SNIFF
I suggest nothing. I only offer the facts.

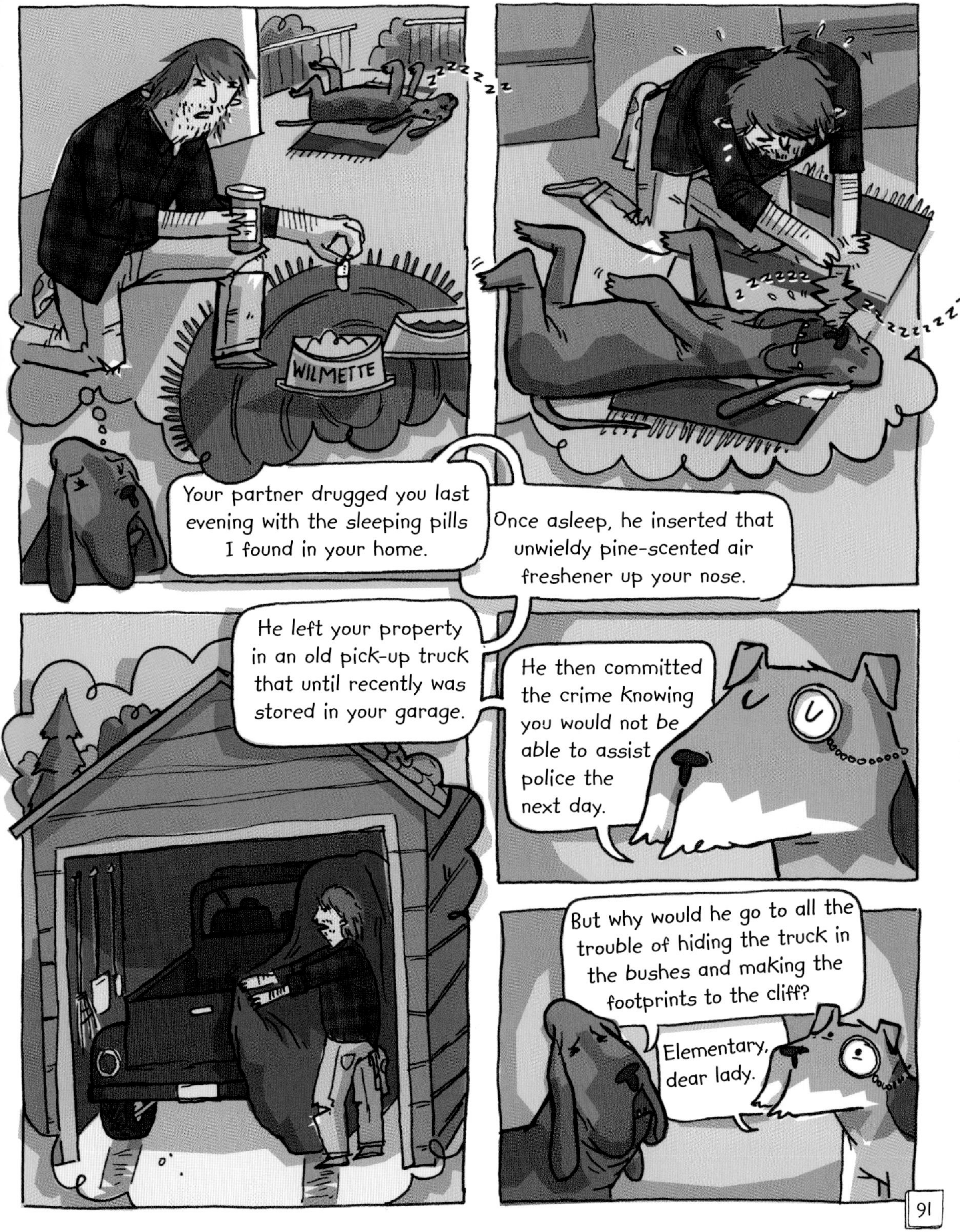
WILMETTE
Your partner drugged you last evening with the sleeping pills I found in your home.
Once asleep, he inserted that unwieldy pine-scented air freshener up your nose.
He left your property in an old pick-up truck that until recently was stored in your garage.
He then committed the crime knowing you would not be able to assist police the next day.
But why would he go to all the trouble of hiding the truck in the bushes and making the footprints to the cliff?
Elementary, dear lady.

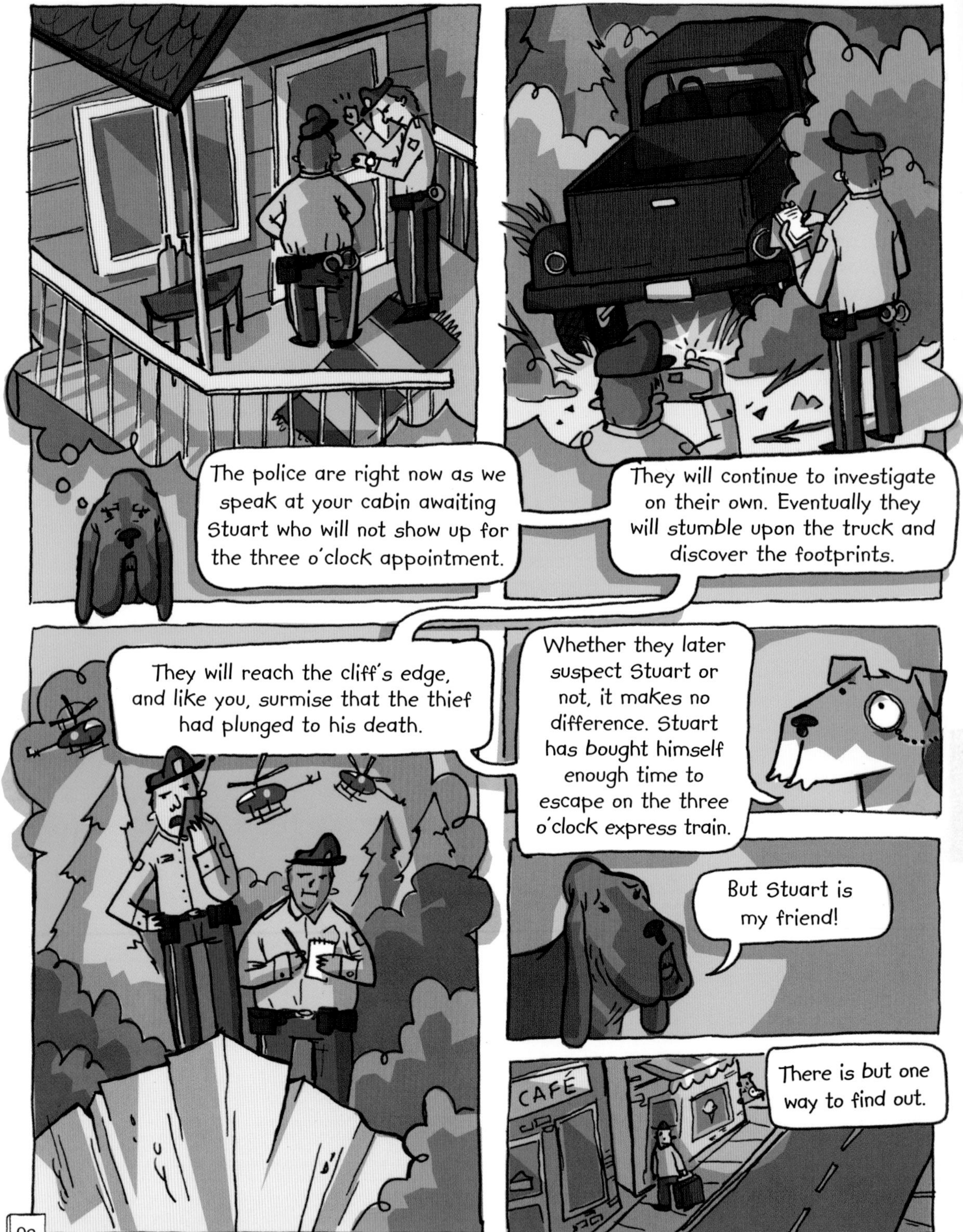
The police are right now as we speak at your cabin awaiting Stuart who will not show up for the three o'clock appointment.
They will continue to investigate on their own. Eventually they will stumble upon the truck and discover the footprints.
They will reach the cliff's edge, and like you, surmise that the thief had plunged to his death.
Whether they later suspect Stuart or not, it makes no difference. Stuart has bought himself enough time to escape on the three o'clock express train.
But Stuart is my friend!
CAFÉ
There is but one way to find out.

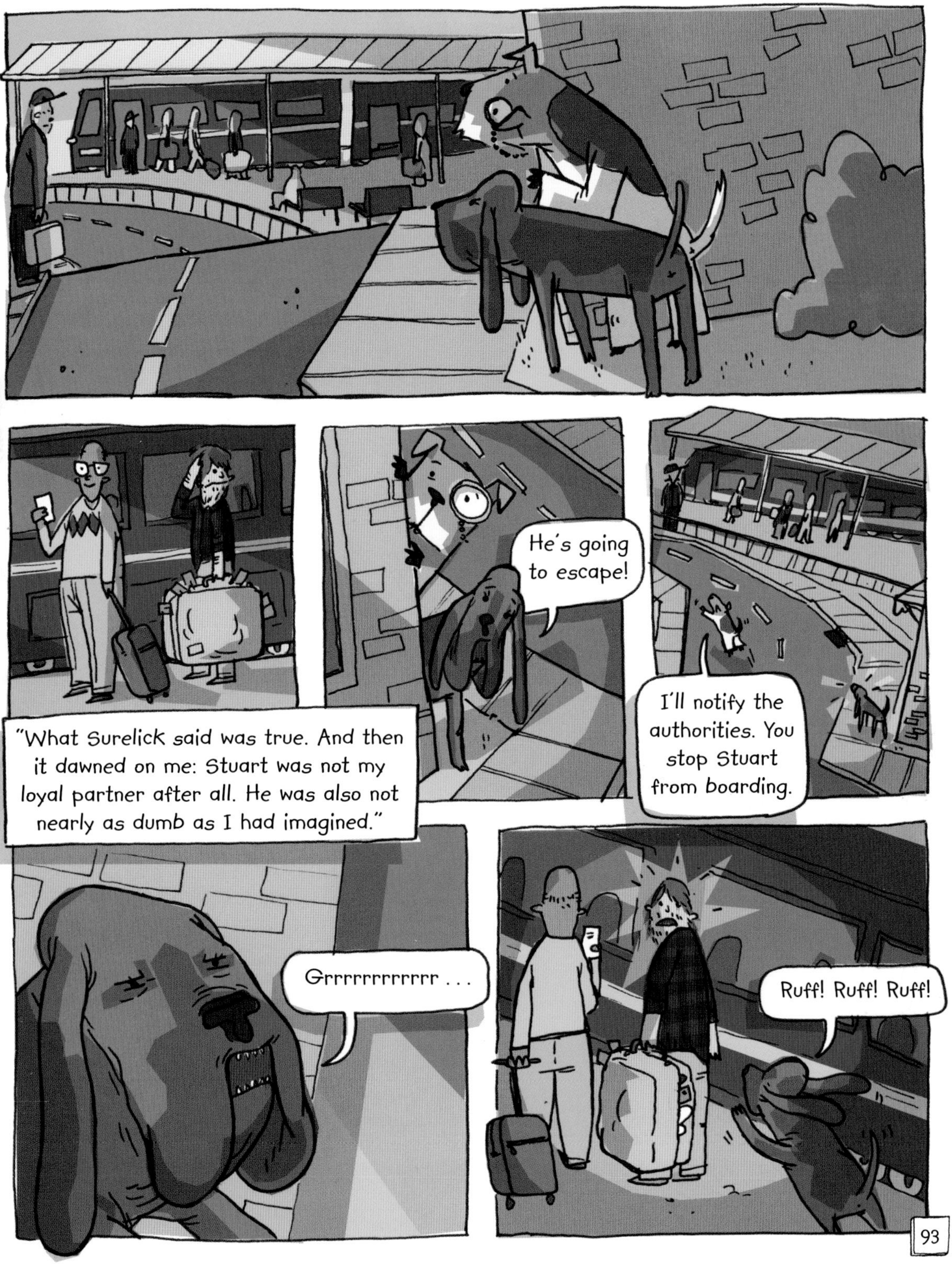

He's going to escape!
I'll notify the authorities. You stop Stuart from boarding.
"What Surelick said was true. And then it dawned on me: Stuart was not my loyal partner after all. He was also not nearly as dumb as I had imagined."
Grrrrrrrrrrr . . .
Ruff! Ruff! Ruff!

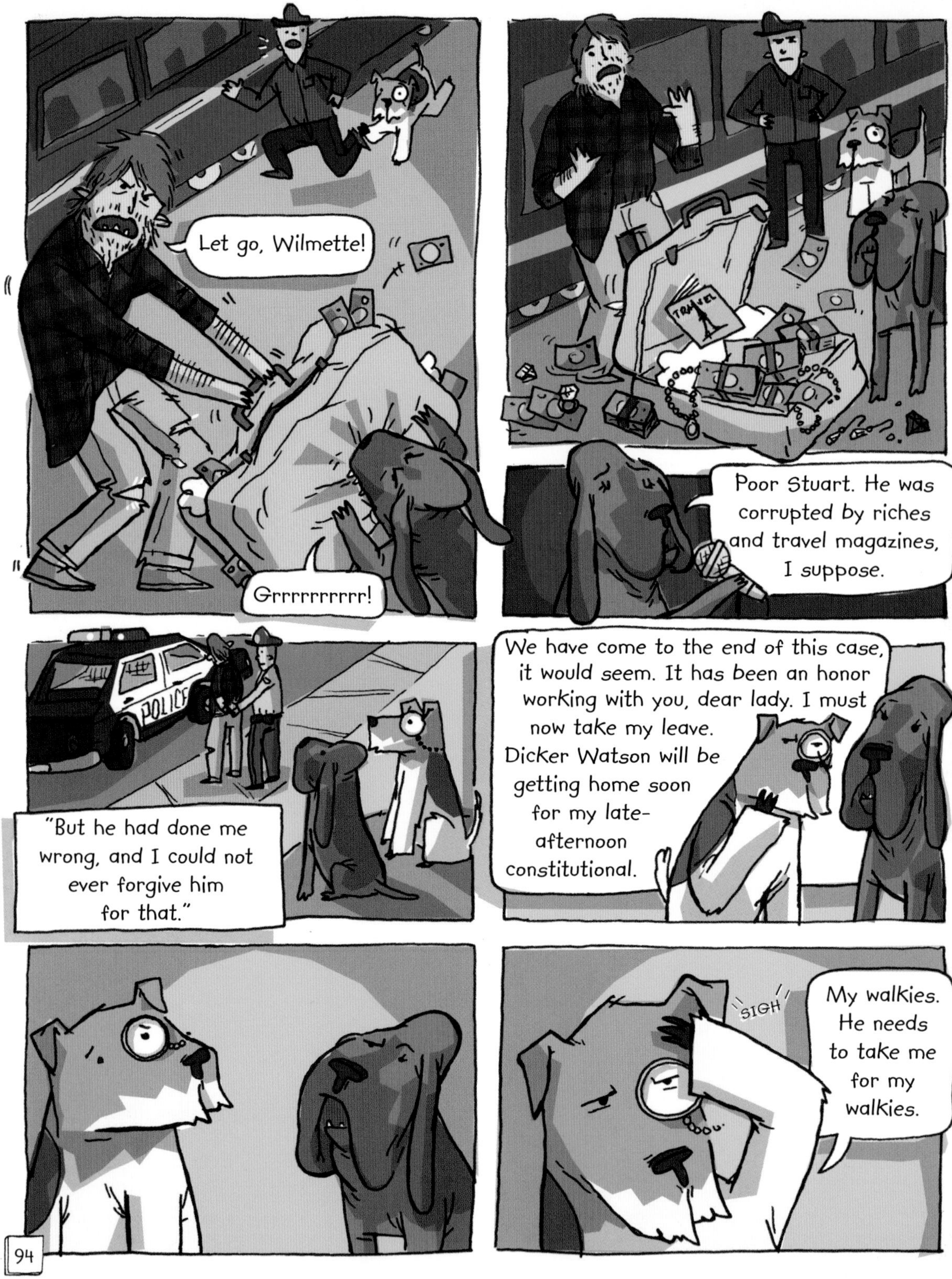

Let go, Wilmette!
Grrrrrrrrr!
TRAVEL
Poor Stuart. He was corrupted by riches and travel magazines, I suppose.
POLICE
"But he had done me wrong, and I could not ever forgive him for that."
We have come to the end of this case, it would seem. It has been an honor working with you, dear lady. I must now take my leave. Dicker Watson will be getting home soon for my late-afternoon constitutional.
SIGH
My walkies. He needs to take me for my walkies.

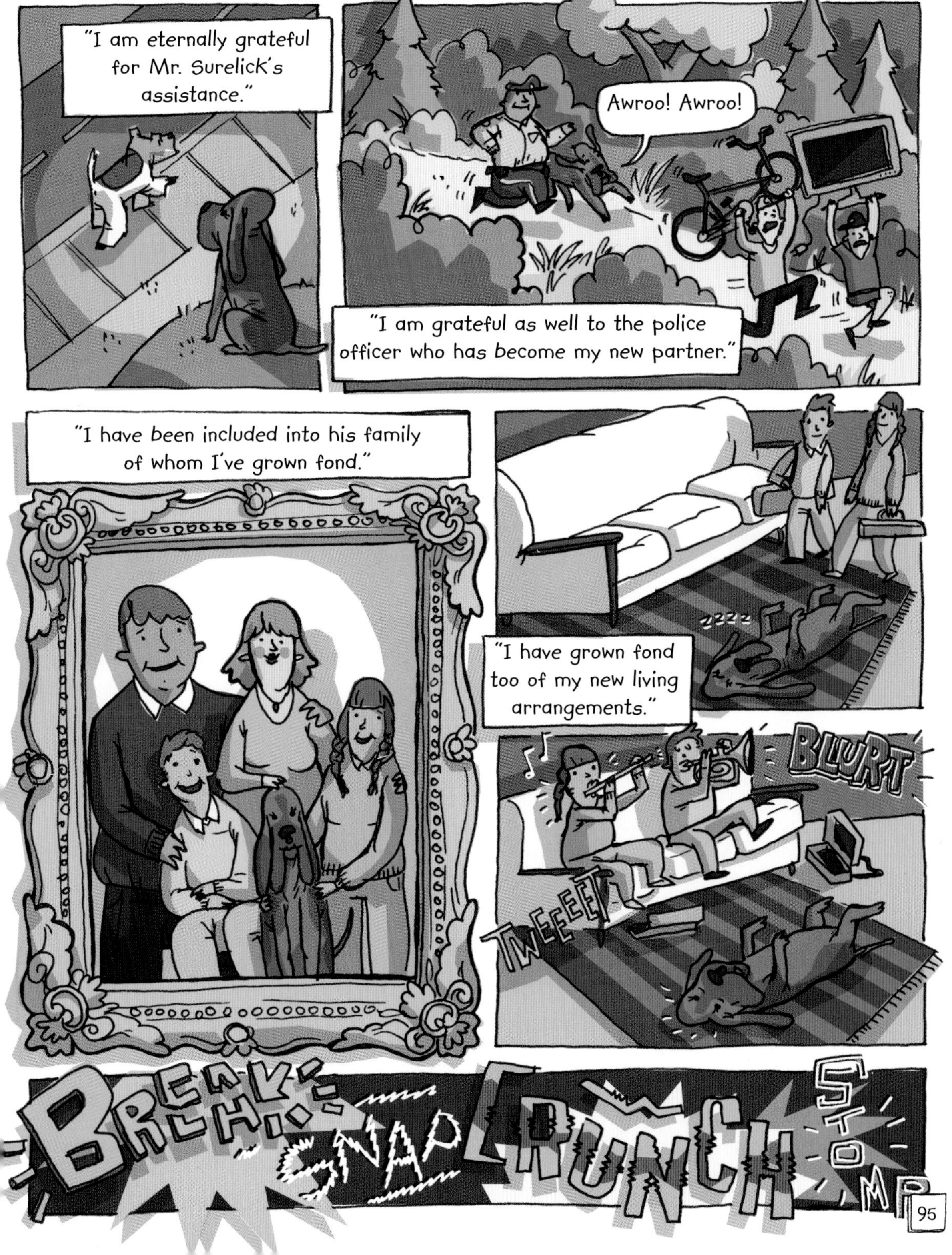
"I am eternally grateful for Mr. Surelick's assistance."
Awroo! Awroo!
"I am grateful as well to the police officer who has become my new partner."
"I have been included into his family of whom I've grown fond."
"I have grown fond too of my new living arrangements."
BLURT
TWEEET
BREAK
SNAP
CRUNCH
STOMP

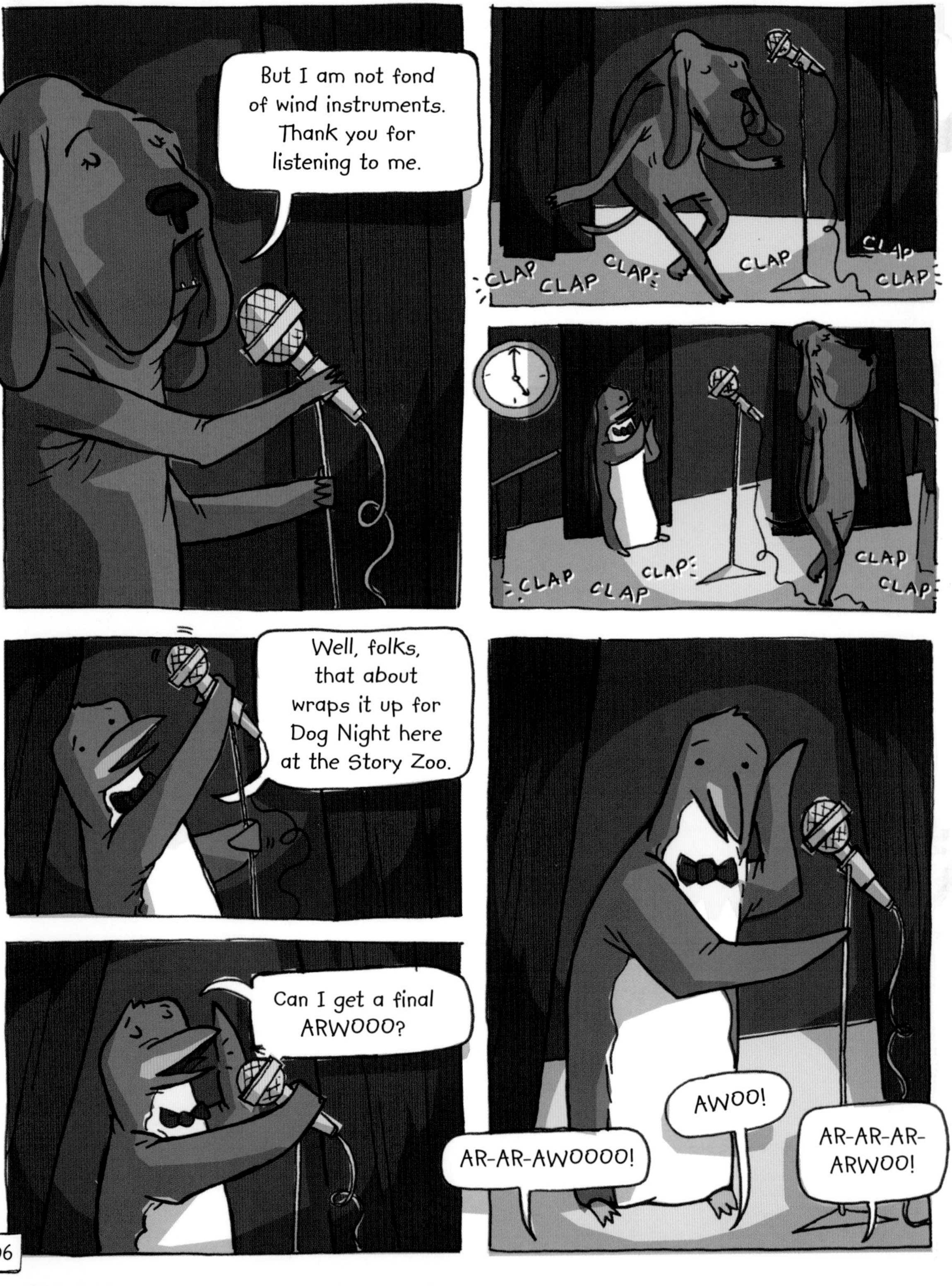
But I am not fond of wind instruments. Thank you for listening to me.
CLAP CLAP CLAP CLAP CLAP CLAP
CLAP CLAP CLAP CLAP CLAP
Well, folks, that about wraps it up for Dog Night here at the Story Zoo.
Can I get a final ARWOOO?
AR-AR-AWOOOO!
AWOO!
AR-AR-AR-ARWOO!

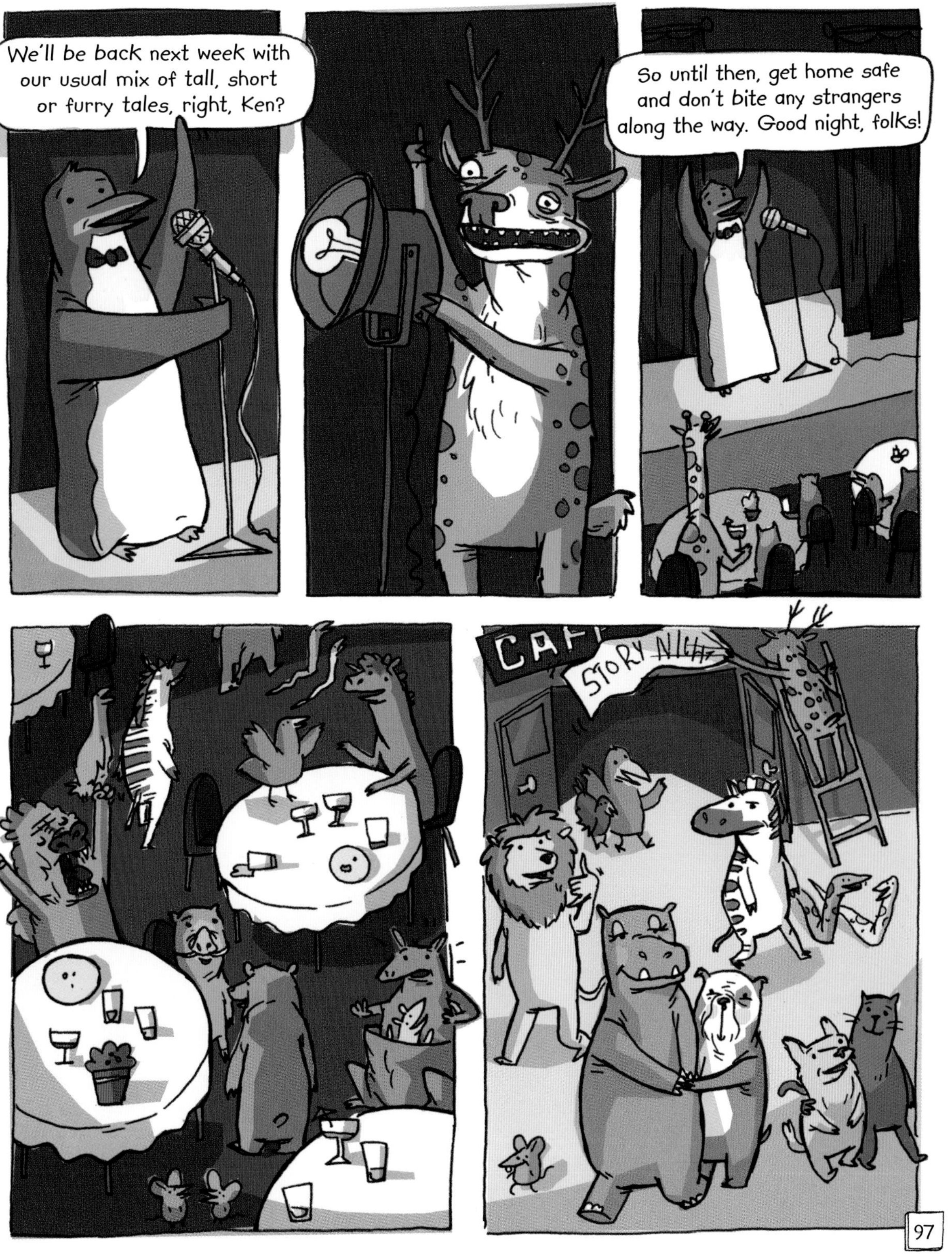
We'll be back next week with our usual mix of tall, short or furry tales, right, Ken?
So until then, get home safe and don't bite any strangers along the way. Good night, folks!
STORY

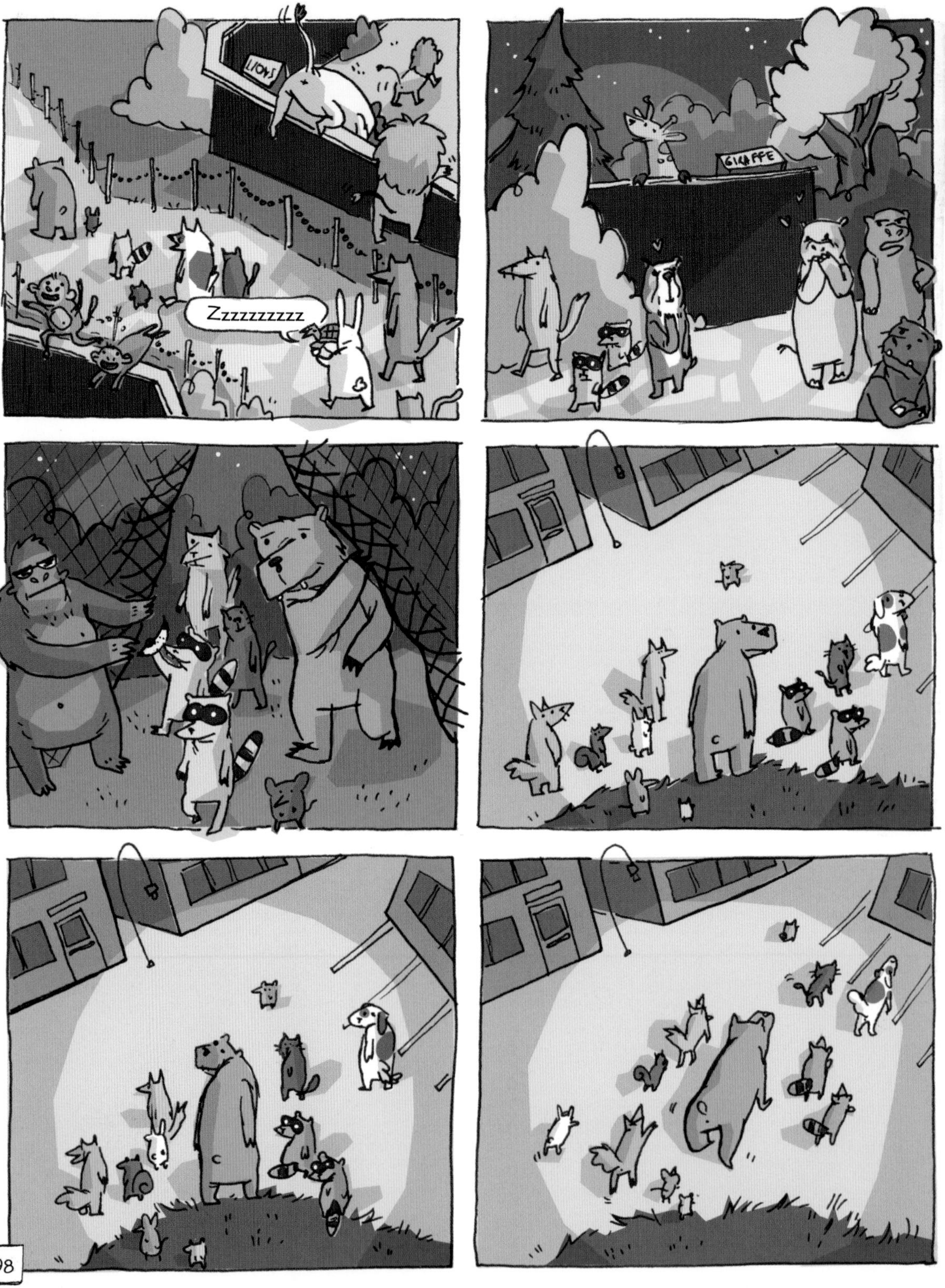
LIONS
Zzzzzzzzzz
GIRAFFE